STALKED

by

JAMES F. BRODERICK

WHISKEY CREEK PRESS
www.whiskeycreekpress.com

Published by
WHISKEY CREEK PRESS
Whiskey Creek Press
PO Box 51052
Casper, WY 82605-1052
www.whiskeycreekpress.com

Print ISBN: 978-1-61160-897-7

Cover Artist: Gemini Judson

Editor: Dave Field

To Jack,
The best Editor EVER!

Dedication

To those who have seen firsthand what can't be explained, this book is dedicated.

I enjoyed writing fiction so much for The MUNDELEIN REVIEW I decided to write this novel. As usual for all things in my life that have gone terribly wrong, I blame you.

Affectionately,
Jim B
Senior Rotary Club Reporter
Mundelein Review

Chapter 1

From the Diary of Clarence Wadsworth Lovelace, Amish Farmer, Indiana Northern Territory, 1827:

September 16. The Lord be praised, I witnessed the miracle of His creation today. Our goat brought forth a kid, the birth wondrous to behold. One must marvel at the simple miracles that surround us. Sunrise and harvest, starry heavens and rainfall. God Bless Us that we might see Thy handiwork in the fabric of daily life. Amen.

Joshua Miller visited after the barn raising. He brought a jar of pear butter from Mrs. Miller, which we will open this Sunday during Feast. We sat for some time at hearth, praying and talking of his land. Joshua hopes to make goodly use of that parcel of swamp behind his field. I told him he'd need to be a magus to turn such terrain to his advantage.

He told me the land is fertile but cursed.

Why cursed? I inquired.

He spake quiet then and seemed at pains to reveal more. I placed my hand on my heart and pledged fealty and he told me a story remarkable.

He sweareth that a creature lived therein, a beast that growled and squealed like the Devil himself, and came out a'sunset to ravage the land. A yard's fabric long with spiky fur, it shows tooth and claw to any poor soul foolhardy enough to find himself alone on that parcel.

And he sweareth too that the animal hideth from the righteous but striketh those whose Faith wavers like the stalks of wheat in the wind. "'Tis danger," he told me, "to traverse that lowland without Bible and candle in hand."

"See it for thyself?" I questioned.

"Did just so, aye," said he.

"And what saw ye, then?"

He fixed me with his good eye.

"'Twas the Devil, sure," he said. "And what I saw chilled m'blood. God protect me, Clarence, from that four-legg'd serpent!"

* * * *

Tossing in her bed, Kelsey squinted at her clock radio: Four-thirty. She'd read that same time on the luminous display too many nights before.

But if it's already so late—or, she thought, *so early—then that means this night, at least, might pass without event.*

She pulled herself up and leaned over, kissing Justin on the forehead. He was breathing easily, freely. Relieved, she snagged a handful of goose-down comforter, pressed it up against her cheek, and rolled to her side, tightly wound in a cocoon of blanket, exhausted by the grip of pre-emptive worry. Soon, the barely perceptible sound of two quietly-sleeping people filled the room, a blissful respite from the previous night. And then suddenly it was morning.

"Put your clammies on, Spinner," her sleep-soaked voice rasped to her son as he climbed out of bed. "The kitchen floor's cold."

"They are not clams, Mommy. They're crabs."

"Right, crabs. I don't know why I always get those two confused." She giggled to herself, oblivious to the eye-rolling of her seven-year-old son Justin. "I guess it's because I never spent much time near the water."

Nonetheless, Justin did as he was told, placing the fuzzy crab slippers on his feet, wrapping himself in a plaid flannel robe and padding toward the kitchen to make himself breakfast. Kelsey lay in bed, thinking she should really get up too, but then she reminded herself that making one's own breakfast breeds independence. She wanted her son to be independent, to be able to handle things on his own, to deal with adversity like the little man he was. Kelsey had a lot of faith in the maxim "What does not destroy me makes me stronger," and she'd been thinking along those lines quite a bit lately, especially during the attacks.

There must be something to it, she reasoned. *Look at him: my warrior, my little guy. I love him so much I'm going to let him continue his quest toward independence,* she said to herself, rolling over to get a couple more hours of sleep.

While Justin filled his cereal bowl with oatmeal and carried it to the kitchen faucet, Kelsey closed her eyes and drifted far away, gently buoyed up by waves, lulled by lapping waters. She was in a small wooden boat, oars extended, bright sunlight refracting off the surface of a lake. She inhaled deeply, a whiff of pine, algae, and mint seasoning the air. She squinted at the sun, and then squeezed tightly her eyes, a kaleidoscope of light and color fragmenting and reassembling with every blink. Her boat and her body were one, riding the surface of the water, feeling the soft undulations of current. A faint breeze brushed her downy arms, lazily extended over the edge of the boat, fingers tracing tiny circles on the skin of the cool water. Languid on the shimmering surface, she felt soft and warm and complete.

She felt the sunshine on her eyelids and her face and she brought her hands up to cover her eyes. She peered out through the lattice-work of her fingers, shafts of brilliant sunlight columning the sky. She lay there, half-dreaming, until the light suddenly faded. A phalanx of cloud now covered the sun, the sky a dark and queasy palate of gray and green. She opened her eyes and a cold terror grabbed at her. The waters had become agitated, waves splashing over the side of the boat, chilling her. She must have fallen asleep while a storm moved in. She reached for the oars and began to row, but the wind and the tide and the force of the waves kept her from moving. She was pulling and pulling but the boat wasn't moving.

As the sky darkened, Kelsey beat wildly at the water with the chipped wooden oars, but it was as if the boat was anchored. It was like something out of a nightmare except Kelsey could feel—pain in her back and arms as she tugged at the oars, blisters on the palms of her hands from the rough-hewn oar handles, a tart chill that ran though her. It was too real to be a dream. A fog had now moved in, shrouding the land and hiding the shore. She yanked and pulled at the oars, but she remained stuck in the water and the fog.

"Mommy!"

Justin's voice, a scream-gurgle of panic, sliced through the air. Kelsey felt the electric shock of terror. She stood up with a jerk, causing the boat to list and almost capsize. She feverishly swept the surface of the water but there was no sign of anyone, just the agitated, nausea-inducing undulations of the storm-stirred lake.

"Mommy!"

Kelsey felt a pounding in her chest and a weakening of her legs. She screamed her son's name as loud as she could. "Justin! Justin! WHERE ARE YOU, BABY?" The boat rocked queasily. A cold rain began to fall. Kelsey stood at the bow and leaned as far over as she dare, scanning the horizon for any sign of her seven-year-old son. Waves now tumbled into the boat and Kelsey was conscious of her feet and ankles feeling wet and chilled and a tingling numbness setting in below her waist. She grabbed an oar and beat at the water with ferocity and panic.

"JUSTIN!"

She could barely get the word out before gagging, gasping for breath, overcome with a wave of dizziness and pain.

I must fight through it.

The rain and sweat and tears coated her body that was so warm just a few moments ago. Her son was out there…somewhere. If there was one voice in the world she knew, in all its volumes and moods, it was Justin's. It was a voice she heard in her sleep.

That's Justin, my baby. I must save him.

She stood up, boat rocking dangerously, gentle winds now replaced by stinging gusts. She looked all around but she could see nothing but the water and the rain and the waves and the boat. She felt like she was about to be sick. With an agonized shout, she tried again to reach her lost little guy before he was lost forever to the unforgiving depths.

"JUSTIN! MY GOD, JUSTIN! WHERE ARE YOU?"

The boat seemed about to be toppled by the increasingly turbulent waters. Kelsey slipped off the bow, cracking her elbow on the side of the boat, a ribbon of pain running through the parts of her body she could still feel. She sat in the boat, curled in agony and despair.

"JUSTIN!" she screamed through the tears, grabbing the side of the boat for support. "BABY, I CAN'T FIND YOU!" She collapsed at the bottom of the boat, certain she was going to be sick, her son's cry for help beating in her brain like a hammer. She continued to call his name, but the wind and the rain overwhelmed her. She thought of jumping, of swimming this way and that, diving under the waves and scanning the brackish waters for signs of her baby. She pulled her head up, looked into the murky waters, and shouted his name once again.

"JUSTIN!"

"Kelsey!"

Kelsey knew this voice, too. It came from the other side of the boat. She pivoted on the slippery surface just in time to see the figure submerge, torso first, then shoulders, then neck, and then chin, and then finally he was gone.

"DADDY!" screamed Kelsey, frantically grabbing at him, reaching out of the boat and falling, falling, through the chilly depths, still reaching out, holding the hand of her sinking father. She squeezed and squeezed but she couldn't pull him up. Still she held on as he pulled her down, deep and deeper. And the farther they fell, the harder she squeezed.

"OW! Mommy! Let go! You're hurting me!"

She awoke to see Justin on the verge of tears from her sweat-soaked grip. He had heard her crying out and was trying to wake her. She immediately released his hand but then she pulled him closer and cradled his head in her arms, tears now filling her eyes.

* * * *

That can't be good news, Kelsey thought as she replayed the message on her answering machine. *Why does Dr. Reeves want to see me "as soon as possible"?*

"Who's that, Mommy?"

"Oh, that's Professor Reeves. I've told you about him."

"The man who's helping you with your book."

"Well, it's called a dissertation, but yeah, it's like a book."

"A BOOK NOBODY READS!" her son shot back playfully, echoing something he'd heard his mother mutter countless times as she plowed through the piles of papers that had taken over much of their small apartment during the last three years.

She turned on her son with pseudo-scorn.

"You promised me YOU were gonna read it, Spinner! Does that mean I've lost my ONLY reader?" She leaned down, grabbed him by the shoulders, and began shaking him gently in mock frustration. "You mean all of my work has been for nothing? Oh, The Horror!" She grabbed him tightly, spun around, and they both tumbled to the floor, Justin—who far preferred the nickname "Spinner" to his given name—and his mother, who now began a ferocious tickling campaign. Paroxysms of laughter erupted from the little man as he half-attempted to free himself from the kneading fingers. Suddenly, she stopped, remembering.

"You okay, Spinner?"

"Mom, I'm fine," he said, squirming free. "What does he want?"

"Who?"

"The man helping you with the book."

"Oh. He said he wants to see me. He didn't say why. That's odd."

"He's an oddball."

"Where did you hear that word?"

"Oddball! Oddball! Oddball!" he shouted riotously, as he rushed his mother and began a tickle attack of his own.

"*You're* the oddball!" she squealed, hoisting his small frame till his feet swung free. "AND ODDBALLS MUST BE DEALT WITH IN THE HARSHEST POSSIBLE MANNER!" Justin's giggling and his mother's mock-growling filled the kitchen, a duet of joyousness that ended only when Kelsey let her mind wander back to the message.

What can he want? The work's done, more or less. I've been working on that dissertation for almost three years, and he's never called me at home. Not once. What the hell does he want now?

* * * *

In less than two hours, she found herself in the oakey office of her dissertation advisor, who gestured to her to sit down as he cradled the phone between his cheek and shoulder and stood at a filing cabinet, struggling to extract a manila folder. Kelsey always liked being here, in the office of a real professor, the room smelling of old, leather-bound books, unlike the graduate student office, with her stressed-out colleagues and the reeking scent of aspiration and resentment. She liked Dr. Reeves from the first time she met him. He'd always been supportive of her, quickly becoming more of a father figure than an academic advisor. She explained at that first meeting her situation: single mother, an asthmatic child, a punishing work schedule—and he listened calmly and he smiled as she spoke. He told her they would work everything out, deal with whatever problems came up, and that the only thing that mattered was that the work progressed. She remembered he'd told her he felt she was capable of great work. She often thought of that, amid the chaos and tumult of her life over the past three years. He believed in her. To the fragile graduate school psyche, belief is manna. When every day brings new reasons to chuck it all, having someone believe in you is more than helpful. It keeps you running.

In the past few years, she'd become used to the scoffing that greeted her answer whenever someone asked "What's your field?" She'd simply smile and say, quite matter-of-factly, "Crypto-zoology," and then, waiting the requisite beat to account for the confused look, she'd add, almost in a conspiratorial whisper, "The study of creatures rumored to exist but never proved." She always wanted to say more: about the rich and complex tradition of myth and folk belief, and about Jungian psychology and archetypes, and the sociology of group-think and patterns of cultural resistance to assimilation, and all the other "serious" aspects of her study. But what people mostly heard when she said "crypto-zoology" was "Bigfoot," and they'd sneer, or tell her to "be careful," or they'd just chuckle and say "Good luck with that" as they walked away, most likely thinking how they seem to give graduate degrees in just about anything these days.

But when she was in Dr. Reeves' office, none of that mattered. He made her feel her studies were worthy, important, even noble. He'd written books on the subject, and he was a highly respected professor. She sat there in his office, remembering the first class she'd taken with him, more than half a decade ago, when she was wondering if this quixotic effort to get her Ph.D. was even worth trying. Those days were hazy in her mind. It was a time in her life when she remembered feeling besieged, dealing with the initial onset of her son's asthma, further tormented by the fearful second thoughts after having just ended a relationship with Justin's father, as well as a naïve understanding of what graduate school was all about. But somewhere along the line, mercifully, it all began to click. Her life got a little easier when she finished classes and had only her dissertation research to focus on. The past three years had been exhausting but also highly satisfying, even if she was only writing a book that nobody would read. And now it was almost at an end. All that awaited was a final polish of the dissertation.

The avuncular Dr. Reeves put down the phone, closed the file cabinet drawer, and walked over to greet his protégé.

"Kelsey, so good of you to come in today," he said, grasping her hand warmly. "I hope my call didn't alarm you."

Well, yes, you sort of scared the shit out of me, she wanted to confess.

"Not at all. I was planning to come by and see you anyway."

The professor looked at her above the top of his reading glasses with a skeptical glance and a wry smile.

"Well then, I don't feel so bad about disrupting your life with this little visit." He sat down behind his desk and opened a file folder, his smile yielding to a look of obvious concern. He was not a man given to dramatic gestures to make a point.

A concerned look must mean there's cause to be concerned.

Kelsey sat there, waiting and worrying.

"Kelsey, as you know, your dissertation defense is scheduled for later this semester," he began.

You bet I know.

The date had been etched in her mind for the past half-year. She'd been told by others in the graduate program that the defense was really just a formality, one last hazing ritual before they let you into the club. She didn't think she had any reason to sweat it. Maybe she was wrong.

"It appears we might have to make a small adjustment to that timetable."

Kelsey felt her heart rise into her throat. She had thought her work was solid. What could possibly be wrong?

"Something rather serious has arisen. A situation, of sorts. It could be a problem for you, Kelsey. To be completely candid, it could threaten your entire project."

A baseball bat between the eyes, a dagger to the gut. All the warmth and comfort and confidence she'd always felt in this setting dissipated like smoke, leaving her exposed and broken.

"But," he said, putting down his glasses and staring at her with earnestness and what she thought might be a touch of envy, "there's a remarkable opportunity here as well."

He reached into his drawer and pulled out a bottle of Napoleonic brandy, and a tray with two small glasses. He filled each about a third of the way, and he handed her one of the glasses. This was a pretty rare ritual. They'd shared a drink and a toast together only once before, when he formally agreed to be her dissertation advisor and they signed the department's official contract. A toast to her success, then. Now, what? Her survival.

"Dr. Reeves, what's—"

"Please," he said, patting her arm in a way that anyone

outside the academy would see as insultingly patrician. “Take a sip.” He clinked his glass against hers, and they both drank.

“Ah. Lovely,” he said, licking his lips unselfconsciously. “Lord Byron is reputed to have said all news of consequence requires an aperitif.” He sat back behind the desk, hands folded.

“Okay, Kelsey. Here’s the situation. As you know, your dissertation deals with several different creatures from the world of crypto-zoology. Your work—impressive work I might add—seeks to establish the root of belief for each of these entities. Yes?”

“Yes.”

“You spend a considerable amount of time discussing one particular creature, the so-called ‘Indiana Corn Weasel,’ an animal of mythic ferocity. Rather silly name for such a fierce creature, huh? You say it can be traced to the Midwest migration of the Amish, and their beliefs in the manifestation of evil in the physical world.”

“Right. Yes I do. I’ve got a ton of research to back this up, and if you—”

“No, Kelsey, I’m aware. I’ve read your research,” he said, pouring himself another drink and then gulping it down in one swallow.

“Your fundamental argument is that this creature exists in the minds of the deeply religious, an anthropomorphic projection of their fear and disdain for the outside, modern world. A kind of mammalian stand-in for the Devil, yes?”

“That’s right.”

He opened the file folder on his desk.

“I have a colleague at a college in Indiana who knows I have an interest in these kinds of things. He sent me these last week,” he said, handing Kelsey the file filled with clippings from a newspaper.

“What is all this?”

“I’ll summarize. There’s a small town in Indiana.

Milton, Indiana. These clips are from the local paper, the *Milton Forum*. They detail—in surprisingly good prose for such an obscure publication—a series of attacks that have taken place the past few weeks. Attacks, Kelsey, which have been attributed to the corn weasel."

"You are kidding."

"Take a look. There are dozens of accounts. Eyewitness testimony. Police reports. Several people have been injured. All the work of the infamous Indiana Corn Weasel."

"Dr. Reeves, that's absurd. We both know—"

"What we know, Kelsey, is that this creature—whose purely mythical status is chronicled in the pages of your dissertation—is wreaking some serous havoc on his home turf."

Kelsey felt uncertain how to respond. Dr. Reeves seemed to be taking all this seriously, and she wasn't sure why.

"If a bunch of religious lunatics want to believe there's some sort of demonic mammal ravaging their cornfields, there's not much I can do about that."

"Think about this, Kelsey. You're about to defend a dissertation that argues no such creature as the Indiana Corn Weasel exists. And while you'll be making that argument, hundreds of people in Milton, Indiana, are locking up their children and refusing to go out after sundown. In the meantime, the local hospital reports at least a half-dozen injuries attributed to vicious corn weasel attacks. This thing—whatever it is—seems to be asserting its existence in a pretty definitive way. You say it doesn't exist, but there's a whole town that seems to disagree."

"So what should I do? Take out that chapter?"

"No indeed. No! Kelsey, isn't it obvious?" He stared at her expectantly while she sat there puzzled, mute. "What you should do is go to Milton, Indiana and find out what's going on."

Kelsey cocked her head, as if she'd misheard.

"Kelsey, this is a terrific opportunity! If it turns out to be nothing—as these things almost always are—you'll have some new information and original research for your dissertation. And if there *is* something going on there—"

"You mean if the Indiana Corn Weasel actually exists?"

"Crypto-zoology has many rewards, Kelsey. Documenting a previously unknown creature is one of the glories of the profession, the dream of every crypto-zoologist. That's the opportunity I was talking about. Think of it, Kelsey. This could be a career-maker for you!"

Seeming genuinely excited at the prospect of her encounter, he refilled his glass and then, with uncharacteristic flourish, raised it, eyeing her.

"To the thrill of the hunt," he said, finishing off the amber contents as Kelsey sat mutely, wondering what to make of the whole situation, feeling a little lost.

* * * *

A light October rain was falling as Kelsey hiked the two uphill blocks from the bus stop to her apartment. The slate gray sky bled into the landscape, bleakly coloring her corner of northern New Jersey. She felt as uncertain as the weather, playing back in her mind the scene in Dr. Reeves' office, wondering if this was some sort of test of her resolve.

Maybe my dissertation committee is just toying with me.

But then she glanced down at the file folder, filled with what appeared to be genuine clippings from a small town newspaper.

Seems like a lot of trouble to go through for a prank.

Still, the whole thing was so far fetched.

Twenty minutes later, stretched out on the sofa bed in the living room of her apartment, reading through the contents of the file folder, Kelsey began to conclude that if this was a clever hoax, it went far beyond her dissertation committee.

Attacked by Vicious Animal, Scout Tells Frightening Tale

By Frankie Auden

Staff Writer

Thirteen-year-old Randy Meyerson rifles through a drawer overstuffed with merit badges, citations, ribbons, and certificates of appreciation. As one of the most decorated members of his local troop, Boy Scout Troop #56, Northeast Indiana chapter, he can point to a whole host of accomplishments.

"That's me and the governor," he says, proudly displaying a photo taken during last year's Founder's Day celebration, Randy decked out in his Boy Scout finery.

"He's one of the best scouts we've ever worked with around these parts," said Regional Scout Master Ernie Coles. "For a kid to be able to track and hunt like he does, it's pretty darn unusual. If I was ever lost in the woods, I'd want Randy with me."

Unfortunately, Randy was alone last Friday, collecting bark samples for his Arbor Badge when, he says, he saw something rustling through the brush.

"Weren't no badger, no raccoon, no possum. I've seen all those creatures, and I know how they act. Weren't nothing I ever seen before."

Randy says he was taking a bark scraping from one of the pines along the old Laudermilk Road when he heard a high-pitched squeal. He says he turned and was suddenly face to face with some sort of wild animal.

"I heard tales of it, but they were just tales. But I know what I saw."

What he saw, he says, was the Indiana Corn Weasel.

"You can laugh all you want. I ain't laughing."

And neither were the emergency room doctors at Holy Cross Medical Center, where Randy was treated for a deep gashes requiring thirty-five stitches, some in his arm, and others above his eye.

"He says it was the corn weasel, so I suppose we've got to deal with that now," said Sheriff's officer Ernie "Bud" Schaffer. "I know him, know his family. They're good people. The kid knows his way around the woods—practically lives out there."

But a corn weasel? Isn't that like some tourist coming back from Scotland with tales of seeing the Loch Ness monster?

"I didn't have a camera, but I saw it clearly," Randy says. "It's just what you hear about in all them old stories. But this ain't no story," Randy adds, dramatically rolling up his pants leg and revealing a red, swollen bite mark.

"What d'ya think done that?" he asks.

No one is really sure. The police classified it merely as an animal attack, and the doctors have begun treating Randy for possible rabies infection. Beyond his description—red, glowing eyes, a raised pelt, high-pitched yelping, highly aggressive behavior, and an almost inconceivable ten-foot vertical leap—there's not much to go on.

The scout's words certainly match the textbook description of the legendary Indiana Corn Weasel, a creature that can be traced back to pioneer days. Though never officially documented, it is said to haunt the woods and

> *cornfields of Northeast Indiana, its bloodthirsty habits—feasting on cattle, protecting its habitat from trappers and hunters by spitting venom, even carrying away infants from their cribs—recorded in legends and folk tales tracing back centuries.*
>
> *Though most dismiss the legend as so much rural silliness, Randy's a believer.*
>
> *"My Daddy says next time I go into the woods, he's gonna get his shotgun and go with me. He says we're gonna have Corn Weasel for supper that night."*

There were other articles documenting other sightings, other attacks. The first clipping was dated July 19, the most recent article almost a month later. What struck Kelsey as she pored through the file was the variety of witnesses who claimed to have seen the creature up close: farmers, store owners, police officers, and in one case, an elderly librarian. As a graduate student, Kelsey had come to rely heavily on librarians—she couldn't count how many times a librarian had saved her from defeat on some line of inquiry.

If a librarian says this creature exists, well then there might just be something to it.

There wasn't a single newspaper article before the July 19 date, and there was nothing covering the last three weeks. Or at least, nothing in the file folder. There was no way to know if the attacks had continued. Kelsey flipped open her laptop and searched for the *Milton Forum* but all that came up was a webpage "under construction" message. A quick search of the White Pages online turned up a phone number for the newspaper's offices, but when she called she was routed to an answering machine. Friday afternoon—why weren't they picking up?

She sat back on the couch and sighed. What to make of all this? No matter what the truth was, Kelsey couldn't just dismiss it as a hoax. Her dissertation was now officially on hold. A three-year paper chase was in danger of being shredded by an angry little mammal in the cornfields of Indiana. Was Dr. Reeves really serious? Going to Indiana to do more research, at this point in her life, was out of the question. She was scheduled to begin teaching next week. She had no place to live even if she went there. And what about Justin? The school year was about to start. She couldn't just drag him along on some academic mongoose chase. The whole thing seemed inconceivable, unworkable.

She brought her hands to her face and pressed her fingertips against her temples. She had a slight headache—was it that drink at Dr. Reeves' office? She tried to relax, reveling in the quiet. She could have slept, but every time she started to drift off she thought of another objection to Dr. Reeves' proposal. Too expensive, too unrealistic, too much to put on hold here.

Doesn't he know I've got a life? Let him spend the fall out in hell's half-acre, chasing weasels.

"Kelsey, this is a terrific opportunity."

It was, for some eighteen-year-old nomad—not for someone in her late twenties, simply trying to finish her dissertation, get accepted into the club, get a teaching job, and raise her son. She didn't want to be heroic, didn't think she could be. Kelsey's battle just to get to this point had challenged all of her insecurities, forced her to be far more aggressive than she would have thought possible, but she was desperate for it to end. She knew that most Ph.D. students hoped to use their dissertation as a springboard to greater success, the opening salvo in an academic firefight. Kelsey wanted to use her dissertation as a shield to protect her from any further battering by the forces of life. Dr. Reeves might have spent his first few decades out of school traipsing through exotic locales, scouring for the remnants of rumored beasts, but Kelsey had her hands full just trying to negotiate the jungle of New Jersey.

She put the file folder on the cheap lacquered coffee table, put her feet on it, and stretched back on the couch, courting rest. In a few minutes, she'd go pick up Justin at the babysitter's.

But just let me close my eyes, just for one minute, clear the fog and empty my mind, she wished. And she drifted off.

She wasn't sure how long she'd been sleeping when she heard the knocking on the door. Still rather disoriented, she stumbled to the door and opened it.

"Mrs. Rausch?"

"Kelsey, it's Justin."

"What's happened?"

"He's having an attack, and we can't find his inhaler. He must have dropped it, or lost it in the park."

Kelsey had dropped Justin off at the Rausch apartment on her way to see Dr. Reeves. It was his usual destination when Kelsey was running around taking care of school stuff. Mrs. Rausch was a recently-retired municipal employee, a careerist in the city clerk's office who was still capable of getting a parking ticket erased or a water bill "re-adjusted." Her daughter, Brittany, was an elementary education student in her last year of college. They were always willing to look after Justin, and because they lived in the same apartment building, it was an ideal situation. Justin often ate dinner there when Kelsey was running late getting back home.

"Okay," Kelsey said, suddenly alert. "I've got one right here." She grabbed the small metal canister and plastic mouthpiece on the coffee table and raced past Mrs. Rausch to the apartment one flight below. Taking the stairs three at a time, she was at 2B in a matter of seconds.

Not bothering to knock, she burst in. Justin was lying on his back on the carpeted floor with his knees bent and sweat beginning to bead on his forehead. She heard the tell-tale wheeze, saw the rapid, convulsive rise and fall of his ribcage as he struggled to fill his lungs with air.

Having gone through this situation countless times, Kelsey knew exactly what to do. Later, when the attack has subsided, after she'd gotten through this latest unpleasant episode with her son, Kelsey would then experience the emotions that always seem to follow in the wake of the attacks: frustration, anger, helplessness. A couple of years ago, she couldn't remember when, exactly, but just after one of Justin's first attacks, an emergency room doctor told her, somewhat patronizingly, that these attacks are worse for the parent, that "It's much harder to watch" your child having an attack than to actually experience the attack itself. She took some comfort in that idea, hoped it was true, but she never really believed it.

"Okay, kiddo. Here's your inhaler. I need you to sit up," she said, pulling him forward. "Now focus, kiddo," she said, shaking the canister. "You're going to inhale as hard as you can." He nodded, still gasping, and pursed his lips around the mouthpiece, ready to inhale a hundred and twenty micrograms of lung-opening albuterol. "Now inhale and hold your breath. Let's make at least ten seconds, okay?" she asked, looking at her watch. She held his hand and counted aloud. "Okay. Great job, Spinner. Now, let's take another spritz, okay?"

As she handed him the canister, she scanned him for clues that the aerosol mist was beginning to work. She listened to his wheezing to determine if it was shallow or deep—a small airway constriction or large airway constriction—looked at his complexion, noticed whether his eyes were glassy, or if he appeared disoriented. When the medicine worked, it usually worked well. But sometimes—rarely, but enough to get your attention—it didn't. That was an emotional challenge of a different order. But he was already starting to breathe easier before even the second dose.

After he exhaled his second dose, he gave her a little nod. She leaned over him and hugged him. "Spinner, you're a brave little man," she whispered in his ear.

"Mom, please," he said, eyes alerting her to his watching babysitters, who were almost as pale as Justin had been a few minutes ago.

Then, rising from her knees, she said to Mrs. Rauch and her daughter, "It's okay now. He's fine. Thanks for coming to get me, Mrs. Rausch. I'll get you a spare inhaler to keep here just in case. Thanks, again." She herded Justin out of the apartment and back upstairs.

Jesus, I really hate these attacks. Why Justin?

But she knew that was a pointless question. It was over, she could relax. She didn't have the energy to climb back into a place of despair. Plus, there was now pudding to be had.

"Tapioca!" Justin exclaimed, licking his lips as Kelsey removed the small plastic containers from the refrigerator. This was their post-asthma-attack ritual: eat some pudding. The doctor didn't include this in his litany of prophylactic measures, but then doctors don't know everything.

"So how'd it go with the professor guy?" Justin lipsmacked between spoonfuls.

"Oh, it was…interesting."

"That's adult for bad," he said, spooning away happily.

How much you know, my little man, thought Kelsey, wondering if things were about to get even more interesting.

Her reverie was interrupted by the doorbell, clanging like a bicycle chain being dragged across a metal cooking pot.

"You expecting somebody, Spinner?" Then leaning in, accusingly, she asked him: "Gotta date?"

Spinner, lapping up his tapioca pudding, looked up mischievously.

"Not telling," he said.

She got up to answer the door, amused at his response. He was turning into a wit.

Hope it sticks.

She peered through the keyhole and sighed animatedly.

"Otto."

Spinner immediately put down his pudding container and ran to the door.

"Otto!" he said as Kelsey opened the door. There he stood, decked out in his purple trench coat and a sock monkey hat, a six-foot-five sad clown with a shoulder bag and a daisy in his buttonhole.

"What would your students say if they saw you dressed like this, Professor Wolcott?"

"Probably, they'd say, 'I can't believe that fashion disaster actually flunked me,'" he said, releasing Justin from his bear hug and leaning forward to kiss Kelsey on the cheek. Then, barely missing a beat, he inhaled dramatically, began fanning himself frantically with his hands, and bellowed, "Speaking of fashion disasters! Where did you dig up this décor? Was there a yard sale at Ward and June Cleaver's house?"

Justin laughed hysterically. He laughed at everything Otto said.

"Don't be too flattered," Kelsey countered. "He doesn't even know what Leave it to Beaver is," she said.

"With a living room like this," Otto said, gingerly uplifting a throw pillow like it was infected with smallpox, "he doesn't need to watch it. He's living it!"

Justin giggled again, and Kelsey felt a momentary rush of gratitude. Otto was a welcome distraction this afternoon. Otto was a distraction pretty much everywhere he went: ostentatious tattoos decorating his ebony skin, a pierced tongue, bleached-blond hair and clothes that would make Mr. Blackwell gag.

Kelsey turned to her son. "Spinner, Otto and I need to talk privately, okay?"

Otto gave Justin a high five as he headed off to his room, and then sat down on the sofa.

"What's wrong? Tell Doctor Otto," he said, patting

the cushion next to him. Kelsey sat down and reached out to grab the file folder. She flipped it open, then closed it, shaking her head.

"Ever heard of Milton, Indiana?"

After a thoughtful pause, he said, "I think I dated him once. Wasn't he that gorgeous guy in Medford's research methods seminar?"

Kelsey shook her head.

"It's a place, not a person. You know…Indiana? A state in the Midwest?"

"That's their problem, Kelsey darling. Y'all got anything to drink around here? I'm parched."

"Help yourself to whatever you can find."

Otto, who always looked like a fish out of water, also drank like one. His capacity to swill cocktails was legendary among his fellow students. Otto would always say that it was a "defense mechanism." As he explained it once to Kelsey, he was convinced that most people were deeply attracted to him at first sight, and that they secretly wanted to get him into bed. He said he was afraid that people would be trying to get him drunk at every party he ever went to just to satisfy their curiosity about what it would be like to be with him. So he set himself the goal of developing the highest tolerance for alcohol of anyone he knew. No one was going to take advantage of Otto—"Unless I want them to!" he confided to her at a graduate school mixer.

Otto's field of study was anthropology. For all his bawdy bluster, he happened to be a first-rate scholar, a fact that surprised most of his fellow graduate students—but not Kelsey. She'd sensed from the first time she'd met him in a study group to prepare for the oral examination that he was gifted, intellectually. All that eye makeup couldn't hide Otto's academic prowess. He practically had a photographic memory. Any piece of information that anyone brought to the study group, Otto seemed to be able to retain, and recall, at will. When he won the Russett-

Langdon prize for the best draft dissertation, Kelsey wasn't surprised. She was, however, disappointed. She thought she had a shot at winning it—Dr. Reeves was on the selection committee. But she couldn't be angry about—or even disagree with—the choice. Otto's work was genuinely impressive, a fact that would almost certainly have been lost on anyone currently watching him dip ice cubes in a jelly jar filled with whisky and then suck on them like a little kid eating a popsicle.

"So tell me," he said, slurping away unselfconsciously. "What's the problem?"

Kelsey told him about her meeting with Dr. Reeves, and how confused and resentful she felt about being put in this position. She still didn't see why something that was happening eight hundred miles away in a rural backwater should have anything to do with her, or her career. The dissertation was done, she thought. Now it appeared the dissertation was undone.

"By a weasel," she said, shaking her head.

"That's no way to talk about Professor Reeves," Otto added, trying to solicit a smile from Kelsey.

"Fucking weasel," she added, oblivious to Otto's attempt at levity. "I think I'll grab a jelly jar and join you," she said.

* * * *

She had a drink coming. The whole graduate school experience had been a tough slog for Kelsey, Otto knew. First her relationship blows up and her partner leaves her, her son develops severe asthma and she ends up doing most of her class prep in the emergency room in the middle of the night, she's stuck spending any free nights and weekends working on her dissertation, and just when the finish line—and some relief—is in sight, it all gets yanked away. By a fucking weasel.

* * * *

She leaned against Otto's shoulder and closed her eyes. He stroked her hair and whispered to her that it would be all right. If only she could believe that.

"So what should I do," she asked, pulling back and looking at him. "Tell me, Otto. What should I do?"

Otto patted her on the check and shook his head sympathetically.

"Girlfriend, you been set up on a blind date with Milton Indiana," he said, grabbing her shoulders and staring directly into her eyes. "And that's one date you got to keep."

In the wake of Otto's departure—he was too dramatic a figure to ever just leave a place, it was always a "departure"—Kelsey sat there, almost as stunned as she had been after meeting with Dr. Reeves.

Is Otto out of his mind? Why do people keep telling me to go to Indiana? I'm trying to write a dissertation and get a job and raise my kid and live my life. She took another sip from the jelly jar she sometimes used as a glass and the whisky warmed her mouth and her throat and she exhaled loudly. Stretching across the sofa, she felt light-headed.

Lots of people are pouring me drinks today. Maybe I'm supposed to get drunk.

She closed her eyes tightly and began to drift off. In a few minutes she was on the water again. This time she was floating on a raft. She could feel the bamboo timbers under her head and her spine and she was lazily hanging a leg over the side, her foot and knee lulling in the cool, clear water, swinging gently like a fleshy rudder. Her eyes were closed but she knew it was sunny; ghosts of shuttered sunlight flitted across the insides of her eyelids. *I could drift here forever*, she felt. There was no sound except her own breathing, deep and restful.

Her mind was empty. As the raft drifted, she felt herself drift further and further from awareness to a kind of lost and dreamy state, and her cares evaporated with the mist nuzzling the surface of the lake. The sunlight caressed her cheeks and her arms and she felt a drowsy splendor that was new and familiar at the same time, the surreal gift of her dream state on the water. She'd heard people talk of "inner peace" her whole life, and she'd even read books about it, and once she took a class at the local YMCA that promised the prospect of just such peace, but it was not to be found there. Not for her. But now here it was, languorous and splendid and dreamy. It seemed like it would never end.

Beneath the surface of the water, just beyond the arc of her gentle swaying foot, it waited, angular snout and razor teeth creating the appearance of a bloodthirsty smile. Its matted fur looked like rows of spiny armor, and its tiny hand-like paws seemed almost human. Kelsey's foot moved, barely, and the water rodent treaded the tide, imperceptible.

Then it struck.

Kelsey gasped for breath, unable even to scream despite the currents of pain pulsating below her knee. The creature's dual rows of teeth had seized onto her flesh with a fierce chomp and were now sawing away slowly toward the mass of bone beneath. Kelsey sat up with a violent jerk, trying to pull her leg up out of the water and onto the raft, but she couldn't budge it. Tears and sweat mixed with a crimson backwash as the creature continued his assault. Kelsey felt weak from the pain and saw in the water her life's blood coating the timbers of the raft and tinting the oily fur of her attacker. The thing bit down even harder now, and the last thing Kelsey remembered was pulling her leg out of the water and confronting a limb vacant from the ankle down. Her foot had been severed, devoured and still the creature was unsatisfied, gnawing now with muted squeals on the raft itself, tearing through the timbers like a circular saw spitting wood dust. Bamboo pulp and blood and flesh and fur mingled in a viscous vortex, and the raft began to disintegrate. Kelsey continued to scream and clutch and bat at the creature, which continued to gnaw and gag on the wood and bone clogging its gullet.

Before she lost consciousness, Kelsey squinted through the deathly tumult and saw, with perfect clarity, the grinning face of a creature she knew well. It was the classic profile, at least as the books presented it, of the Indiana Corn Weasel.

She woke up, her heart still beating wildly. She knew exactly where she was but she still looked down at her feet and counted her toes: there were ten. Her breathing relaxed a bit but the sweat was still beading on her forehead. As she calmed down, she stared up at the ceiling and sighed to herself in disbelief, then muttered, "Now *you're* after me, too."

Maybe it was a sign. Kelsey's research had introduced her to myriad folk customs that believed profoundly that dreams were omens, prophecies of things to come—good and evil.

Maybe this dream is a prophecy and I should shred the chapter on the Indiana Corn Weasel like he just shredded my raft and be done with it, forever. The academic in her turned over the parts of her dream, one by one. Maybe, she reasoned, the raft represented graduate school, a place where she always felt slightly out-of-place, a pretender. Maybe the dream was a sign that her attempt to become Doctor Kelsey Kane was doomed, destined to be washed away like so much driftwood. Or maybe it was a dare, a subconscious challenge to uncover the depths of truth at play in the cornfields of the Hoosier state.

Her analytical reverie was interrupted when Justin bounded out of his room and landed on the sofa next to her. He stared at his mother, squinting.

"Whatcha looking at, Spinner?"

"When I grow up, will I be as pretty as you?"

"Well, boys don't grow up to be 'pretty.'"

Justin thought for a moment.

"What about Otto?"

Kelsey laughed to herself.

That's a good point.

"Otto is an exceptional case."

Justin seemed satisfied. He molded himself into the bend in her elbow and put his head on her shoulder.

"I'll always be here for you, kiddo," she whispered. "You always be here for me too, okay?" She choked back a few tears and kissed his wispy, straw-colored hair.

"Where you go, I go," he said, crossing his arms. Kelsey liked the sound of that. But she wondered if he'd really be happy following her to the place she felt herself inexorably being drawn to, like a piece of driftwood surrendered to the tide.

Chapter 2

"Nope, sorry. No copies of the *Milton Forum*," the portly middle-aged man in the checkered shirt told her. "It's just not important enough."

"Well it's becoming pretty important to me," Kelsey muttered, more to herself than the librarian. "You don't have a single copy?"

"Miss Kane, you've spent enough time around here to know how it works. If a publication is deemed to be of sufficient academic interest, we'll make it available, either in print or on microfiche. We simply don't have the resources—or the space—to catalog every newspaper in the country. To tell you the truth, it's the first time I've even heard of Milton, Indiana."

"Yeah. Sorry, Mr. Klausen," Kelsey said. "I didn't mean to get snippy."

He patted her hand the way he'd done so many other times before when Kelsey was facing an I-NEED-IT-NOW! crisis. He spared her the speech about how lack of planning on her part didn't constitute an emergency on his part. Mr. Klausen liked Kelsey. She might have been impatient, but it was the impatience of the learner, rather than that of some arrogant snot who thought a couple of graduate courses made them better than the "moles." That was the grad students' nicknames for the library staff.

"Nothing on the internet?"

"Nothing I need. Just the homepage of their offices. No back issues."

"Well, I could contact an affiliated library. Let's see," he said, the scrolling of lighted text reflected in the spectacles yoked to the folds of his sharpei-like neck by a thin chain. "Hmmm. Not familiar with… Okay, here we are. There's a library in South Bend that has copies of the *Milton Forum*. Would you like me to make a request?"

"How long would it take?"

"Well, if they have to make microfiches, it might be three, four weeks."

Kelsey shook her head. "Thanks anyway. This is kind of a rush job."

"What, in the last three years, has not been a rush job, Ms. Kane?" he said, peering over the tops of his eyeglasses, head cocked slightly. But then his prosecutorial gaze softened. "Let me know if there's something else I can assist you with."

Prowling around down here in the grad school library would be one of the things Kelsey would truly miss—if she ever managed to graduate. It was here in this musty catacomb of learning that Kelsey Kane began her re-birth as a scholar. From the almost-accidental withdrawal of a few books on mythic creatures and folklore—someone had taken out the books on the topic she had originally come in search of, linguistic patterns of rural Appalachian peoples—a new life had begun for her. It might not have been an annunciation worthy of the fabled phoenix but it offered her a path she'd never expected to travel, a life she was still trying to imagine. As Mr. Klausen told her at the end of her orientation tour of the library several years ago, she wouldn't be leaving the way she came in. It took Kelsey a little while to catch his drift.

Having concluded that a trip to Indiana was unavoidable, she was now trying to re-capture some of the zeal that had drawn her to graduate study in the first place.

She'd already told Dr. Reeves—"Never doubted you for a moment!" he announced—and had begun making preparations to take a leave of absence from her teaching assignment, to sublet her apartment, and to get all of Justin's medical records in case she needed to keep him with her for a longer period of time than she expected. She thought briefly about how she might go to Indiana without disrupting his life too, but she couldn't think of a single option that would allow her to leave him behind.

For a fleeting moment, she thought of Justin's father, but even registering that thought made her wince, a psychological shooting pain jabbing her memory. Kelsey had met him while she was still trying to find herself, working as a waitress in a small music club and bar in lower Manhattan. He was a keyboard player in a neo-psychedelic band called *Boot the Gong*. He turned Kelsey on to both hashish and Hendrix. They had a tumultuous tear through a three-month relationship while the band played a circuit of music clubs in the Northeast. But when the smoke cleared, Kelsey discovered he was no more committed to her than he was to any of the other drug-addled groupies he'd met before she came along. Once his band was booked for a series of West Coast concerts, she knew she'd never see him again. And she was prepared to let him go, she thought. End on a high note, part friends, stay in touch, all those other clichés derived from the triumph of hope over sense. She really did think they could make a clean break. But then she made the mistake of telling him her next move.

"I think I want to go back to school," she said hopefully, on the last afternoon they ever saw each other as he disassembled his keyboard equipment, packing it away into gig bags. She was hoping he'd say something to make her feel affirmed in this decision, something like what she'd said to him every night as he came off the stage. True, Kelsey didn't immediately appear to be academic material, but she'd grown tired of watching a parade of bands night after night at the club where she worked, driving crowds into a frenzy, realizing their dreams while she stood on the sideline, bar towel in hand, flailing.

He looked over his sunglasses at her and said the thing she'd never forgotten: "I've played a lot of colleges, Kelsey. Trust me—this," he said with a sweeping gesture that took in the empty bar room, "is a much better fit for you."

Even if she did have other options, she knew she simply couldn't stand to be away from Justin. She'd rather not even finish the dissertation if it meant being away from her son for any length of time. That's how it was between them, for better or worse. And when she told Justin the news, he reacted exactly as she hoped.

"Sounds fun, Mommy!"

Kid's got a weird sense of fun, she thought as she hugged her excited little boy, lifting him off the ground. *And where we're going he's going to need it.*

* * * *

She'd hoped to see Otto before they left for Indiana but he was away, delivering a paper at an academic conference in Orlando, Florida. "Going down there to work on my tan!" he'd joked with her before he left. The past week had been a blur. What normally would have been filled with back-to-school preparations for her, and for Justin, was spent making plans to relocate her life eight hundred miles west. She'd made arrangements with Justin's school to remove him for an unspecified period of "guided study," a sort of home-school protocol that would satisfy the school board when he eventually returned. Kelsey was relieved they'd been able to work things out, but in truth, this new arrangement wouldn't be too terribly different from what happened last school year. After Justin's asthma worsened, he was forced to miss almost a month of school, and Kelsey was forced to juggle. But in some ways, it was easier to have him home: no lunches to pack, no buses to run for, no pickup to arrange for after school. Any concerns she might have had about the impact of all those missed school days vanished early last year, when she discovered that her son loved to spend his free time, most of all, with a book in his hands. Justin was a natural lover of learning, and he seemed just as able to keep up with his schoolwork at home, on his own, as he did at school.

As she packed up the last of her suitcases and prepared for the long train ride the next morning, she decided to call Otto—mostly because she really needed someone to talk to. Everything had happened so fast, and she was still feeling rather unwound. Otto had a way of making the tumultuous seem normal.

"Hello, sweetie!" he shouted to her, picking up his cell on the first ring.

"Hi, Otto. Sorry to bother you—especially when you're working so hard," she said sarcastically amid the throbbing music and discordant chatter in the background.

"You have no idea how draining these kinds of events can be," he countered.

"Yeah, I'll bet. What's the panel you're currently attending? How to solve the crisis in anthropology studies one martini at the time?"

"Oh, Kelsey Kat, you wound me. Here I am, trying to advance the cause of human knowledge, and you just...hold on a minute..." She heard him say, "Hello there! Cocktail weenie person! Over here, please!" There was a pause, and then Kelsey heard a muffled "Thank you…and more champagne please!" before he resumed their conversation. She realized he was talking to a waiter.

"The lengths you go to stay on top of your discipline, Otto, are truly impressive."

"The study of man is a tireless pursuit, sweetie. But what am I telling you? You're about to embark on a pretty fierce pursuit of your own."

"Yep. Sure am," she said, trying to muster enthusiasm

but betrayed by her own serious misgivings about whether this was really the right thing to do. Otto picked up on her anxiety.

"You listen to me, Kelsey soon-to-be-doctor Kane. Everything is going to work out. Wanna know a secret? I'm envious, girl. You're going to have a real adventure! And when it's all over, and you catch your weasel, and you defend your dissertation, we'll go out and get rip-roaringly drunk. Even Spinner!"

Kelsey laughed.

"Thanks, Otto."

"You bet. Good luck in those cornfields—and don't forget to spend all of your grant money!"

Given the fairly small grant Dr. Reeves was able to cobble together at the last minute, Kelsey didn't think she'd have any problems achieving that. But she played along.

"Might be hard, Otto. Not much to do in Indiana except sit around and watch the corn grow, I suppose."

She waited, but there was no reaction from Otto—he'd disappeared into the ether. The silence was jarring and felt a little lonely. They had been abruptly cut off. It was an awkward reminder of how quickly a void can consume what once seemed so inviolable.

* * * *

In 1852, a decade before the Civil War severed the fabric of national unity, an escaped slave named Cedric Horne fought his way north from his plantation in Savannah, Georgia. Guided only by his survival instincts, and his fear, he somehow managed to evade packs of hunting dogs and posses of slave-chasing—well, they were really chasing profits—white men, as well as the elements encountered over the unforgiving terrains of swamps, forests, and swollen rivers. In an odyssey that took him several months, begun in blistering heat and ending in bitter snow squalls and punishing cold, Cedric Horne persevered. In the few stolen quiet moments on the plantation, as he dreamed of freedom, he'd heard stories from his fellow captives about other escaped slaves and their quests, and his spirit was buoyed by tales of a so-called "underground railroad" that gave aid, comfort, and shelter to runaways just like him. If there were such places, such people, he felt obligated to try to seek them out. As his trek north, which began on August 14th—the date his mother, who had long since been sold to a slave owner in Richmond, Virginia, had told him was his birthday—unfolded, he was dejected to discover the reports seemed to be false. He couldn't find aid and comfort anywhere. The signs he expected to find—secret markings along the highway, rocks positioned into arrows along well-worn paths through the woods, even celestial signs guiding his journey, were absent. The more Cedric stared up into the night sky, scouring the heavens for the fabled "drinking gourd," the more he just saw a bunch of stars, luminous but random.

Except for one: the North Star. That was his compass. He reasoned that as long as he kept heading north, he'd eventually make it to one of the free states. He learned to hide himself by day, often buried in leaves, twigs, and mud until the dusk, when he would begin anew his adventure, guided by the North Star and his faith in God—a faith that would be even more severely tested than it was on the plantation. Cedric Horne believed in a loving God, a God who answers prayers. And just when Cedric seemed on the verge of starvation, a rabbit or a wild turkey would appear in the woods, and Cedric would have food for another few days. And just when thirst threatened to claim him before the slave-chasers and the hound dogs could, Cedric would stumble blindly upon a hidden lake, stream, or small pond. As he pounded his way north, his faith in the underground railroad diminished but his faith in God almost never wavered.

After several more months of fearful struggle, and after a particularly grueling few weeks trying to survive amid snowfalls and early evening deep-freezes, Cedric, exhausted and debilitated by the pangs of hunger, was now showing the dire and predictable symptoms of malnutrition, as well as frostbite and infection from a deep gash suffered when the spike of a rusted rotor plow hidden under the snow pierced the flesh on the underside of his foot. Cedric, more worried that the blood drops would give away his position than about any possible medical consequences, had at last concluded that perhaps God had not wanted him to survive after all. Pushing blindly ahead in no particular direction, and asking God to please have mercy on his soul when he died, Cedric was granted a vision of a farmhouse in a clearing. Unsure where he was—he had no idea if he was still in slave territory or he'd made it to a free state—he concluded that he had no other options. He had to approach the farmhouse. Putting his fate in the merciful hands of Jesus, as well as whomever was likely to answer the door, Cedric waited until dusk, and then dragged himself across a slumbering cornfield, praying earnestly that the Lord would provide, oh please Lord, provide for thee.

Cedric looked in the window. A gas lamp flickered inside. Outside the house was a lone cow, and what looked like a couple of donkeys tied to a post in a small, fenced-off stable next to the house. Behind the house was a small barn. The rest was darkness.

The runaway slave took a deep breath, said one more silent prayer, and knocked on the door.

"Who the hell's that?" bellowed a slurred voice.

Please God Please God Please God, thought Cedric.

The door swung open, and standing there was a man holding a jug of corn liquor and a shotgun.

"I said, who the hell are you?"

Cedric quavered, unable to speak. He looked at the gun, and his thoughts evaporated. He said the only thing he could thing of: Psalm 23. Falling to his knees, he clasped his hands and began reciting what he expected to be his final words.

"Though I walk through the valley of the shadow of death, I fear no evil for thou art with me…"

The man was almost as speechless as Cedric.

"Bless my Soul!" he said. "A Christian pilgrim, right here at my door! Come in, my son!" He wrapped his arms around Cedric, lifting him up, and pulling him into his house.

"Here you go!" He offered Cedric the jug of corn liquor. Cedric took a tiny sip. Then, looking to see if it was okay, took another."

"Good lord, man, drink up! You a mess! Let's get you some vittles!"

And the man, who said his name was Julius Augustus Milton, made Cedric supper. It wasn't much: some potatoes, a little corn mash, some salted beef, but Cedric ate it with tears in his eyes and disbelief swelling his heart. Over the next few hours, Cedric revealed himself to this good and Christian host, and the gentleman farmer-merchant offered Cedric every hospitality. Food, drink, medicine, and a warm bed in which to begin his recovery.

Over the next week, Julius Augustus Milton oversaw the resurrection of Cedric Horne's body. The host went into town and purchased clothes and medical supplies for Cedric, and he fixed up a small room in his house for the former slave in case anyone came to visit the farm house unexpectedly.

"Even in Indiana, you coloreds gotta watch out for yourselves," the older man told Cedric.

Indiana—a free state! I made it!

Thoughts of his extremely uncertain future were pushed out by thoughts of his immediate present. But Julius Augustus Milton, a self-professed Christian man, assured Cedric he would take care of everything. "You juss get your body back to where it was 'fore you made it out of them swamps of Georgia."

* * * *

After about ten days, Cedric's condition had improved substantially. He offered to help with chores around the farm, but his offer was declined.

"No, son, you still need to rest," he was told. "Soon enough you'll be able to work. Ain't no need to go rush. Like the good book says, patience is a virtue," said the older man, between spits of his plug tobacco.

And Julius Augustus Milton's patience was about to pay off. At the end of the second week, after sunset, three men visited the farmhouse. As they made their way across the still-heavy blanket of snow on the ground, Cedric reacted with alarm, but he was told not to worry. "I know these men. They're good Christian people." But he said Cedric could wait in the room they had fixed up for him if he wanted to. After the men came in, there was the usual talk about crops and the weather, and the passing of the jug, and then a knock upon the secret room door.

"Come on out here, Cedric. Some people I want you to meet."

Cedric stepped cautiously across the threshold.

"Come on. They ain't gonna bite."

As Cedric advanced, the other three men got up out of their chairs, and each reached out to shake Cedric's hand. "Ain't he got a strong grip!" one of the men noted to the other two. They sat back down, still sizing him up, as they rocked slowly, Cedric still standing amid them, feeling awkward and uncertain about what to do next.

"You done a good job, Julius," said one of the men. "He's in fine shape."

"Course he is. Shoulda seen him when he got here—nothing but skin and bones!" he said, and they all laughed a little. "But as you can see, I done fattened him up."

"Done a real good job," said one of the other men.

The rules to this game I simply don't know, Cedric conceded to himself. He turned to tell his host he was going to return to his room when he was shocked to see a shotgun barrel aimed directly at his heart.

"Cedric, these men here come to get you, take you back to Savannah, Georgia. I'd be right smart and do what they say, lessen you wanna die right here at my fireplace." The three men then pounced at him, punching him and kneeing him and forcing him onto the ground, tying him up with rough-hewn hemp rope so he couldn't move his arms or legs. After the brief struggle, Julius Augustus Milton walked up to Cedric and spat in his face.

"Running away from a good Christian master!" he said, shaking his head. "What an evil and ungrateful sinner you are. Cedric I hope this Christian charity I done showed you these last two weeks will profit you. I know for sure," he said, looking around the room at the merry faces of the other men and smiling broadly, "it sure gonna profit me!"

* * * *

It did, handsomely. There was money to be made returning fugitive slaves to their masters. Most of the time, what the plantation owner got back was worth a fraction of what he lost—but not in Cedric's case. He was rested and fattened up and commanded a tidy reward upon his return. An entrepreneur, Julius Augustus Milton made money any way he could—corn liquor, horse thieving, selling bogus property claims. And now he could add slave trading. In the years leading up to the civil war, as this Northeast parcel of the Free State of Indiana welcomed Mennonites, itinerant farmers, fugitives from the law, cattlemen, soldiers, and railroad workers, it seemed there was always somebody new to take advantage of. "The Lord tells us to prepare the way for the Kingdom. I 'spose I'm just trying to bring the Kingdom a little closer, is all," Julius used to say.

Over the decades, he built a small kingdom. When the Civil War hit, he sold corn liquor to the Union Troops and fugitive Confederate soldiers to the U.S. Government. By 1870, he'd amassed an impressive amount of wealth and property. And when the Mennonite leaders who represented the largest population of the region decided to build a church, it was Julius Augustus Milton who provided the funds.

"Always happy to do my Christian duty," he proclaimed at the dedication of the cornerstone.

In gratitude, the elders of the Church agreed to name their newly incorporated town after their benefactor: Milton, Indiana.

* * * *

Kelsey wouldn't find Cedric Horne's story in the official history of Milton—or even in the unofficial history she'd been able to cobble together over the past week. The thin file folder Dr. Reeves had given her with a few articles about the alleged corn weasel attacks was now stuffed with lots of scholarly odds and ends: photocopied maps, articles downloaded from the internet about the history of Indiana, a cheesy brochure from the Indiana State Tourism and Visitors' Bureau— "Hoosier best bet for vacation fun? We are!"—notes rescued from her dissertation-writing days about the behavior of weasels, a few pages from the Old Farmer's Almanac, and the name and phone number of a real estate agent provided by Dr. Reeves, who cautioned Kelsey that *"apparently, there's not a great deal to choose from, shelter-wise."* These scraps offered some hints of what she was headed toward, but hints only—nothing substantive. As the train pressed westward and as Justin pressed up against her, Kelsey poured over these disparate pieces of paper, aware that even if she knew how to arrange them, they wouldn't form much of a picture.

She again began to feel the tug of insecurity. It wasn't supposed to be like this. After years of graduate study she was supposed to have reached a comfort level in life, the reassurance of her presumed expertise. When she taught her classes she generally felt confident, and if she wasn't a certifiable expert yet, she certainly knew enough to impress a classroom full of undergrads. Even in her discussions with her fellow grad students, or with Dr.

Reeves, she often felt a warm surge of relevance, of genuine belonging. The tentative apprentice who couldn't figure out the grad library's classification system, or didn't know the difference between a "bibliography" and a "works cited" page had gradually been supplanted by a seasoned scholar. She'd thought her days of having to fake a sense of confidence were over but with every mile further she felt like all she knew was dissipating, disappearing into the prairies whose barren stalks and grasses offered only a bleak, teasing promise of welcome.

"Kelsey, this is a terrific opportunity!"

Dr. Reeves had seemed so genuinely excited for her. Otto too. And her fellow graduate students actually congratulated her—as if she'd done something commendable. At the informal going-away party they hastily threw for her in the grad student lounge, she realized how much she'd come to enjoy the academic life—or at least life on the fringes of academia. The rest would come later. She flattered herself thinking that she even belonged among such intellectually ambitious people. But when she opened the gift they gave her—a corn cob pipe and a pair of denim overalls—she realized they knew as little about Indiana as she did, falling back on cheap, retread stereotypes of the rural Midwest.

She mentally ran through the litany of reasons—well rehearsed by now—that she *ought* to be more excited: here was a chance to do ground-breaking research, finish her dissertation, maybe even make a name for herself in the world of crypto-zoology. Besides, she'd never had the time or money to travel, and though it wasn't exactly Disney World, at least it was someplace. Justin deserved a vacation—even if it was just Milton, Indiana. A bright kid like him ought to see the world, she thought.

Okay, so I'm going to show him some of it, and together we'll make it an adventure. And if he's bored or offput by the whole Midwest experience, well then perhaps he'll have a new appreciation for his New Jersey roots.

Really, what is there to lose by doing this?

Outside the train, cool autumn winds massaged tree limbs as the moon rose over wide open fields. Kelsey knew she should try to sleep. Justin had no trouble falling asleep in his berth, lulled by the rhythmic swaying of the rail cars rolling through the night. She looked down at her son and wondered what he might be dreaming about. After she told Justin that they'd be taking this trip, he reacted like she'd just told him they were going to the corner to mail a letter. "Okay, let's go," he said. That was it. They talked a little bit about why they had to go, but Justin didn't seem bothered in the least that their lives were about to be completely disrupted.

Boy, I wish I could be like that, Kelsey thought.

She stared outside the train window and saw her own anxious glance reflected in the glass. In a few hours, they'd be pulling into the train station in South Bend, Indiana, and then they'd clamber onto a bus headed south, past small towns with storybook names and honest-to-goodness main streets. Wouldn't it be funny if she and Justin ended up liking it there? Kelsey never imagined she'd live anywhere but the city. There was too much she loved, too much she depended on. If she wanted to order Chinese food at three in the morning, she could. "I wonder if they even have Chinese food in Milton?" she said aloud, amused at the question.

Well, if that's my biggest problem, I guess things might not be too bad, she reasoned.

Propping her jacket between the window and her head, she closed her eyes and tried to clear her mind.

Better get a few hours of sleep at least, she concluded. *Life might be a lot slower there, but we have much to do when we arrive.*

She reached out, put her hand on her son's foot, closed her eyes, imagined she smelled a plate of Kung Pao chicken, and gave herself over to the cold quiet of the night....

* * * *

"Mommy, wake up! The man says we're here!"

Can't be morning already. Can't be.

Kelsey squinted, blinked away the night, and found Justin's beaming face welcoming her to Indiana.

"We're here? Really?" She half-stretched, and then twisted around to look outside. The train had indeed stopped, and a skinny conductor with a handlebar moustache was walking through the corridor of cars, shouting, "South Bend! Station stop South Bend!"

"Come on, Mommy!"

Justin tugged at her with mock ferocity. But his enthusiasm was just what she needed—that, and about sixteen ounces of strong black coffee. Before she knew it, they had disembarked from the train and were climbing aboard a bus. They found a seat in the back, and Justin took the window side. While he stared out at the rolling landscape, Kelsey rifled again through her notes. She found the number of the real estate agent Dr. Reeves had told her about, and she took out her cell phone and called the number. Before the phone even rang, she was re-directed to voice mail.

"Umm, hi. This is Kelsey Kane. I'm the graduate student Dr. Reeves told you about, I think. My son and I are here, in Indiana, and anyway, we're headed to Milton. We'll be there in about…um…actually, I'm not sure. Hold on a second." She turned to the passenger across the aisle from her, a young man in his early twenties, in military fatigues, and asked him how long the ride would take.

"Hour, thereabouts," he said without any detectable emotion.

"Okay, thanks. Hello? Hi. Sorry. We'll be at the bus station in about an hour, and then we'll hop a cab to Milton, so I'd say around ten. I'll call you when we get there. Thanks again for your help. We really need it, by the way. My son and I have no place to stay." She ended the call and joined Justin as he stared out the window, gauging the suitability of his new, temporary home.

"What d'ya think, Spinner?"

"Look at that, Mommy! Cows right here in the city!"

Sure enough, there was a pasture, and a picturesque farmhouse, only minutes away from the bus station.

"Sure, cows. What did you think we're gonna see here, kiddo?"

He leaned in and whispered, mischievously: "Weasels!"

Kelsey laughed and hugged her son.

"With luck, maybe we'll see some," she confided to him, and then leaned in and said, also in a whisper: "I know a special weasel call. Makes them come right to your door!"

"You do *not*!" he said, laughing. That's how they passed the rest of the ride, staring out the window together, Justin looking for weasels, Kelsey scouting for Chinese restaurants.

In less than an hour, the bus rolled into Warburg, a town about ten miles from Milton. Kelsey had hoped to arrange to have a taxi waiting in advance of their arrival, but no one at the bus station seemed particularly aware of how to go about that. So when they got off the bus, Kelsey scanned the depot for taxi cabs. She didn't see any, but a leather-jacketed man noticed her looking around, and he approached.

"Need a ride, Missy?"

He was a surprising candidate for a taxi cab driver. An elderly man, skeleton slim, with a New Testament jutting out of his pocket, he offered her his hand. Somewhat taken aback, she took it.

"Milton, Indiana?" she inquired.

"It's where I live," he said, picking up her luggage and carrying it around to the trunk of his car. "Have you there in time for morning services. Yours?" he asked, pointing to Justin.

"Spinner, c'mon. Our ride is here."

The man scrunched up his face, inspecting Justin over his bi-focals.

"You her husband?"

Justin giggled.

"Get you there before you know it, Missy. Name's Chester, by the way."

"Hi, Chester. I'm Kelsey. That's Justin."

"A pleasure, master Justin. Climb aboard."

And with that, the beat-up, makeshift taxi belched into gear and wended its way through the barren landscape of northeast Indiana. Chester, a retired welder who now spent his time ferrying the occasional passenger between bus stations, lit a cigarette and blew plumes of smoke through the small gap in the window as farm houses and corn fields raced by.

"You got kin in Milton? Not too many tourists come round here."

"Nope. Just visiting," Kelsey said.

"My mommy's here to see the weasel!" said Justin, innocently.

Chester's demeanor changed, and he pulled the car over abruptly, idling the cab on a gravelly shoulder. He threw his cigarette out the window, then turned to them in the back seat, fixing them with an icy glare.

"You don't want to be jokin' about that," he said, with a look to match his threatening tone. "You folks ain't from around here, so take a little friendly advice: Don't be thinking about poking around where you don't belong." His bony, nicotine-stained finger shook as he pointed first to Kelsey, and then to Justin, frightening him. "Sure would hate for anything to happen to good Christian folks like you." His face churned from a rather stern scowl to an indulgent half-smile. Still, it unnerved Kelsey. "You folks are Christian, aren't cha?"

Kelsey wasn't sure how to respond. She didn't want to lie in front of her son, who hadn't seen the inside of a church since they ducked into one during a surprise rainstorm a few years ago. He loved the stained glass, but said he thought the place "smelled funny". Yet here they were, hostaged on the side of a lonely road in rural Indiana.

What if he only transports Christians? What then? Will we have to walk the rest of the way?

Justin looked up at her, expectantly.

Kelsey reached out and patted the man's hand. "You won't find two people more devout in their beliefs than us," she said, reassuringly. He seemed mollified, and he turned forward to put the car in drive and resume the journey. Kelsey winked at Justin, and they both settled back, still somewhat anxious. Kelsey wanted to ask more questions about the weasel, and she guessed Justin would too—but they both kept silent, except for occasional nudges of acknowledgement as they passed a picturesque grain silo or corral of horses.

If there was a "Welcome to Milton" sign, Kelsey missed it. Chester turned the car into the parking lot of a bait and tackle store and then turned to them, announcing in hushed tones, as if imparting some piece of secret wisdom: "You've been delivered." Justin bolted from the car as soon as they came to a stop, obviously eager to check out the local attractions, but Kelsey lingered for a moment. She wanted to ask Chester some questions about the Indiana Corn Weasel. He seemed just like the kind of "folk" who could shed some insights into folk beliefs. The old man seemed to sense what was on Kelsey's mind, and he beat her to the punch.

"It don't care who you are, Missy," he said, his mournful, aged eyes softened a bit by a reflection of the morning light. "It don't care what you know. Ain't no amount of education gonna protect you," he said, holding her with his gaze. "Or him," he said, nodding toward Justin, who was busy pressing the buttons of a bait vending machine.

Kelsey was briefly stunned.

How does he know I'm a graduate student?

And then she remembered he helped her with her bags.

He must have noticed my laptop computer and notebooks among the bags when he loaded up the trunk. Of course.

"It just don't care," he said again to her, slowly, directly. And then, as if some spell had suddenly broken, his whole expression changed, and he bounded out of the car with a vigor that belied his age. He removed her suitcases and backpacks and closed his trunk. Kelsey dug in her pocketbook to pay the fare, but as she turned around to ask how much the ride was, Chester was already back behind the wheel, the car suddenly peeling off at a high rate of speed, heading back the way they came. She caught a glimpse of the old man's bony hand waving as he drove away. One cab ride: no charge, with a little free advice thrown in.

"What's wrong, Mommy," said Justin, noting the troubled look on his mother's face.

"Nothing, Spinner. It's just—he wouldn't take any money for the ride."

"Wouldn't take any money?"

"No," she said, shrugging it off and starting to collect her belongings off the ground. "I guess it's true, Spinner—Midwesterners are just more willing to help out than we're used to."

They gathered their stuff into a small pile near the entrance to the bait store, and Justin climbed on top. Kelsey took out her cell phone and called the real estate agent. This time, the agent picked up right away.

"We're here," Kelsey announced. "We're homeless, and tired, and hungry, but we made it." She looked over at Justin and shot him a thumbs up, which he returned from atop their small mountain of belongings. The agent said she would swing round to pick them up. Ryerson's Bait and Tackle was only two minutes from the real estate office, the agent said, so don't get too comfortable, she cautioned. Kelsey looked around at the gravel parking lot, the vending machine that dispensed yogurt-sized containers filled with live grubs and nightcrawlers, and her son, sprawled across all of their worldly belongings they felt they'd need to survive here.

No chance of that happening.

Sure enough, before Justin had a chance to steal enough change from his mother's purse to purchase a small bucket of bloodworms, a ruby red pickup truck rolled into the parking lot.

"You must be Kelsey—and Justin," said the polyester pant-suited, forty-something blonde woman walking across the parking lot.

"Right. That's us. You must be Mrs. Langston."

"Patsy, please."

"Okay. Thanks for coming to get us."

"Oh, it's no problem—I've got a great place picked out for you. We can swing by and look at it, and if you like it, you can sign the papers."

"Well, you know we're just here for a little while."

Patsy waved away Kelsey's concerns. "It's an old converted barn—but don't let that scare you. It's really quite nice."

"All right! We're living in a *barn*!" Justin blurted.

"Not so fast, Spinner. We have to take a look at it."

"I've seen it—it's lovely," Patsy affirmed.

"What are the terms?"

"Well, as I mentioned to you, it's pretty tough to find sublets around here. Most folks, when they decide to give up a property, they just put it on the market, sell it, and they move on. But I'll tell you, there's not much of that, even. People come, they stay. I don't handle much here in Milton. In the trade, this is known as an 'extremely static' market. Very little turnaround. That's why I was so excited to find this property."

"Sounds intriguing," Kelsey said.

"Very intriguing," said Justin, crossing his arms and mimicking his mother's tone. Patsy laughed.

"Aren't you quite the little...well, I don't know what!"

Trying to remain open-minded, Kelsey imagined an elegant and historic façade giving way to a fully functional living space: Town and Country classic, with a touch of modernism. It could work, perhaps.

It's only for a little while—and Justin loves the idea of living in a barn.

When they pulled up to the property ("Just a minute's drive from Main Street—or a nice country walk, depending," Patsy offered somewhat enigmatically), Kelsey said the only thing that she could think of: "It's a barn, all right."

And so it was. The outside of the structure lacked any of her hoped-for pastoral charm—it looked quite shabby, actually, as if a good stiff wind could sweep it away, scattering its unpainted, weather-beaten boards across the adjoining field. But the inside was a little surprising. The actual living space was much smaller than one would expect—the interior had been framed out to accommodate no more than two or three people. There was a separate bedroom, but it had no door, and it was difficult to determine where the living room ended and the kitchen began. But the place was clean, at least, and surprisingly warm.

"I expected something draftier," Kelsey confessed.

"The owners of the property, the Millers, converted this space for an elderly relative, Eileen Miller's mother," Patsy said. "That's where they've gone, to her home for a couple of months. When they all come back, she'll live here. And Eileen insisted that this be the warmest residence on the whole property. It's triple insulated. That's means no drafts—and believe me, it can get pretty cold and windy in these fields."

There was running water and electricity and heat and

even an old-style rotary phone. Kelsey picked it up. There was no dial tone. The bathroom tile was two or three generations out of date, and the clawfoot tub was so old it was now stylish.

"I don't mean to pressure you, but given your price range, this is about as well as we're going to do."

A barn on a farm in the middle of nowhere. That's the best we're gonna do.

"What d'ya think, Spinner?"

"If you're looking for weasels, a barn seems like a good place to live," he said.

Patsy was startled by his wit. "How old is he, did you say?"

"Seven."

"My goodness. I'll have to remember that about weasels. The girls at work will get a kick out of that. Isn't he precious! So, shall we sign the papers?"

They spent the rest of the day unpacking.

Chapter 3

By nighttime, they were exhausted but at least a little more settled. Kelsey had commandeered a couple of unused planks she found lying outside the barn and turned them into bookshelves, the centerpiece in her new makeshift workspace. Justin had unpacked most of his stuff as well and he seemed content—no, he seemed really *happy*—with the new arrangements. But Kelsey felt they could both use a bit of a break, so after a quick dinner of mac and cheese, they took a walk to explore, for the first time, what the locals called "Downtown."

It wasn't much to behold. Milton's population was barely more than a thousand people, and most of those were scattered among the farmhouses on the fringe of town. There were only about a dozen businesses along Main Street that Kelsey counted as she and Justin strolled along. The setting sun threw the shadow of the town's lone steeple across Main Street like a huge pointer, a shadowy partition dividing light from dark and the righteous from the evil.

On the same side of the street as the church was a diner, a flower shop, a pharmacy adjoining a doctor's office, an insurance agency, the Milton Town Hall, and set back from the street about a hundred feet, the public elementary school. Across the street was a trophy and sporting goods store with Little League uniforms hanging in the window, a small grocery store, a funeral parlor, a gas station, and further down the road, the bait and tackle shop that marked the beginning of the "business district." At the other end of the road was a small outpost of the country sheriff's office. About a quarter mile away was a huge grain and feed store, a farm supply depot, and, at the very outskirts of town, near the county line, a nearly-abandoned U.S. military base with a handful of cinder-block office buildings, a barracks, and some sort of medical facility. While researching Milton's history, she learned the base had been targeted for complete shutdown several times over the years, but it managed to survive with a skeleton detachment of civilian employees. During the Cold War, the military complex had been a thriving operation, boasting several thousand enlisted personnel and officers. Now it was, to all appearances, a heavily gated ghost-town.

She noticed some sort of commotion at the church. At first Kelsey thought it was a funeral, but who has a funeral at night? She and Justin crossed the street to get a little closer and see what was happening. There was a sign on the small patch of lawn in front of the Church, which was named "Jesus the Redeemer," listing the weekday and Sunday services. This building had long ago overtaken the Mennonite Church as the spiritual center of Milton, she would learn. But tonight something was happening there. Kelsey scanned the sign listing the services, but there was nothing special scheduled.

"Let's check it out, Spinner," Kelsey said. "And don't forget to make a wish." Kelsey couldn't remember who told her to always make a wish when you entered a new church, but the idea had somehow stuck with her.

"That's just superstition," Justin said.

"Of course it is," Kelsey said. "But let's check it out anyway."

Kelsey would have liked to survey the church without

any people in it, to have a chance to study the iconography and the architecture. But what she was now in the midst of offered her far greater opportunities for scholarly excavation: the good, God-fearing people of Milton, Indiana. She had stumbled upon an unscheduled service (convened, she later discovered, after an urgent petition of parishioners demanded somebody—namely, Minister Lawrence Croydon, spiritual leader of the congregation of Jesus the Redeemer church—do *something* about what was happening to their town).

Kelsey and Justin slid into one of the long wooden benches in the back row, still shrouded mostly in darkness. The lights hanging above the front half of the church were on dimly, and Kelsey could see that almost every space was taken. There was a slight draft, and Kelsey felt a little chilled sitting there waiting. Everyone sat attentively, expectantly, quietly, but Kelsey couldn't figure out what they were waiting for. Was this some sort of church committee meeting, perhaps to plan an upcoming bazaar or field trip? A meeting to discuss fund raising, or some rebuilding campaign? A memorial service for a recently deceased but dearly beloved longtime member of the church? A devotional of silent prayer and reflection?

Kelsey and Justin just sat there with all the others, removed but still a part of the gathering, allied with their new neighbors in anxious uncertainty. Kelsey was about to lean over and whisper to Justin that they'd leave if nothing happened soon, but before she could tell him anything, all the lights in the church went out, and they sat there in darkness and mild trepidation. For minutes it remained dark, and despite the size of the crowd, the church was remarkably silent. Kelsey held Justin's hand and they sat there waiting, scanning the dark for some clues as to what was happening, wondering what they had gotten themselves into. Were they supposed to be praying? Meditating? Chanting to themselves? Once again, Kelsey was preparing to get her son and head out the way she came when she noticed a pinprick of light coming from the front of the church. Barely visible, it wavered a bit, moving from the side of the church to the center. Fixing her gaze on the flicker, she realized it was a candle, a lone tiny flame struggling heroically to offset the vast darkness. Then there was another, and another, and soon a row of thirteen candles formed a small gateway of light. And now she could see the figure behind the light, or at least an outline, head and shoulders. As he moved closer to the light, she could make out the contours of his face, but just barely.

And then a voice disturbed the quiet.

"It is written that the righteous shall be tested, so that they shall stand known," stated a breathy, steady voice rising just above a whisper. The candles cast a dim halo, an azure arc of light framing the speaker, whose jaw and cheeks shone vaguely in the glare.

"And the agent that separates the evil from the Godly shall be fearful, and loud lamentations shall herald its arrival, and blood and tears shall soften the ground." The speaker paused, and those who filled the benches said not a word. Justin looked up at his mother in the darkness, and she put a finger to her pursed lips.

"My brothers and sisters in Christ, I believe I know your hearts tonight. I know your fear and doubt, I know your confusion. But you need no longer be confused, for the hand of the Lord bests the claw of the beast, and the tongue of the Holy Spirit is mightier than the jaws of the demon."

Still no one else in the congregation so much as murmured. Kelsey's eyes had begun to adjust to the dark, and she could see that the very few empty spaces of the church had been mostly filled in. Suddenly she was aware of bodies coming nearer to her. Someone entered the back row of benches, nudging Kelsey and Justin toward the middle. She squeezed Justin's hand and together they shuffled toward the center, making room for others whom they couldn't quite see.

"A rabid beast feasts upon doubt in the hearts of man," the voice announced, its controlled quaver never breaking, its tone never modulating. "Fortify yourselves and you starve the beast." Another pause—and then a shattering call from the pulpit, startling the congregants and cracking the cool quiet.

"FORTIFY YOURSELVES!"

Kelsey squeezed Justin's hand. A murmur now began to pass among the gathered, churning through the rows, a mumbling of assent. "Yes," it began. "Yes we must. *We must.*" As it leapt amongst the rows of parishioners the murmuring grew louder and more forceful, a wave of acknowledgement and affirmation. And then the voice was renewed with aural vengeance.

"The weak shall perish by the poisoned bite of Satan! Surely shall you perish also unless armed in righteousness! Go forth as Christian warriors and let not your faith be shaken!"

And here the voice returned to its former subdued tone, still breathy but with a pleading, expressive quality that suddenly made it personal. "Else your soul will be lost as easily as a flame in a cyclone." With that, the candles' flames seemed to leap, illuminating for the first time, and for the briefest of moments, the face of the speaker. Kelsey thought she could make out the man's face, spectacled, high-cheeked. But these impressions passed quickly, for no sooner did the candlelight erupt excitedly than it died away, leaving a spectral afterglow and a church full of silent and rattled listeners.

As the gatherers sat in the dark, there was an audible heaving, deep breaths emanating from the flock as if they had all just gone through some sort of personal trial. And then it began—slowly, softly at first, from the front of the church to the back, row by row, person by person, each grabbing the shoulders of whomever they were next to, grasping them firmly as they spoke the words echoing in a cacophonous blessing that bounced off the walls: "Fortify yourself!" Each person there was instructing, emboldening his brothers and sisters, each making flesh the abstract spiritual call to arms. "Fortify yourself!" commanded the person next to Kelsey, whom she still couldn't see completely in the darkness but who had found her and was holding on to her shoulders with slightly tremulous hands. But the grip was strong, and the voice was calm but potent. It wasn't a scold—it was a plea. "Fortify yourself!" Kelsey nodded reflexively, and then turned to Justin. She grabbed her son's shoulders gently, leaned down, and repeated to him, as it had been repeated to her: "Fortify yourself, Justin."

And then it began to dawn on her what they were all doing, what they were really saying, what they were fortifying themselves against. And for the first time, in the darkness and the cavernous space filled with strangers who she could feel but not see, she understood the fear they must all be living with. More than that, she actually felt it. "Fortify yourself!" bellowed a parishioner behind her, standing, who leaned in, eager to share in this summoning of will, startling her.

She was a little freaked out at how vulnerable she felt herself becoming. It must be fatigue, or the stress of relocating, or the simple power of suggestion, she would later conclude. But as she stood there in the darkened enclave of Jesus the Redeemer church in Milton, Indiana she finished in her head the sentence no one else felt necessary to say aloud:

Fortify yourself against it, the creature, the Indiana Corn Weasel. Fortify yourself—or else!

Hours later, as Kelsey lay in her bed, the first night of being sequestered in her Indiana barn, she tried to be analytical about what had happened in the church. The social scientist in her, the trained Ph.D. candidate, had already catalogued and critiqued the experience in her mind. It was, to use a phrase that would be completely at home in a paper on the phenomenon, a manifestation of mass hysteria. That's the simple and intellectually defensible interpretation. But it didn't completely explain what happened to her, what she felt while she was sitting in the back row of that dark church, her imagination massaged by the stark oratory and the candles, and the chanting, and the touching. She felt a jolt of something vaguely threatening. She wouldn't call it hysteria. It was closer to a kind of controlled anxiety. She was aware at the time of her heart beating faster, and of a slight sense of impending dread. How could it be that the simple recitation of a few austere and threatening words could conjure those feelings? Kelsey knew—she really *knew*—that stories of the Indiana Corn Weasel were just that and nothing more. She also understood mass hysteria. What she didn't understand was why she felt a genuine trembling, for just a brief moment, in the wake of the service, or why she felt such relief when that stranger grabbed her by the shoulders. For an instant she felt first fear, and then comfort—the comfort of another.

That's so odd, Kelsey thought. *It's Justin who should have been frightened—not me.*

But Justin seemed just fine. On the way back to their farmhouse, he kept talking about how cool he thought the trick with the candles was, how weird and wild that chanting in the darkness was. She remembered squeezing his hand in church, but now it dawned on her that she held him tight not for his sake, but for hers. Anyway, something chilled her there, an irrational tinge of fear, a feeling of foreboding. She felt there was something she should be worried about, a formless cold caress squeezing her nerves. But what?

It's all superstition. Better get some sleep, she reminded herself. *All this cogitation is making me a little nutty,* she concluded. She closed her eyes and fell quickly into a merciful slumber, so completely exhausted by the day's events that she didn't even hear the clawing at the hard earth just outside the farmhouse door.

* * * *

The oversized pages of what municipal clerks call a "Platte book"—really just a bunch of maps and blueprints collated and bound—spilled over the edge of her reading table on the second floor of the Milton Town Hall. Kelsey was flipping the pages of yet another volume, trying to get a sense of the town's geography, and how the town might have changed since the time of its founding. Though she was not particularly skilled in cartography, she was able to conclude that not very much had changed at all. She kept coming across the same landmarks and property lines, year after year, in the county's annual survey of property required by the local tax assessor's office.

From the first official, though very rough, sketches of Milton to the latest satellite-generated images, she noted a daunting uniformity to the town's topography. Borderlands comprising farms, a small lake in the northwest quadrant of town, a mild sloping landscape that resulted in a series of drainage ditches along the eastern border, and the fringes of a thick forest starting just at the edge of the town's southern terminus. Nothing about the town's landscape seemed to have changed in the last couple of centuries. As a student of crypto-zoology, Kelsey had learned early in her studies to acquire knowledge of habitat. In this case, it seemed pretty straightforward. She already knew that weasels—the genus Mustela—and particularly the least weasel, or so-called "dwarf weasel"—Mustela Rixosa—were indigenous to this part of the state. And the actual, scientific, observable weasels did bear some resemblance to their mythic cousin, the Indiana Corn Weasel. But the latter was far more vicious, and was said to possess almost supernatural abilities—not uncommon in the creation of figures from folklore. The Indiana Corn Weasel was rumored to be up to three feet long—an absolute impossibility, Kelsey's research had shown her—and could leap several feet through the air, as well as jump into tree branches or, even in some cases, climb onto roofs. It emitted a high-pitched, ear-splitting squeal. Actual weasels are notoriously shy, Kelsey knew, and difficult to study in the wild because they recoil at the slightest noise. But not the Indiana Corn Weasel, which according to legend, actively seeks out human contact—usually with disastrous consequences. In one scientifically significant way, the real weasel and its fictional doppelganger were alike: both were carnivores.

Kelsey concluded that her study of the town's geography wasn't really getting her anywhere. Her appointment with the local newspaper reporter who'd been writing about the weasel sightings wasn't until six p.m. so she decided to pop in on Justin and see how he was doing on his first day of school. She'd been able to arrange for him to temporarily attend the local elementary school—although the paperwork the school district required was only slightly less than what Kelsey had generated when she was applying to graduate school. Still, it was an immense relief to know that he'd have some sort of stable routine while her life veered further and further from any kind of established order.

She hiked over to the school—it was clear that if she was going to spend much more time here she'd need, somehow, to find a car—and walked up the half-staircase to the principal's office. It struck her as odd that the doors of the school were kept open and anyone off the street could walk in. It probably would have struck them as odd that Justin's school in New Jersey not only kept its doors locked and under constant video surveillance but also that all the students had to walk through metal detectors before entering the building.

"He's doing just fine," said Mrs. Hochstetler, the principal. "Though I'm afraid there are some things we have to hold him back from, like recess and gym class, because of his health history."

"Oh, don't worry about that. He's used to it."

"How's your book coming along?"

Okay, so Kelsey exaggerated a bit when she said she was in town to finish up her book. But it might be published, one day, conceivably.

"Not very well, I'm afraid. Not yet, anyway. I've mostly spent the morning looking at old maps. According to them, nothing has changed in this town since, well, ever."

Mrs. Hochstetler smiled. "Well, it *is* a small town. But you know what might be helpful to you? Let me see here…" She flipped through a plastic box of index cards, some of them yellowed and fraying at the edges. She pulled one out and copied the information, handing a piece of ruled notebook paper to Kelsey.

"We used to have a gentleman who worked as a part-time custodian here. He was retired and looking to be…what was it he said…looking to be 'of use' I think is how he always put it. He's been around this town a long time. A sort-of local historian. If you like, I can see if he'd be willing to talk to you. Maybe he can help you out."

"Thanks," said Kelsey, a little surprised.

Is this woman being helpful because she's a school principal? Or is this just how small town people are?

Either way, she was grateful for the lead.

"I could call him, save you the trouble? Do you have a number?"

"Oh, I'm afraid that's impossible."

Kelsey gave her a puzzled look. She looked at the paper Mrs. Hochstetler had handed her, and all it had was an address, no phone number, or employment history, or any other personal information.

"You say he was a custodian?"

"Oh, well, he did a little bit of everything. I think the children loved him because they often don't get to see the Amish people up close. They tend to be a little, well, *closed off*. But Mr. Yoder, who is Amish, was a bit more approachable, and used to even tell the children stories about Milton in the olden days. That's what made me think he might be of use to you."

"Thanks," she said, getting up. "I'll pick Justin up after school."

"He'll be fine. Good luck with your work."

She turned to leave, but stopped. "Oh, one more thing. Since you've been so nice, I was wondering if you might be able to offer me one more piece of advice."

"I'll be happy to."

"Do you know where I can get a car really cheap?"

* * * *

Several hours later she found herself back where her journey began, at the bait and tackle shop, milling conspicuously with the fishermen and farmers who spend their autumn mornings congregating among the rods, reels, and night crawlers, talking about the weather, the harvest that just passed, or the expected price for a bushel of winter wheat or grain sorghum on the commodities market. But this morning they were speaking about something else.

"D'ja hear about Jason Taylor?" one man asked. Kelsey couldn't help but overhear. The store was small, and as hard as she tried to look interested in the Styrofoam bait boxes and shimmering minnow lures, she knew she must have stuck out pretty badly. But she was captive there, however, until Mrs. Hochstetler's brother arrived. He was in the towing business, she explained, but he also ran a used car business on the side, mostly consisting of cars he'd hauled out of ditches or had been abandoned along the side of the road, whose owners simply walked away. After Kelsey had told her she needed a car, the principal dutifully called her brother, who happened to have "the perfect car" for her: a high-mileage sub-compact with "a little rust but a lot of get-up. And for a friend of my sister's, I'll let it go at cost," he assured her. "An absolute steal." Kelsey was sure of that. Apparently, used car salesmen sound the same no matter what state you're in. But Kelsey needed a car, so she wasn't in a position to haggle. So there she stood in the bait and tackle shop, trying to look interested in the current issue of *Fishing Facts* and stealing glances at her watch.

"Yep. Heard ol' Jason got himself a good look at our little buddy," said another of the older farmers, who chewed tobacco as he spoke, pausing between sentences to spit into an empty soda can that he carried with him for just such a purpose.

"That's the first time he's been seen west of the crick," said the first farmer. "Ain't too far from the Miller place. With that corn silo stuffed to the rafters, reckon they might be next."

Kelsey's ears perked up. The "Miller Place" was the property she and Justin were living on.

"Anybody but ol' Jason tell a story like that, I don't give it no mind," said one of the men, who was holding a steaming mug of black coffee with a picture of Porky Pig and the words "Th-th-th-that's MY coffee!" written across the front. "But he ain't no liar. I figure he saw somethin', whether it was our boy or not, I can't rightly say."

Our boy. Our little buddy. They had already begun turning this mysterious menace, this darkly mythic creature into a figure of bizarre familiarity. Kelsey had seen this pattern many times in her study of folkloric beings. She had once interviewed a fellow in the Pacific Northwest who swears to this day it was Bigfoot who overturned his car one night while he was in it on the side of the road, sleeping off a bender. The rolling over of the car resulted in a near-paralyzing case of whiplash. How did he deal with this trauma? He set up a T-shirt-and-trinket stand selling Bigfoot memorabilia to state park tourists, posing for pictures in his "I Met Bigfoot and Survived—Barely" T-shirt. One man's terror is another's punch line.

Kelsey listened, hoping to hear more. What were the details? Was anyone injured? What did ol' Jason Taylor really see? Was he sober at the time? Are there any footprints? Tufts of fur? Bite marks? Did he fill out a police report? Specifics were hard to come by among the laconic farmers, whose conversations consisted of as many silent nods and long pauses as actual speech. The leisurely pace of life out here had leeched into their speech patterns, informing their linguistic code with a vocabulary of slight head bobs, heavy sighs, the occasional groan, and the rhythmic expectoration of tobacco juice. Kelsey had taken enough courses in socio-linguistics to recognize that she wasn't going to get much more verbal confirmation from these wizened rural congregants. But then she was surprised to hear something that might actually be useful to her.

"Jason's son gonna be up at Mercy a few days," said one of the men between spits.

"Ain't much they can do, 'ceptin those nurses might be able to leave a few bite marks of their own," another said. "Take your mind offa what put you there." Muffled laughs. Groans. Sighs. Spit.

Kelsey recognized the reference to Mercy. It was the county hospital—technically "Mother of Mercy Medical Center". It was one of the first things she checked out before agreeing to come to Milton. In case Justin needed emergency room care—*when* Justin needed emergency room care—she wanted to know how close, and how good, the nearest hospital was. The verdict was mixed on how good the place was, but it was pretty close. And apparently, the son of ol' Jason Taylor was admitted because of something that happened when he encountered "our little buddy." Was it a case of shock? Rabies treatment? Tissue or organ damage? She made a mental note to try to find out exactly what happened.

Her eavesdropping was interrupted by the intrusion of a bellicose man shouting as he entered the store. "Who here's looking to steal a car this morning?"

Kelsey was a little surprised to find that the brother of such a pleasant and helpful woman could be such an obnoxious, self-serving oaf. Ernie "Bud" Hochstetler was every used car salesman cliché wrapped up in greasy overalls and topped off with a pompadour. "You'll be sittin' pretty in this here ride, little lady," he told her as she checked out the car.

Little lady? Let's just finish this transaction as quickly as possible, Kelsey told herself. There was no haggling—Kelsey had enough discretionary income from her grant money to pay cash for the car. Plus, the vehicle was pretty much a disaster. It didn't appear likely to make it through another harvest season. That was just fine with Kelsey. That meant it could be had cheap. She needed only to get through this fall and then she'd do what the last owner of the car no doubt did: abandon it on the side of the road.

As she drove along the short swath of Milton's Main Street, Kelsey felt an unexpected sense of normalcy. Having been forced to walk everywhere proved not to be the quaint and somewhat romantic experience she'd originally envisioned. She'd thought that traipsing around in her hiking boots would somehow bring her closer to the land, the people. Instead, she felt vulnerable and dependent. Perhaps the original settlers of Milton trudged mostly on foot over its dusty paths to get where they needed to go, but without a car, Kelsey simply felt restive. Now, even in this junker she'd just purchased in the parking lot of the bait store, she felt re-invigorated. Having a car, she thought, would allow her to travel further into the recesses of the town, plumbing its hidden and uncharted byways, even though its mere handful of paved roads seemed rather unpromising as portals of discovery. As a scholar, Kelsey knew that it was the detours one takes that often yield the freshest and most surprising results. Surely it was that, she reasoned, and not the prospect of quick and easy escape from this place that explained her newfound contentment as she perched behind the wheel, headed to Justin's school to pick him up.

"Spinner'll be surprised to see me in *this*," she said aloud as she cruised past the small handful of storefronts populating Main Street. Kelsey couldn't shake the feeling that she was on a movie set every time she was on Main Street. The more she studied the facades of the town's "downtown," the more she tried to pierce the patina of Mid-American normalcy that Milton's Main Street presented to the world. She remembered a scene from a Sherlock Holmes story she had read in graduate school, with Holmes getting a shiver while passing through some rural English village in a cab with his trusted companion, Watson. When Watson asked what was wrong, Holmes told him something about how the pastoral beauty of the English countryside masked far more villainy and evil than even the roughest London neighborhood.

But what Kelsey saw as she drove along generated no thoughts of villainy—just a grudging respect for the people who could live so simply, and a wonder about how they kept from going crazy with so few outlets. "And not a single Chinese restaurant," she said to herself. "How do they do it?"

Her reflecting didn't last long—Main Street quickly disappeared as she rolled along toward the school. After Kelsey picked up Justin, she'd have to get him back to the farmhouse for a quick bite and then she'd head off to meet the reporter from the *Milton Forum* for dinner. She was looking forward to that dinner—or more accurately, the dinner conversation. In her first days in town, she'd sensed that everybody seemed to believe in this fictional creature, the Indiana Corn Weasel, from the spooked-out parishioners at last night's church service to the men at the bait shop this morning. It would be nice to talk to what she presumed would be a fellow skeptic who might be able to help her understand how so many people could be so gullible.

She pulled the car around to the side entrance of the school and parked. It wasn't dismissal time yet, but she was hoping they'd let her spring Justin a little early. She walked into the building and headed to the principal's office. As she passed a few of the classrooms, she peeked in, noting with a wry smile how enthusiastic and happy the students seemed. Of course, the school year had just started, but Kelsey got the same feeling when she used to pick Justin up from his elementary school last year, a regular and necessary reminder of how fun it used to be just to learn, how eager to try new things little people are. Kelsey was poised at the opposite end of the spectrum—her schooling about to come to an end, desperate for it to come to end. She tried to remember what she was like as a student when she was seven, what she felt, but she had almost no memory of her years of school at that age. Instead, she mostly saw herself reflected in Justin, imagining that she must have been like him—inquisitive, precocious, hopeful, eager to try new things. As she turned the corner to head to the principal's office, she passed the school nurse's office. Mrs. DeVore, the nurse, saw her and immediately beckoned to her: "Mrs. Kane! Mrs. Kane!" Kelsey had told her when they first met that she was Ms. Kane, not "Mrs.," but in Milton, Indiana "Ms." was a foreign word.

"Yes?" said Kelsey, peeking in, preparing to be scolded for not having turned in some vital piece of paperwork among the dozens of documents she'd already submitted.

"Mrs. Kane. Please, come in. It's about Justin. We tried to call you."

Kelsey drew in a breath. Nothing in Mrs. DeVore's manner suggested this was about a paperwork problem.

"Mrs. Kane, I want you to know he's going to be okay. The paramedics said—"

"Paramedics? Oh my God…what's happened?"

As Kelsey's heart raced, Mrs. DeVore explained that Justin was outside with the other students in his Life Science class, picking wildflowers in the field just behind the school.

"They were going to press the flowers in a book," Mrs. DeVore unhelpfully began. "One little girl found a particularly beautiful flower, and another kid wanted it and started chasing her, and then pretty soon all the kids were running around the field, and Justin was running along with them too. It seemed harmless enough to their teacher, just a bunch of kids happy to be outside, playing in the sun and the dirt. But then she noticed Justin hunched over, on his hands and knees, and when she went to check him out, she could tell he was having trouble breathing."

"Asthma attack," Kelsey said, rising. "Where is he now?"

"Please, Mrs. Kane. Stay calm. He's fine. School regulations require we call the paramedics for any potentially serious medical situation. We called, and they came right away. He's at Mercy Hospital. I just talked to them, and they said he's—Mrs. Kane? *Mrs. Kane!*"

Kelsey was gone, down the hall, down the half-staircase, out the door, in her car. Mercy Hospital was close. She'd be there in a few minutes. She tried to stay calm. She gave herself the speech that she usually reserved for Justin. "Relax. Breathe in—hold it. Count ten. Release. Then another good, deep breath. Focus." Soon she would see Justin and discover that he was perfectly fine, and that the attack wasn't serious, that he was only doing what he was supposed to do when he felt his chest getting tight: stop running, get down on the ground, relax, tell someone where to find his inhaler, then take a puff, hold his breath, exhale, repeat. But as she raced to the hospital, heart still beating furiously, Kelsey mentally scolded the school for letting him run around in a field of wildflowers. Then she scolded herself, wondering why the hell she dragged him halfway across the country. What was she thinking?

Later, she wouldn't remember parking the car, entering the hospital, talking to the woman at the reception desk, or riding the elevator. All of that was just a blur. What she remembered was seeing her little guy lying in a hospital bed in one of those paper gowns, looking small and a little lost. When he saw his mother, he broke into a broad smile.

"Spinner!"

"Hi, Mommy!"

After she finally released him from her clutch, she asked how he was feeling.

"Oh, I'm fine. I tried to tell them to get my inhaler out of my cubby, but Mrs. Shelley told me just to lie still, not to move, and she started yelling for the nurse. Next thing, some guys came and then I ended up here. Mommy, I rode in an ambulance!"

"Way to go!" she said, high-fiving him while also choking back a few tears.

Justin's fine, just fine. He handled this episode better than the school. Better than me. It's much harder to watch.

"Hey, nice gown. Where can I get one?" his mother joked. Justin giggled, and then told her he had something to show her. He picked up a remote control and pressed a button. Suddenly, the foot of his bed began to rise.

"Awesome, huh?"

"Maybe we can get one of these for the farmhouse," Kelsey said. "In the meantime, stay put while I figure out how we can break out of this joint, okay, Spinner?"

"Okay, Mommy."

Kelsey found a nurse at the reception area, and told her she was ready to take Justin home.

"I'm sorry, ma'am. We can't release him for twenty-four hours. State law."

Kelsey thought she was joking—Justin was clearly fine. But as it turned out, that was indeed the law. If a patient who is a minor is transported by emergency personnel, the hospital must keep the young patient for a minimum of twenty-four hours. It had more to do with potential insurance liability than medical care, but regardless, Justin was stuck there overnight.

"I'm sorry. He's a cute little boy. We'll take good care of him, don't worry."

Kelsey was still reeling from this new development when she explained to Justin that he'd be staying.

"Cool!" he exclaimed.

"Hey, why not? You've got a magical bed, your own television, and nurses who fawn over you. Pretty nice set-up, little man."

Kelsey was starting to feel a little foolish that she'd panicked on the ride to the hospital. Justin never seemed happier.

"Hey, kiddo. You'll be okay here by yourself for a little while? I've just got to get to our farmhouse and take care of some stuff."

"Can you bring my books when you come back?"

"Of course. And I'll bring a cake with a file in it."

"I'd break a tooth, Mommy!"

"You need to watch some prison movies. We'll cover that later," she said, leaning over his forehead, kissing him gently. "Don't drive the nurses too crazy."

"'Bye, Mommy," he said, as he flipped through the channels on the television set hanging on the wall.

You promised him an adventure, Kelsey reminded herself as she headed toward the exit. And then, recalling her own adventure, she paused for a moment, and turned back to the reception desk.

"Can you tell me the room number please for Jason Taylor's son?"

* * * *

It turns out that he did indeed have a first name: Reggie. Kelsey felt a bit apprehensive walking around the hospital looking for his room, but somehow the fact that her son was a patient there made her feel a little less sneaky. If it didn't turn out well, if Reggie didn't want to talk to her, she'd just head back to Justin's room. "Just stretching my legs," she'd tell any suspicious hospital personnel.

She found room 217 at the end of a hallway. A middle-aged doctor in a white coat carrying a clipboard walked toward her, gave a vacant, practiced smile, nodded, and continued on his way. She peeked in the room, and saw that the bed was empty. She wondered if the attendant had given her the wrong room number when she heard a flush from the bathroom. She stepped back out of the room for a moment, heard the bathroom door open, and waited half a minute before re-entering the room. She hadn't given any thought to what she should say. She considered briefly her alternatives. *"Hello, Reggie. You don't know me, but I'd very much like to see your bite marks."* Or how about *"Reggie, my name's Kelsey, professional weasel hunter. I understand you might be able to give me a lead on one of these pesky buggers."* Then there was always the undercover approach. *"Mr. Taylor, I'm with the state weasel bureau. I'm afraid I need to ask you a few questions."*

"You waitin' on me?" Reggie had beaten her to the punch. He hadn't climbed back into bed, but rather grabbed a pair of crutches and was leaving the room when he almost ambled into her.

"Me? I was just…um… You're Reggie? My name's Kelsey." She awkwardly stuck out her hand. He grabbed it and offered a shy hello of his own. She tried to focus on why she was there—this might be her only chance, and she didn't want to blow it. "Reggie, I was wondering if I could ask you a few questions."

"Well, if it's bout the insurance, you gotta talk to my Pa."

"No, Reggie, I'm not with the hospital. I'm a…naturalist. I'm researching local wildlife in these parts. I just want to ask a few questions about what happened to you."

"Don't know as there's much to say. Wouldn't even be here 'ceptin' for my own clumsiness."

"I'm not sure I understand."

"It's just like I told 'em when I come in here last night. I'm working in the barn, I heard my Pa holler, so I run out to the field to see what's going on. I run out there so fast, I tripped over a spool of bailing wire, twisted my ankle pretty bad." And then in a sort of conspiratorial whisper, he leaned in and added, "Ain't even s'posed to be out of bed, but I just couldn't stand laying there all day. Don't report me, okay?"

Kelsey nodded. "Your secret is safe with me. Now can *you* keep a secret?"

Reggie gave her an "aw, shucks" smile that suggested he'd kept secrets before.

"I'm trying to find out what it was that your father saw that made him yell out."

"That ain't no secret. Not 'round here, anyways. He seen one of them weasels."

"The Indiana Corn Weasel."

"Ain't no need to be so formal. Pa just calls 'em our old friend. Ain't too friendly though, if you ask me. Them things is downright dangerous."

"You've seen one?"

"Shoot, ain't nobody lives in Milton can't tell you a story about the Indiana Corn Weasel."

An orderly pushing a double-decker cart filled with what appeared to be cafeteria trays passed them without comment, but Kelsey felt her interrogation might be better conducted in a less public place. Reggie was one matronly nurse away from being busted for going AWOL, and that might mean the end of any corn weasel stories he might be willing to share.

"Would you be more comfortable back in your room?"

"Shoot no. I was going crazy layin' around. I figured if I told 'em I was going to chapel, they wouldn't make much of a fuss."

Chapel. Perfect. It'll definitely be quiet there, and if we have the place alone, Reggie might feel more like talking.

"Great idea. I was going to pop in there myself." Kelsey had no idea where the chapel was. She didn't even know the hospital had a chapel.

Mother of Mercy, Kelsey. Of course there's a chapel.

And it was really pretty striking, Kelsey thought. The

sterile, off-white corridors of the hospital gave no hint of what was to be found through the stainless-steel-handled wooden door marked simply "Chapel." The afternoon light streaming through stained glass mosaics of St. Francis feeding the birds and the Virgin Mary clasping the infant Jesus cast swirled shadows of purple and rose and royal blue. There were fresh flowers along the perimeter in simple glass vases with polished pebbles at the bottom, and padded benches with kneelers on either side of the room. There was no altar, but there was a raised platform at the front of the church. Toward the front of the platform was a lone kneeler facing a wall-sized crucifix, draped in a white linen shroud. Just off to the side of the platform was an elaborately carved mahogany rack with a half-dozen copies of the *Holy Bible* and other religious pamphlets displayed behind its varnished slats. And just off the entrance was a leather couch and an end table, perhaps for those less religiously-inclined souls who merely wanted a quiet place to meditate, or forget.

"Why don't we sit back here?" Kelsey said, pointing to the couch.

"All right," Reggie said. "Just give me a minute." He hobbled up to the front of the sanctuary and, casting aside his crutches, knelt on the padded kneeler. He clasped his hands together and bowed his head. For a couple of minutes he remained silent, eyes closed, lips barely moving. Immersed in prayer, apparently convinced that whomever he was speaking to was listening, Reggie gave the appearance of the most devout communicant.

Wonder what he's praying for, Kelsey thought.

She'd long-since given up the impulse to pray, and even when as a little girl she brought her hands together and knelt at her bedside, it was mostly for show. The last time she remembered doing that was after she'd done something wrong—she couldn't remember what, exactly—and she heard her father coming toward her room. She jumped out of bed and fell to her knees, the picture of a sincerely sorry soul.

Dad can't get too mad at me if he sees me talking to God, telling him I'm sorry, she thought.

She was right. She remembered her father coming in to her room, kissing the top of her head, and then leaving, never saying a word about whatever it was she'd done to drive her to faux repentance.

It was only a few days later, Kelsey remembered, that the accident happened. With no father around to mollify, she never again climbed out of her bed to fall on her knees in prayer. Of course, losing her dad the way she did didn't do much to reaffirm her belief in God. Mostly it just made her angry—an anger she'd never really moved past. But lots of people do move past their anger, Kelsey knew. Maybe something bad happened to Reggie in his life, something he blamed God for. And yet, there he was, on his knees, eyes tight, mouthing silent solemnities, a true believer.

He made the sign of the cross and reached out for his crutches, joining Kelsey on the couch. Kelsey hadn't expected to conduct any interviews here in the hospital, so she hadn't brought her notebook and pen with her. Instead, she grabbed a small wooden pencil and a few sheaves of note paper from the stack where worshipers were encouraged to write down their prayer requests and put them in a small, locked wooden box.

"Mind if I take a few notes?" she asked Reggie.

"This ain't for the paper, right?"

"No, it's just for me. I'm doing some research."

"You a scientist?"

"Well, sort of," she assured him, stopping just short of confessing "I'm almost a doctor." Instead, she told him to just say what he saw on the night he was injured.

"Didn't see nothin'," Reggie said. "After I tripped, I just laid there on the ground. Pa came over, still holding his shotgun. He got off a couple shots, but he didn't hit nothing. He told me what he saw, but I didn't see it."

"What did your father see?"

"Biggest damned corn weasel you can imagine."

"Did he describe it?"

"Didn't need to. Everybody knows what he looks like."

"You've seen the Indiana Corn Weasel?"

"Sure, I saw him once. Got a real good look at it."

If Kelsey hadn't witnessed him in prayer just a few minutes ago, she would have suspected he was lying to her, putting her on, having a little fun at the city girl's expense. But Reggie spoke so openly, so unselfconsciously that she was inclined to believe that he really believed.

"Can you tell me about it?" she asked.

"Well, ain't nothing I ever told nobody. I was in the barn with Wendy Jergens. This was, I guess, about a year ago. We was up in the loft, you know, messin' around. It was Friday night, the football game was over, and we had a bottle of hootch up there with us."

"Hootch?"

"You know…home brew?"

"Home made liquor?"

"Shoot, everybody round here knows how to make hootch. Corn liquor, I s'pose is the proper name. We're up there in the loft, drinking it and havin' a little fun and then Wendy just starts screamin'. Pretty near busted my ear drum. I turned around to ask her what got her so riled up and then I seen right away what it was."

"Yeah?" said Kelsey, scribbling away on her prayer request sheets. "What did you see?"

"I looked into the reddest eyes I ever did see on any creature. It was about three feet long, had yellow fangs, and was making this high-pitched squeal. I grabbed the only thing I could get, the bottle of hootch, and I threw it at 'im. He made a hissing sound—a terrible sound I ain't never heard 'fore or since. Anyways, I threw the bottle at him and he flew over our heads, out of the loft, and onto the ground. In another second, it was gone. Fastest damn bugger I ever saw."

"He flew?"

"Yes, ma'am. He flew like he had wings. I didn't see no wings, but there's some will tell you they seen one with wings. Well, we was kinda shook up, so we put ourselves together, if you know what I mean, and got out of that loft. Ain't but a few seconds later, I heard Wendy scream again. I raced over to her and I saw what it done. That Corn Weasel had mauled one of the goats we kept tied up in the barn. More than mauled it. He gone clean through it."

"Gone through? What do you mean?"

"I mean there was a hole in the middle of that goat, right in his middle parts, like somebody hollowed him out. The thing had gone through Betsy like he was burrowing through straw."

"A hole? In the middle of the goat?" Kelsey had a little trouble imagining what that must have looked like, or how that could happen.

"That creature went through him like a jackblade through a block of lard," Reggie said matter-of-factly, a poetic phrase in its way that Kelsey quickly wrote down on the prayer request.

"What happened then?"

"Well, Pa come out and seen what the screamin' was all about. We didn't tell him we was up in the loft. I left that part out. But he seen the goat. Pa reached down and put his fist through the hole, and then he looked me, and then he told us to go inside and not to come out. He grabbed his shotgun, but he couldn't find nothin' the rest of the night. It's been a year and we ain't seen it since, 'til last night when Pa saw 'im again."

"He said it was the same creature? The Indiana Corn Weasel?"

"Naw, Pa just said 'he's back' is all. But I knew what he meant."

As Kelsey scribbled away, an elderly woman in a

black shawl entered the chapel. She paused, crossed herself, and walked gravely forward to take her place in one of the front benches. Kelsey stopped writing and watched her as she pulled a strand of rosary beads from a hidden pocket. Bowing her head, she began mumbling softly, conveying beads between her crippled fingers. Like many people who are cynical about religion, Kelsey was also a little envious of the truly faithful. For this woman now engaged in deep prayer, the world and its problems have been reduced for the moment to a series of polished glass beads and memorized phrases, chanted over like incantations. Another true believer.

"I better be getting back," Reggie said, pulling himself up on his crutches.

"Right. Can I help you?"

"Naw, I can manage it."

Kelsey held the door open and Reggie pivoted himself through, back into the cold, clinical light. "Thanks again for talking to me."

"Wasn't nothing," he said. "Good luck."

They shook hands, and Kelsey watched him hobble along the hallway and turn the corner, disappearing. She took her handful of notes, folded them, and stuck them in the back pocket of her jeans. She was about to head down the hallway herself when, for reasons she didn't completely understand, she felt compelled to return to the chapel. Opening the door almost guiltily, she stepped back inside. The elderly woman was still lost in her devotions. Kelsey sat back on the bench, exhaled deeply, and stared up at the stained glass mural. She recognized the figure of St. Francis of Assisi. In the red and green and blue and golden shards comprising the glass mosaic she saw the familiar image, birds perched on his outstretched robed arms, squirrels and rabbits congregating at his feet, a doe unafraid, approaching.

I wonder what he'd do if he saw the Indiana Corn Weasel.

Laughing aloud, she shook her head and wondered

what it was that people were really seeing. Could there really be a giant, yard-long, red-eyed, yellow-fanged squealing weasel that flies through the air and leaps through farm animals? Sure, she concluded, staring up at St. Francis. The world's full of wonder. That's always what her father told her. She was drifting back in time, her mind in another place, her eyes closed, when she heard a rattling. She opened her eyes and noticed the old woman had dropped her glass rosary on the marble floor and was having trouble bending down to retrieve it. She got up and walked toward the bench where the woman was sitting. She reached underneath, snagged the rosary, and then reached out toward the woman.

"Excuse me. I think you dropped this."

The old woman looked at Kelsey, but it was more like she looked through her, past her, like she was seeing something behind Kelsey's face. She said nothing at first, but she wrapped her hands around Kelsey's hand, which still held the rosary. Though her hands shook, her gaze was steady. Then she leaned in close, her mouth near Kelsey's ear.

"At the finish, everything looks different."

She released her grasp, leaving Kelsey holding the rosary. The old woman rose and walked out, never once looking back. She crossed herself at the door, and disappeared into blinding institutional florescence. Kelsey remained there in the dark and quiet, the strange words echoing in her mind as she absent-mindedly fingered the beads, rolling them slowly between fingers, her flesh warming the polished glass.

Chapter 4

Justin was glad to get his books, and he didn't seem fazed at all when Kelsey told him she was going to spend the night at the farmhouse. She told him she'd be back to pick him up in the morning. In the few hours she was there with him, the nurse must have come in half a dozen times to check on him. There would be no shortage of attention paid to her little man. And Kelsey was grateful for the break. So much had happened, so quickly, that she really needed some time to be alone and sort things out.

Kelsey decided to spend the evening poring over her dissertation notes and re-reading some of the material she'd collected over the years on the Indiana Corn Weasel. Well, that was her plan. Instead, she fell asleep. With her hot cup of tea and a stack of books at the ready, Kelsey closed her eyes ever so briefly, and then she was out. She had no idea what time it was when she heard the pounding at the door. Trying to regain her wits, she stumbled toward the knocking, issuing a raspy "Who is it?" as she looked around to get some indication of what time it was.

"It's Frankie Auden."

It took only a moment for the name to register.

"Oh shit!"

Frankie heard her through the door.

"Not exactly the reaction I was hoping for, but not one I'm altogether unused to hearing either," he quipped.

She opened the door.

"Usually you have to get to know me a little better before feeling that way."

"No, I meant 'Oh shit! We had an appointment tonight.' Right?"

"About four hours ago, to be precise. But after three and a half hours of waiting, I left. I have my pride, you know."

Kelsey was a little surprised to hear him speaking so glibly, so casually, considering this is the first time they'd ever actually met. But they had spoken on the phone several times since Kelsey decided to come to Indiana, and she found Frankie to be, at least over the phone, easy to talk to and, for her purposes, extremely helpful.

"I'm so sorry," she said, though she could tell he was miffed by her mental lapse. But she regained the upper hand quickly.

"My son's in the hospital," she said bluntly.

His whole demeanor changed, a sudden shift from wronged party to sympathetic friend.

"I'm sorry. What's wrong?"

"He had an asthma attack at school, and they kind of freaked out. They called the paramedics, and now he has to stay there overnight."

"How's he doing?"

"Oh, he's fine. In fact, he's better than fine. He's loving all the attention he's getting."

"Yeah, Mercy has some good people. Its finances are a mess—it's criminal what's going on with their Medicaid payouts—but the staff there's really good." He spoke exactly like a newspaper reporter, Kelsey thought.

"Well, anyway, his being there really threw me off my schedule. I should have called. I'm sorry."

"No problem. I've been eating alone at that restaurant for years."

Kelsey glanced over at her kitchen clock. It was almost 10 p.m. She'd napped for three hours, out like a light.

"I hope you don't mind my dropping by," he said, walking around the room, seemingly absorbed by the odd architecture of the place. "By the way, for a barn, this is a pretty nice setup. Not what I was expecting."

Kelsey didn't mind him dropping by at this hour. She'd been keeping graduate student hours for the past several years, and between all-night sessions working on her dissertation and unscheduled parental emergencies, Kelsey was a friend of the night. But she did think it a bit odd that he came out to see her without even calling.

"Should I be worried?" she asked him jokingly. "You're not a stalker, are you?"

"Reporter—which is essentially the same thing," he said. "You still want to go somewhere and talk? There's not much open at this hour. Actually, there's nothing open at this hour."

"That's okay, we can just hang out here if you like."

They ended up talking as easily as they had on the phone. Frankie, like her, was a city kid. He was born and raised in St. Louis, and when he graduated from college, unlike his friends who sought out jobs at large metropolitan dailies, Frankie decided he wanted a different experience. He saw an ad in a journalism trade journal for a reporter for a small Midwestern weekly and thought he'd give it a shot. That was four years ago. Expecting to stay only six months, he was surprised at how happy he was covering 4-H fairs and the annual gladiola festival.

"I've got friends who I went through J-school with, and they're already burned out," he said. "Twelve hour days, fighting for scraps among the other metro reporters, police scanners that never quit squawking, politicians who won't talk unless you've got a TV camera pointed at them…a couple years ago they were crusading idealists. Now they're all looking for cushy P.R. jobs."

"You're not job searching?"

"Why should I? I've got a pretty good gig here, I figure. The pace is manageable, I get to cover pretty much what I want, everybody in town reads the paper, so I'm sort of a mini-celebrity, and I'm not too stressed out at the end of the day to work on the Great American Novel, which I expect to finish in another year or so. After that, I'll retire as a gentlemen farmer-writer. Maybe run for Mayor of Milton, just for kicks."

Kelsey was a bit puzzled. Frankie was well-educated, eloquent, literate, and yet content to spend his days stomping around this dusty burg, chasing stories about chicken theft and barn raisings.

"You really like it here?"

Settling into an easy chair, Frankie grabbed a book off the top of the stack on an end table and examined it. "I love it," he said, flipping the pages. "It's like some strange, alien world I've been transported to. The crew I ran with in St. Louis thinks I've lost my mind. But I feel like Eddie Albert in Green Acres. Remember that show?"

Kelsey shook her head.

"It was about this big city lawyer who moves to the country, and he's surrounded by all these hicks in a farm town called Hooterville who drive him crazy. But the weird part is he absolutely loves being a farmer, and he grows to love the town. That's pretty much my story. I could have stayed in St. Louis and written about municipal corruption and tax levies and some new pitching prospect for the Cardinals, but I came here. You know what story I wrote today? A feature about a kid who lives over in Dorchester Fields who grew a squash that has the face of Jesus on it. I find that refreshingly bizarre."

Kelsey found *him* refreshingly bizarre. He made a face as he looked through the book he was holding.

"The encyclopedia of crypto-zoology. Speaking of bizarre."

"Don't be fooled by the cheesy cover. The chronicling

of crypto-zoological creatures is a legitimate scientific endeavor."

"I'm sure it is, Professor," said Frankie, somewhat mockingly. "So how'd you get sucked in?"

She got up off the book-filled crate she was sitting on, walked over to a kitchen cupboard and took out a bottle of scotch whisky—a parting gift from Otto. She poured herself a glass, and catching Frankie's eye, pointed to the bottle. He nodded, so she grabbed a second glass and filled it. She walked back into the room, handed him the drink, and sat back down on the crate. She took a gulp and looked off into the distance, into the past, distracted, even a little haunted.

"I was seven. Same age as Justin is now. Anyway, my dad used to tell me all these stories at night before bed. Monster stories. I was one of those weird kids who loved getting spooked. He'd tell me about Bigfoot, and vampires, and since we lived in New Jersey, he had all these great stories about the New Jersey Devil. But my favorite was the Loch Ness Monster. I had a fish tank in my room, and I used to imagine how freaked out the fish in my tank would be if they ever saw Nessie." Kelsey took a gulp of scotch. She still had a faraway look in her eyes.

"There was this lake about a half hour away from where we lived," she continued. "My dad used to tell me that Nessie had a sister, Bessie, and that Bessie lived in that lake. He'd tell me all kinds of stories about Bessie. I even used to make these sketches of what she'd look like. I had them taped up all over my bedroom walls. Some just of her, some of Bessie and me, the great monster hunter."

"Your father must be proud of you now. Look at you. A real life monster hunter."

She looked at Frankie with a mix of scorn and regret, and swallowed the last gulp from her glass.

"I kept pestering him to take me out to this lake so I could see Bessie. I guess I knew she didn't really exist, but I was seven. You know how when you hear for the first time that there's no Santa Claus, but you still sort of believe anyway? The residue of all those nights, clutching belief, keeps you hopeful. My dad used to show me pictures of Nessie in a book, but no one had ever taken a picture of Bessie. I was going to draw her. I was going to be famous."

Frankie nodded and took a sip, his reporter's instincts apparently aroused.

"So we drive out to the lake one day, just him and me, and he actually rents a rowboat for us. I've got my sketchpad and dad has this fishing net, and we launch our boat. It's a gorgeous day. There's no wind at all, and the water is smooth like ice. And we row out to this little secluded part of the lake where there's a little cove near a kind of a peninsula, or half-island, with these great white cranes that come flapping in and diving for fish, and Dad tells me that's where Bessie like to swim because the water is a little shallower and that sometimes she even crawls up onto shore and looks out at the water from the land. So I ask him if he thinks she'll come up on shore today, and he says maybe she will, but if she doesn't, he has a plan. He says he'll jump in the water and swim around and scare her out of the water, and that when she comes up, I should be ready to draw her picture right away because she's really fast and I might miss her if I'm not looking closely. So I put my sketch pad on my lap, and Dad's in his bathing suit, and he takes off his sandals and his shirt and stands at the front of the boat, and I'm really excited because the afternoon just had a magical feel to it, with the sun and the cranes and the cool water and my dad and me, and everything was just perfect, you know? Just absolutely goddamned perfect."

Kelsey stopped abruptly, dropped her glass, put her head in her hands, tears already dampening her cheeks and fingers.

* * * *

Frankie wanted to do something to comfort her, but he didn't know her well enough to put his arm around her, or hug her, or rub her shoulders as she sat there, sobbing. He sensed how the story was going to end, and he wanted to tell her she didn't have to finish. Amid the flurry of tears, she reached out and grabbed his hand and whispered, "I'm sorry."

He squeezed her hand and told her it was all right. She continued looking down, tears trailing her cheeks, trickling. "He dove into the water, Frankie. He dove in head first, and he must have hit his head on a rock, one of those totally freak accidents you hear about, and he was paralyzed and couldn't move. But he didn't come up to the surface. I sat there in the boat, with my sketch pad, and this expectant smile on my face, waiting. And I just kept waiting, and then I started calling out, and then, after a few minutes, I started screaming. I don't remember what happened next—I must have passed out from shock, or something. The next thing I know I was on the shore, and there was a state trooper there, and I was wrapped in a blanket, and they were taking me into an ambulance, and I remember asking where my dad was, and I'll never, ever forget the look in that trooper's eyes. He didn't want to tell me that he drowned, so he just kept saying in a low voice, 'Try to relax, honey. Try to relax.' I curled my hands into a fist and cried harder than anybody's ever cried. While I was having my meltdown, they pulled the boat out of the water, checked the paperwork at the boat rental place, found out who we were, and they called my mom, who came to get me at the local emergency room. An hour later, the police divers found my dad."

She looked right at Frankie. "In his bathing suit pocket, they found two triangular pieces of polished green glass. He must have slipped them in there before he jumped. He used to tell me that Bessie had scales that shined and sparkled in the sun like emeralds. I think he was planning to tell me that he saw Bessie, she got scared and swam away, but he managed to grab her by the tail and grab a couple of her scales. I know my dad. He loved doing that kind of stuff. He always…" She was unable to finish, her composure undone by the daggers of memory. She sat there shaking in the living room of the farmhouse, holding her head in her hands, shedding fresh tears for a decades-old wound. "I haven't told that story to anybody in years," she said. "I guess it still gets to me pretty good. I'm really sorry."

Frankie nodded, went to the cabinet where she'd gotten the bottle, and took it down. He brought it into the living room and generously refilled their glasses. He lifted his glass and said, warmly: "To your father." She clinked glasses with him, grabbed his hand and squeezed, and said in a quavering voice, "To my father." And then she drank, the tang of saline flavoring the grainy amber liquid.

* * * *

The more time Kelsey spent in Milton, the more she wondered if its idiosyncrasies belonged to it alone, or if all small, rural towns were odd in the same way. For all of her urbanity and her advanced learning, Kelsey was discovering that she really knew nothing of the world outside Northern New Jersey, and certainly nothing of what is affectionately called "the Heartland." She thought her study of folk legends had acquainted her with the mindset of people such as those who live in Milton, but much like the prize-winning onions that grow to softball size in their fields, these folks had layers. For days, Kelsey had driven around town, talking to farmers, senior citizens hanging out at Town Hall playing checkers in the rec room, and truck drivers passing through town, stopping only long enough to sop up some of Flo's biscuits and gravy at the diner.

"Don't go native on me!" Otto had said to her in his most recent email. There was no danger of that happening. But Kelsey was aware of a shift in the way she felt, a slight change in her understanding of things. The gnawing anxiety of the unfamiliar she felt in her first few days was gradually being replaced, supplanted by a kind of respect as she penetrated the veneer of her now-fellow Hoosiers and came to know them a little better. But she also felt she could only get so close. There was some sort of barrier between her and her new neighbors that geography could only partly explain. The phrase that came to mind when she thought of the people she'd met here was "defiantly hospitable"—always willing to grant her time or some request but also subtly conveying the sense that it was their Christian obligation that was motivating them rather than genuine personal curiosity.

She'd never met so many people so intensely interested in small talk. But when it came to the larger issues, a sort of wall went up, as if to announce, *"Advance no further."* This was different, Kelsey knew, from the way she interacted with people back home. In fact, it was the opposite. Her New Jersey friends hated small talk, couldn't do it, didn't want to waste their time. Their tendency was to ignore you altogether, whereas in Milton there was almost a pathological necessity to break the public silence of a grocery checkout line or a bus stop with talk—doesn't matter what about. But within her social circle in New Jersey, when they did grant you access, they skipped the preliminaries. And then they went deep. In Milton, the depths were clouded, shifting, perilous, off limits. People here would truly give you the shirt off their back but then turn inward and a little defiant if you asked them about their beliefs, or why they held them. Anytime Kelsey mentioned her son's asthma, she received immediate unsolicited medical advice—mostly folk remedies—from everyone: farmers, teachers, even the mailman. But ask them about something meaningful, like God, and if they've ever had any doubts about His existence, and a disdainful quietness descended. She got the same reaction when she asked them about the Indiana Corn Weasel. People believed. They believed mightily, but they just weren't going to talk about it with you. Whatever they thought deep in their hearts appeared to be as undiscoverable as the proof Kelsey had come here to unearth.

"It's Reverend Lonnie," Frankie had told her during lunch at the diner. "He's got 'em all worked up. They think the weasel is some sort of punishment for their sins. No wonder they don't want to talk about it," he added. "It's all part of the nexus of sin and guilt and shame."

"How do you know all this?"

"I go to Sunday services. I never miss. It's great fun. Now pass the ketchup."

Frankie could be awfully glib about the religious zeal of Miltonians, but he might have been on to something, Kelsey concluded. That's why she found herself driving over to see Reverend Lonnie for an interview. He agreed to meet her in the church offices. As she pulled into the church parking lot, she had a vision of the good Reverend lit only by candles, breathlessly exhorting his flock to reform their lives and purge evil from their world. Now she hoped to get some of that on tape.

Kelsey wanted to walk through the church rather than use the side entrance. She hadn't been inside the building since that night she and Justin stumbled upon the impromptu service, and since she spent most of that night in the dark, she hadn't gotten a good look at the place. A carved limestone archway and white-gray slate pathway led up to a pair of sliding wooden doors that looked like they had come from someone's barn, criss-crossed with mahogany beaming, the wood grain lightened by years of bleaching sunlight.

The interior of the church was comprised of rows of wooden benches—Kelsey had been in the back row on her previous visit—that ended in a series of red-carpeted steps leading to a raised platform stage of veined marble. As she walked down the center aisle, she studied the life-sized Jesus figure splayed against an elevated wooden cross. His eyes were open, and his face appeared serene, conveying no sense of agony, his hands and sides and feet pierced in the familiar places. There was a swatch of linen discreetly tossed about his midsection. Kelsey's research into religious iconography had taught her that the loin cloth was a fiction. Most crucifixion victims were naked, since it was a form of public humiliation as well as torture. Though the "historical Jesus" camp had made great strides in altering contemporary Christianity's understanding of Jesus' authentic life and times, that realistic detail was probably just a bit too much for people to handle at nine a.m. on a Sunday, Kelsey figured.

So she stood there, looking up at Jesus aboard that giant cross, shrouded by the midday light seeping through the open transoms along the church's side walls. Kelsey stood there for a long time, thinking, wondering why she was never stirred by this image that has moved millions, called forth something within their souls, even sent them to die for their faith. She saw a man in a pretty desperate situation. "But that's all I see," she said aloud, to herself, almost as if in reproach.

"Then stop looking with your eyes."

She was briefly startled, but she recognized the voice, that same buttery tenor that had worked the congregants into such a frenzy on her first night in town. She turned to find the Reverend Lawrence Croydon, known throughout the town as Reverend Lonnie, standing at the edge of the raised platform.

"You're looking for signs of suffering, wondering how a man being tortured to death can be so serene," he said to Kelsey, as if he could read her thoughts. "To the true believer, Ms. Kane, the flesh is only a vessel, a disposable container for the eternal soul."

"Yeah, but it still had to hurt," Kelsey noted.

"You know," he continued, still looking up to the crucifix but now walking towards her, "there have been some martyrs in the church's history whose faith seems to have made them impervious to pain. There's a story told of my own patron saint, Lawrence, a third century martyr who defied the Emperor Valerian. The emperor was a particularly cruel tyrant, even by the standards of Roman emperors. To punish Laurence and to get him to renounce his faith, Valerian had him stretched out on a gridiron and literally roasted alive over an open fire. Do you know what Lawrence's last words were?"

Kelsey shook her head.

"You can turn me over now. I'm cooked on this side."

Kelsey released a chuckle but then saw that Reverend Lonnie wasn't laughing. She quickly re-assumed a posture of respectful composure.

"He really said that?"

"Well, he said it in Latin. *Assum est. Versa et manduca*. That is an impressive degree of faith in the eternal soul, don't you agree?" the Reverend said. "Come. Let us talk."

He led her from the front of the church to an anteroom where two upholstered parlor chairs faced a polished cherry-wood desk. He directed her to one of the chairs, and he sat behind the desk, turning on a floor lamp and leaning back in a manner that reminded her of Dr. Reeves. It wasn't a posture of smugness but rather one of surety, of total comfort with one's station in life.

"Thank you for seeing me," Kelsey began, somewhat formally. "As I explained on the phone, I'm here doing some work for my doctoral dissertation."

"Crypto-zoology," interrupted Reverend Lonnie. "Widely discredited, though still a fascinating field with which I have some familiarity." He leaned back in his chair, his pressed fingertips forming a fleshy tent.

Widely discredited. Have I just been insulted? Kelsey wondered.

"Well then, you can perhaps appreciate what I'm up against here."

"Oh yes. You are looking to prove that something that

people believe exists doesn't, in actuality, exist at all. You hope to show that it is all a figment of their overactive imaginations, a false impression formed by an almost primitive clinging to outdated beliefs."

"Well, yes, I suppose that's right," Kelsey said, somewhat defensively. Something in the way he characterized her position—though accurate—made her uncomfortable. "What I'm looking for is the truth."

He raised his eyebrows slightly at her assertion, and then leaned forward in his chair.

"The truth, Ms. Kane? That's what you're seeking?"

"Please, call me Kelsey."

"Of course. Kelsey. As an educated woman, you are surely aware that greater minds than ours have spent their lives in a quest for 'the truth.' Many is the scholar whose lifetime journey to seek the truth ended in the belief that no such thing exists. For some, that way lies madness." His desktop was clear except for a black leather Bible and what he now held in his hand: a skull.

"Memento Mori," Kelsey whispered.

Reverend Lonnie looked at her with admiration. "Very good. You know your church history."

"I had a graduate seminar in Medieval literature. We learned about the monks who kept skulls on their writing desks as a constant reminder of their final end. The memento mori—'reminder of death.' I haven't thought of that in a while."

"You've been busy pursuing other mementos," he said, returning the skull to its resting place atop his polished cherry-wood desk.

"Mustela nivalis."

"Excuse me?"

"It's the scientific name for weasel."

Reverend Lonnie smiled and leaned back.

"But not just any weasel, yes? A very special creature."

"That's a good way of putting it," Kelsey said, trying

to return to a businesslike posture. "Anyway, what I wanted to ask was, I was in church last week, during a service that you had, around about seven p.m., and I was wondering if that was related in any way to this recent round of sightings."

He assumed a paternal tone, reassuring in its certainty, persuasive in its clarity.

"Kelsey, when people are frightened, or disturbed, or confused, they often turn for guidance to their spiritual source. Which, in the case of many people in town, is this particular church. Is there something wrong with seeking comfort in the communion of other like-minded souls?"

Why does everything I'm saying come out sounding like an unfair attack and everything he's saying sound like an eminently logical defense? Maybe they teach you that at minister school.

Breathing deeply, she took another tack. "It appeared from where I was sitting—"

"Back row."

"Yes. That's right." She was a little thrown by that. How could he have possibly noticed her, an unfamiliar face, in the distance and the darkness.

"Anyway, you kept telling people to fortify themselves. Against what, exactly?"

He nodded, his forefinger pressed up against his lips, his eyes closed.

"The most powerful force in the world, I believe, is love. But a close second is fear, and we know fear leads to sin. We must all fortify ourselves, everyday, against the temptations of the modern world. Me, you, and those people who assembled here that night, many of whom came here in fear. Would you have them leave here still fearful? As their spiritual leader, was it wrong for me to point them to peace of mind and clarity of thought? Surely even in your atheism, Ms. Kane, there is room for the comfort that fortitude provides."

Ms. Kane again. Maybe ministers aren't allowed to be

on a first-name basis with atheists.

She wasn't expecting to be drawn into a theological debate. She was trying to get a few simple answers to what she thought were pretty simple questions. She tried again, this time taking the blunt approach.

"Do you believe the Indiana Corn Weasel really exists? I don't mean as an entity in people's imaginations, or on some metaphorical level, but actually, provably, scientifically exists?" She was trying to knot up all the loopholes before his sophistry found an escape route. But she missed one.

"If I only believed in the existence of those things which could be proved scientifically I wouldn't be of much use in this position, would I, Kelsey?"

As she drove away, the church's steeple still prominent in her rear view mirror, she couldn't shake the nagging feeling the Reverend Lonnie was somehow connected to the recent spate of sightings of the Indiana Corn Weasel. His answers were just a little too glib, his manner a bit too guarded. Something inside told her that the Most Reverend Laurence Croydon knew much more about her prey than he let on. The faithful and God-fearing people of Milton might look to him for guidance, but Kelsey was starting to think he might be as much a part of the problem as part of the solution.

* * * *

Tonight, no more interviews. It would just be her and Justin, hanging out. Kelsey had already filled several notebooks—and most of her evenings in Indiana—talking to locals, trying to make some progress in her investigations. Her results thus far had been disappointing, mostly second or third hand retellings of weasel sightings, nothing nearly definitive enough to use in her dissertation. Tomorrow she was planning to meet the farmer Yoder whom the school principal had told her about. He had been ill recently and had put off her initial interview request. But tonight it was catch-up time with Justin, who had been pretty busy himself trying to get into the flow of the new school year in such challenging circumstances.

The surprise wasn't that Justin was doing well in school. Kelsey knew he was a smart kid, and she figured he'd adapt well enough in the short term. The surprise was that he was enjoying it as much as she was. Kelsey chalked some of that up to the extra attention he'd been getting from his teachers after his asthma attack and hospitalization. Having the paramedics haul a kid to the hospital was a pretty big deal to the school's faculty, but to Justin it was just a fast ride through all the red lights. He was a little slow making friends, but Justin was always a bit of a loner. Also, Kelsey noticed, none of the other parents seemed all that interested in setting up "play dates." Most of the kids just went home after school and stayed there. Their houses were isolated, and most kids went home to working farms where the list of "chores" that needed to be done annihilated the possibility of wasting time playing video games or hanging out in front of a big screen television. Kelsey actually felt great relief from the guilt she usually experienced when Justin was in school that she wasn't doing enough to "socialize" him. She always thought that was a rather nonsensical modern obsession, and in Milton, Indiana, she found a place that seemed to agree.

"Don't forget to squish, Mommy."

Justin had been put in charge of dinner. His edict: spaghetti and meatballs. And now, as they shaped the ground beef into meaty golf ball-sized globs, Justin was exercising quality control.

"I am squishing, Spinner. You don't like?" She held out her latest effort, which he inspected with great seriousness.

"It looks like an egg," was his verdict. "Supposed to be round. You know, meatball shaped."

Kelsey laughed. "You're a tough critic. Okay, show me how it's done, master chef." Justin grabbed a palm-full of meat from the mixing bowl and began pressing it into a glob, and then—"here's the important part," he announced—he placed the meaty orb on one upturned palm and rolled it quickly and lightly with the palm of the other outstretched hand.

"There," he said, showing her this thing in his hand like he was revealing a rare bird's egg or a valuable jewel. "See? It's round!"

"What's the difference?" said Kelsey, taking the philosophical approach. "We're just going to eat them anyway."

"Sheesh," said her little guy, shaking his head, and Kelsey laughed again to herself. *What an interesting person you're turning out to be,* she thought. Even if her research proved to be a bust—a prospect she was growing more fearful about by the day—she was beginning to think that this Midwestern sojourn might turn out better for him than she'd imagined.

The spaghetti and meatballs were delicious. Nestled on a cold autumn evening in their converted barn, Kelsey and Justin felt surprisingly at home. The tumult of their first few days was subsiding in memory, and as they drank hot chocolate and listened to the wind howling across the prairies of Indiana, a sense of unexpected calm took hold of them. They talked just as if they were back in New Jersey—about school, work, familiar things. Standing at the sink as they finished up the dishes, Kelsey and Justin were like a Norman Rockwell tableau.

"Do you like it here, Mommy?" Justin blurted out as his mother handed him a plate to dry. Kelsey thought about it for a few moments before answering.

"I like some things about being here, Spinner" she said. "What about you?"

"I like it," he said, pausing before asking, "Do you think Otto would like it here?"

"Maybe." She tried to imagine a flamboyantly gay black man with multiple body piercings and a wardrobe that a drag queen would die for standing around the bait and tackle shop, attracting sneers as he held the shiny fishing lures up to his earlobes, asking "Does this go?"

"Maybe we should invite him here," Justin said.

"Well, I'm not sure we're gong to be here long enough, Spinner."

She thought he actually looked a little disappointed.

"Are you almost done with your work here, Mommy?"

Good question.

She'd come here with a great deal of trepidation but also with the hope of finding some answers about what was going on in these fields and forests. So far, not much. She didn't see the value in hanging around indefinitely.

"Well, I've gotten a few things," she said. "Not what I needed, though."

"Don't worry, Mommy. You'll get it. And then you'll be as happy as a pig in shit."

Kelsey stopped rinsing, put down her plate, mouth agape.

"What did you say?"

"You'll be as happy as a pig in shit. The kids say it all the time in school. Leonard Smalley says that when Christmas vacation comes, we'll all be as happy as a pig in shit."

"I see." What could she say? He had a good ear, and a good memory. "Let's just say that I'd be very happy if I could dig up some more information about our friend, Mr. Weasel." She laughed to herself as she grabbed the last plate, conceding in her mind that yes, if she could get what she needed to finish her dissertation, she *would* be as happy as a pig in shit.

Warmed by the memory of Justin's unorthodox vocabulary lesson, Kelsey slept well that night. She was so deeply immersed in her slumber that she didn't hear a thing until Justin was practically on top of her.

"Mommy! Mommy!!"

Oh no—another attack.

Adrenalin surging, she immediately snapped into action.

"Okay, Justin. Try to relax, and focus. I'll get your inhaler."

She was halfway across the room before she heard his protest.

"No. Mommy! I'm fine! But something's out there!"

Kelsey groped for the table lamp on the nightstand, and turning it on, saw that Justin was indeed fine—scared, but fine. He showed none of the tell-tale signs of obstructed breathing—but he was clearly agitated. She reached out and grabbed his hand.

"Okay, kiddo. Tell me what you heard."

"There was scratching, Mommy, and then I heard hissing. I think it's him!"

Kelsey knew what he meant, of course, by "him"—the Indiana Corn Weasel. She pulled him close, hugged him, felt his heart racing. They stood there in the dimness, Kelsey listening for whatever he heard, Justin still shaken up, clutching his mother. There wasn't a sound, inside or outside the barn. The two stood there for several minutes in the silence. Kelsey knew well the terrors and the seeming reality of nightmares, and she was thinking that all their talk earlier in the evening about the Indiana Corn Weasel had unsettled him.

"Hey, Spinner, I've got an idea. Why don't you climb in bed with me? There's plenty of room, and besides, the bed was getting a little cold."

Both lies—the mattresses were much smaller than Kelsey was used to, and she was actually a little too warm under the blankets in their triple-insulated bedroom-within-a-barn. But Justin jumped at the chance, nodding fervidly in agreement. She could tell he was still agitated by his dream. "How about a cool glass of water before bed?" Kelsey asked.

"All right. I can get it, Mommy" he said, courageously. He padded off to the bathroom to fill a glass as Kelsey rearranged the blankets for two. As she smoothed the goose-down quilt that came with the place, she thought she heard Justin turn on the shower.

"Hey Spinner, what are you—"

He was standing right next to her, glass in hand, a look of terror etched across his face. It wasn't the shower Kelsey had heard, but a hissing sound that now filled the barn.

"Mommy, what is that?"

Kelsey had no idea. The wind? The water pipes that criss-crossed the barn? A gas leak? While she wrapped Justin in her arms, she cocked her head and tried to locate where the sound was coming from but she couldn't. It was a generalized noise that seemed to fill the place. Kelsey held Justin's hand as she walked slowly toward the front door, turning on all the lights as she went. Still the hissing continued, interrupted only by brief pauses. Justin was freaked out. She could feel him shaking. Kelsey was perplexed. The noise continued, growing slightly in intensity and then subsiding, starting again, measured, persistent. But Kelsey had been through far too many anxiety-inducing nighttime episodes to be undone by merely a noise in the night. She turned to face her son, grabbing his shoulders.

"Spinner, there's absolutely no reason to be afraid. We'll figure out what this is—and it'll turn out to be nothing. Well, nothing scary. Maybe a pipe burst and it's leaking steam, or water. Maybe there are a few loose boards outside and we're hearing the wind howl as it squeezes between the cracks. But I'll find it, okay? I'll bet it's something that happens all the time and if we lived here long enough we wouldn't even pay it any attention!"

Justin nodded but he was obviously unconvinced. Kelsey, emboldened by her own reason and her calmness in this situation, walked bravely toward the door, put her ear against it. The hissing wasn't any louder outside than inside, but as she listened closely she could hear now a kind of rising and falling intensity in the noise. And then there'd be a pause, for just a second, and it would start up again. She looked up at the ceiling to see if there were any leaks coming through or any water spots. She looked at the curtains to see if a draft was billowing the drapes. But everything was the same as always. Except for that damned noise.

She stood poised at the door, her hand on the knob.

"Mommy! Don't open it!" Justin blurted, his sobs now muffled as he burrowed more deeply into her robed midsection. Kelsey squeezed him, felt his fear. Still she listened closely, and still the hissing filled their rooms, filled their heads, a noise as diffuse as light, permeating the barn.

Despite Justin's protests, she knew she had to open the front door. She'd steeled herself to slowly pry it open when the sound suddenly stopped.

Just like that.

And just like that, Kelsey and Justin found themselves standing at their front door, shaking, puzzled, anxious, without any answers. They waited a few moments before moving, half-expecting and fearing that the hissing would begin again. They both looked around, not sure what they were looking for, exactly. Waiting.

As they climbed into bed, Kelsey didn't expect that either of them would get much sleep. As she gently brushed Justin's wispy hair, and whispered that it would all be okay, she went through a checklist in her head of all the possibilities behind that unnerving hissing sound. First thing in the morning, she decided, she'd call a plumber and get him to come over and check the pipes, as well as scouting around for loose boards or large cracks around the barn. And she'd ask her neighbors if they heard anything strange. She would be logical. She'd check all the possibilities. She'd be scientific about this. She went over the list as she drifted off to sleep, half-consciously adding one more item before sleep completely claimed her.

Check for footprints.

Chapter 5

The next morning on the ride to school Justin was quiet, and Kelsey knew he was still anxious about what happened. They talked about it over breakfast, and Kelsey promised him she'd figure out what had made that hissing sound.

"You don't think it was him?"

"Justin, there is no Indiana Corn Weasel," she said, a bit more fiercely than either of them expected. What did it mean that her own son, who'd heard her dismiss such legends for years as modern fairy tales, could be so easily convinced by a few scary stories told by some school mates and some unexplained noises in the night?

But he's only seven years old—just a little kid, really. He gets a pass.

What really bothered her were all those adults she kept running into who believed there's this large rabid beast with supernatural powers who has chosen Milton, Indiana, as the site of his unholy terror campaign.

"Have a good day, Spinner," she shouted after him as he climbed out of the car and ambled up the walkway to school. He waved to her, and then she watched him lose himself in a crowd of his schoolmates, a restless and naïve corps of believers who were helping spread the legend like so much fertilizer across the fruited plains. "Don't be swayed in your beliefs, little man," she said to herself, clutching the wheel and turning her car toward sunrise, squinting at the Indiana morning and feeling acutely the need for a good strong cup of coffee.

As she stepped out of the car, she remembered what Mrs. Hochstetler had said and she dug her tape recorder out of her bag and threw it onto the front seat of her car. No tape recorders, no cameras. Only a note pad and a pencil—she was told that even a ball-point pen would be frowned upon. Setting up the interview with Benjamin Yoder had given her some glimpse of what the actual experience of meeting him might be like. She wasn't able to call him—the Amish didn't allow telephones, televisions, even electric lights—so they communicated like a couple of junior high students, passing notes back and forth to Mrs. Hochstetler. Kelsey had tried several times to initiate contact, but every time she went to the address on the paper Mrs. Hochstetler had given her and knocked on the door she got no answer. Yet she could clearly see someone moving around inside the large farmhouse.

Kelsey was half expecting the same response this time when, to her surprise, the door opened before she even knocked.

"Good morning. Mr. Yoder? I'm Kelsey Kane." She extended her hand. He inspected her for a moment, nodded silently, reached out not so much to shake her hand but merely to pat it, as if to acknowledge the gesture. He said nothing, but stepped aside. There was an awkward moment where Kelsey waited for him to say something like "Come inside," or "Welcome," or "Nice to meet you." But he just stood there, still as a statue, an expression neither welcoming nor withering.

Kelsey didn't want to push her luck, but somebody had to say something.

"Nice place you've got here," she said to him, as she rocked back and forth on her heels, still waiting for some sort of cue. "Is the inside as nice as the outside?"

"Clever girl," he said, sweeping his left arm in a gesture of invitation. She nodded and walked inside the entranceway of a vast farmhouse. What first struck Kelsey was how bright the place was. Living in her dark barn had accustomed Kelsey to expect dimness and shadow, but here was grand illumination. Light seemed to stream in from unseen corners and nooks. Ben Yoder's dark clothes—and the well-established religious conservatism of the Amish—had led her to expect darker accommodations.

He guided her through what she took to be a sort-of living room, or family area. The place looked like a showroom for unpainted furniture. Everything appeared to be made of wood—the chairs, tables, floors, cabinets, window frames. Yoder himself moved rather stiffly, as if living among all this wood had affected his physiognomy. He continued guiding Kelsey wordlessly through a room she took to be a sewing room, and then into a sort of school room with smaller benches and wooden desks and old fashioned slates, each with a string holding a piece of chalk tethered to its wooden frame, and then finally a small room with a few rocking chairs and a Bible resting open on a simple reading stand. He indicated a chair, and Kelsey sat. He sat also, facing her, and he began to rock mechanically, back and forth, like a human metronome, wordlessly, eyes fixed on some distant spot on the wall behind Kelsey. As she was thinking of some way to break the ice, Ben Yoder spoke up.

"Skunks, as a rule, are not unwelcome visitors on a farm."

Kelsey wasn't sure if she had just been insulted. But hey, it was an opening, and she was eager to get some conversation going here.

"They're not? Hmm. I would have thought they would be."

"No, that's city-folk thinking," he said. "Skunks eat grubs, slugs, and lots of other insects that could harm the crops. The skunk can be the friend of the tiller. When you make your living off the land, you need all the help you can get."

"But what about the smell?"

He stopped rocking.

"Met some people in my life who stink a lot more than skunks, young lady."

Okay. Now we're getting somewhere. No idea where that might be, however, she acknowledged silently.

"But you're not here to talk about skunks, Miss Kane, isn't that right? Or perhaps one of their relatives?"

Is he talking about people? Is he saying someone in particular is a skunk? Or does he actually know that skunks are scientifically classed as a member of the weasel family?

She had no idea, but she decided to try to guide the conversation rather than just play along in this sort of weird guessing game.

"Mrs. Hochstetler said you might be able to fill me in on some of the history of Milton. She says you've been here a really long...well, what I mean is—"

"I'm old, and I've seen a lot. 'Tis no sin to be old."

"Right. Well, I'm trying to learn a little more about the town, and you know, any big changes that might have taken place. For instance, the Amish settled this town, right? But it doesn't seem like there are that many around? Even the old church—"

"Fellowship Hall."

"Excuse me?"

"The Mennonites—of which the Amish are a branch—call their places of worship 'fellowship halls,' not churches."

"Oh, okay. Thanks. So what happened to the Amish? The old church off Main Street—I mean, sorry, the fellowship hall—looks like it hasn't been used in years, but the other church, Jesus the Redeemer, is packed every Sunday. So what happened to the Amish? Did they...I mean, if you don't mind my asking…" Her voice trailed off—she was unsure how tactful she needed to be.

"Did they die off? Is that what you mean?" Kelsey nodded. "No, God be praised, we're still around. The Amish community still exists, Miss Kane. Have you been to Shipshewana? Or Elkhart? You'll find quite a vibrant Amish community—many of whom used to live in Milton."

"So what happened?"

"Adolph Hitler happened."

"Adolph Hitler? I'm not sure I understand. I know he went after the Jews. I didn't know he tried to exterminate the Amish too."

At this, Ben Yoder smiled.

"I'm not trying to rewrite history, Miss Kane. What I meant was World War II happened, and the military built a huge munitions factory in Milton, and later, a training base and officers' installation. At one point, almost half of Milton's land was owned by the U.S. Army."

"You mean they kicked you off of your property? That's awful."

"No, Miss Kane. Most of the Amish people left on their own. Willingly."

"Why would they do that?"

"In today's world, I can see where it might be difficult for you to understand," he said, no longer rocking, no longer gazing above her head but starting directly into her eyes, seeking her understanding. "We are deeply committed to our principles. Our religion is founded upon the idea of non-violence. War is unjust. For many of my brethren, there was no way they could live in a community that had become a facilitator of war. Military men in uniform were everywhere—it was as if our whole town had been seized by a crazed, evil impulse. Convoys of jeeps trampling the farmlands and cargo trucks carrying bombs across our plains. It was too much to bear. In protest, in the name of preserving their own religious convictions, they moved away. Not all, of course. My family decided the better way to protest was to dig in, try to persuade by example, pray. But we're one of the few Amish families left in Milton. At the end of the war, there were all these empty farmhouses. Slowly, they filled up with other God-fearing Christians, but by then most of the Amish had resettled elsewhere. Those who arrived to take their place were of many denominations. They built Jesus the Redeemer—which was quite modest at first. Now, it's the largest non-denominational church in the county."

"Yeah, I met Reverend Lonnie. I interviewed him last week."

Ben Yoder said nothing, but the look he gave her suggested mild contempt for the reverend in particular, maybe the church in general as well. Ben Yoder had, no doubt, never expected to spend his elder years as the object of public curiosity, but as one of the last Amish families in Milton, that's exactly what he and his fellow believers had become. She wanted to bring the conversation around to the Indiana Corn Weasel, but he seemed determined to continue plowing the same furrow.

"The military," he said, now somewhat agitatedly, as if Kelsey had reopened an old wound. "What they did out there, becoming an engine of war and death, was horrible enough. But when the war ended, they should have too. They're still at it. There's something going on out there, something not right."

Still at it? At what, exactly?

Kelsey was confused. "The base has been deserted for years, right? It doesn't look like anything is going on out there nowadays," she said.

He paused, began to rock a bit more quickly, and then stopped suddenly and fixed her with his steady gaze.

"Do skunks hibernate, Miss Kane?"

"Skunks? Well, not really. None of the weasel family hibernates," explained soon-to-be-Doctor Kelsey Kane. "But they give the appearance of hibernating. From what I know about weasels, they dig these shallow burrows and pretend to hibernate, but in fact, they remain conscious and ready to spring to action in a moment's notice. It's a predator's trick."

For the first time during their whole conversation, Ben Yoder laughed out loud.

"It's good you know your skunks!" he said, still laughing to himself. "That's *very* good!" he said, his laughter echoing off the wooden floor and walls as Kelsey smiled along dumbly, feeling a mix of pride and confusion.

* * * *

Everyone seemed to be talking in riddles to Kelsey lately. She'd come to town with what she thought was a pretty clear objective: find out the truth behind these reported attacks of the Indiana Corn Weasel. What she was filling up her notebooks with, however, wasn't clear evidence of anything—just rumor, speculation, religious and agricultural metaphors, and thinly-veiled warnings. She was starting to wonder if she'd ever get the pieces necessary to put the puzzle together when her cell phone rang.

"Hey, Kelsey, it's Frankie."

"Hi, Frankie. What's going on?"

"We just got word at the paper of another sighting. I'm on my way to talk to the witness. Thought you might want to tag along."

"Really?"

"Sure. I figured you'd want to hear about it from the source, rather than read about it in next week's paper."

"Come on, I don't read that rag," she said, but then she quickly backtracked, not wanting her cheap attempt at levity to cost her this chance. "Seriously, thanks for the heads up. I'd love to come along. Where should I meet you?"

"I'll pick you up at the diner in ten minutes. Then we have to swing out to Mercy."

"The victim's in the hospital? What happened?"

"No, she's fine. She just happens to work there. X-ray technician. I'll pick you up."

In a small town like Milton, you're never more than a few minutes away from anything, so Kelsey knew she had plenty of time to get to the diner. She turned her car around and headed north towards Main Street. When she got there, Frankie was already waiting.

"I thought carpooling might give us a chance to compare notes, go over some questions," Frankie said. "Besides," he said, eyeing Kelsey's bargain-basement clunker, "I get the feeling your car's about one large possum away from getting knocked out of commission."

"I appreciate your concern," she said sarcastically, but she really did appreciate his concern. He was doing Kelsey a huge favor by letting her sit in on the interview and get some much-needed first-hand information. Being able to talk to a credible witness could be a huge help, Kelsey hoped. Unfortunately, that wasn't going to happen for a couple of hours. When they got to the hospital, they learned the X-ray technician had a solid roster of patients and wouldn't be free for a while. So Kelsey and Frankie decided to kill some time in the hospital's cafeteria.

"So guess who I talked to this morning?" Kelsey asked her lunch companion, who was looking rather derisively at his meal of meat loaf and mashed potatoes.

"The highway supervisor who provides road kill to the cook at Mercy?"

"Don't be so snarky," Kelsey said. "The food here isn't bad. I had a couple of meals in this cafeteria when Justin was here."

"How's the little guy doing?"

"Oh, he's fine. I'm still trying to figure out why he likes it so much around here. I thought he'd be pining to go back home by now, but he's actually digging it. His science teacher has them collecting bark samples. He's really into it."

Frankie swallowed a forkful of his lunch and shrugged.

"Tell me who."

"The science teacher. I don't know his name."

"No, tell me who you talked to this morning."

"Oh. A strange—but in an interesting kind of way—older farmer named Yoder."

"Ben Yoder? He's a trip, all right. I'm not really in with the Amish crowd. After three years of chasing stories, I still can't get them to return my calls."

Kelsey nodded and continued eating.

"That's a joke, Kelsey. Return my phone calls…the Amish…"

"Oh, I get it. They don't use phones. Very funny, Frankie."

"Yeah, I don't get to tell too many Amish jokes around here. People can be pretty sensitive."

"And just plain weird. I'm still not sure if he liked me or hated me."

"If he opened the door to you, he liked you, believe me. They let almost no 'outsiders' into their homes. Did he give you anything useful?" Frankie's stated distaste for Mercy Hospital's food didn't keep him from shoveling it in.

"Take it easy, Frankie. Remember, you hate this stuff," said Kelsey, grinning. "I have no idea what he told me. Something about a skunk, and also about the military base in town."

"The base?" Frankie dropped his fork and grabbed his reporter's notebook. "What did he say, specifically?"

"Nothing. Nothing at all, really. I just got the impression he doesn't like that place, even though it's deserted. Why? What does he know?"

"It's not deserted, Kelsey. There's a skeleton crew that works there. Three shifts a day. You can see the cars come and go along Edgemont Road every eight hours. But nobody really knows what goes on there, how many people work there, what they do. It's pretty mysterious. The high school kids will tell you lots of wild stories about that place, things they've seen, or heard."

"Why don't you check it out?"

"I'd love to, but my publisher won't let us. We're not allowed to write anything about the base. He doesn't want to piss off the military with bad publicity. Afraid they'll close it, sell the property."

"So what?"

"Kelsey, that base takes up almost half of the land in town and pays two-thirds of the property taxes. If they go under, there goes Milton. The stores downtown couldn't afford to make up that tax revenue. Homeowners would see their taxes triple overnight—and most of those folks are barely getting by now. There'd be a mass exodus, foreclosures, then it's goodbye advertisers, goodbye readers, goodbye *Milton Forum*. They won't let anyone on staff get near the place. We haven't even mentioned the base in the paper in, like, years. It's ironic—it keeps the town afloat and we pretend it doesn't exist."

"What are they afraid you might find out?"

"Who knows? Maybe there's a brothel being run out of the barracks, maybe they're dealing drugs. For a while, the rumor was that there were aliens locked underground in one of the medical facilities. Whatever it is, they want us to keep hands off. Which is just fine by me. I like my job." He swallowed a heaping spoonful of translucent lime-green Jell-O and looked at his watch. "Let's get back down to radiology. I don't want to miss our chance."

"What did she see, anyway?"

"Not sure. She talked to the police last night. I haven't seen the report, but Smitty gave me her vitals."

"Smitty? Vitals? I feel like I've stepped into a detective novel."

"Smitty's the dispatcher. Good guy. I take him out in my boat sometimes. We go fishing."

"You have a boat?"

"A speedboat. You and Justin should come out with me sometime."

"I don't do boats," she said flatly. Frankie nodded.

"Anyway, Smitty tips me off to stories. He gave me her name, told me where she works. He said she filed a report, but he hadn't seen it. So we'll get to find out together."

Kelsey nodded, picked up her tray and followed Frankie out of the cafeteria and toward the elevators that would take them down to radiology. She loved this part of the dissertation process: the digging, the research, the sleuthing. She always felt she would have made a great reporter. Of course, she would prefer sifting for clues in some large, gritty, bustling metropolis. But even in an out-of-the-way hamlet like Milton, research had its rewards. She was fervently hoping her interview with the x-ray technician would prove to be one of them.

When they entered the radiology waiting room, Kelsey took a seat while Frankie went up to the reception desk and signed the roster of patients.

"One way or another, we're getting in to see her," he told Kelsey. "Even if we have to get x-rayed ourselves."

"I'm not putting on one of those paper gowns that leave you exposed," Kelsey countered.

"Really? I think that'd be a good look for you."

Kelsey laughed it off, but then she began analyzing Frankie's comment.

Just what does he mean exactly? Those gowns are not flattering, but they do leave your rear end pretty much out there for the world to admire. Is that his idea of a compliment? Is he saying he thinks I have a nice butt? That he wants to see more of me?

Kelsey hadn't thought of Frankie at all in romantic terms, but now it occurred to her that maybe she was being myopic. Romantic relationships were so far down on Kelsey's priority list that she was unprepared to even think in those terms. But why not? And why not Frankie? He was smart, reasonably attractive—even if he was barely her own height—funny, and a writer. If Kelsey was the kind of person who made lists about her ideal mate, Frankie would probably rate pretty highly. Her life over the past few years was so dominated by her research and her son that matters of the heart had been closeted, boxed up like so many dissertation notes. But here comes this guy, making this ambiguous comment that probably means absolutely nothing, and though it might not have woken up that part of Kelsey that had been slumbering for so long, it gave it a nudge. She made a mental note to pay more attention.

It was another twenty minutes before the nurse called Frankie's name. They both got up and walked to the examining room. "It's okay if she comes in too," he said to the nurse, pointing with his thumb to Kelsey. "She's my sister."

Sister. So much for romantic fantasies.

The x-ray technician, a woman in her mid thirties named Sheila Walters, was looking through some paperwork. She looked perplexed.

"I don't see your chart here. Did the admitting nurse take your paperwork?"

Frankie spoke up.

"I'm not here for an x-ray. My name is Frankie Auden. I'm with the *Milton Forum*. I left a message on your voice mail. I wanted to talk to you about last night."

Sheila Walters put down the clipboard and sat down on the little padded stool on wheels. She glared at Frankie.

"Who is this with you, really?" she said, pointing to Kelsey.

"I'm his fiancé," Kelsey chimed in.

Try that on for size, brother.

"Yes, that's right," he said, without missing a beat. "We were here anyway to get our blood test for the marriage license, so I asked her to come along while we talked. I hope that's okay."

Kelsey made a mental note to add "unflappable" to the list.

The technician looked at Kelsey, and then at Frankie, her stoic expression still intact.

“Congratulations. Now ask your questions. I’ve got a full slate of patients.”

“Can you tell us what you saw?” Kelsey asked, beating Frankie to the punch. He shot her a look of mild irritation.

She told them how she was driving home last night from work when she stopped her car near Lofton’s field, just outside of town.

“I’m a photographer. I’m always on the lookout for great pictures. So I’m heading home and there’s this magnificent sunset. I pull over, grab my camera, get out of the car, and that’s when I heard it.”

“Heard what, exactly?”

“Well, I’m focusing on the sunset, looking through the lens, trying to frame it all and at first it sounded like someone was letting the air out of my tires. It was this really loud hissing sound. I walked around to the back of the car, and there, in a ditch along the side of the road, I saw this…thing.”

“Tell us about it,” said Kelsey. Both she and Frankie were taking notes.

“At first I thought it might have been a dog, but it was way too skinny. It had reddish eyes that—this is going to sound weird—were kind of glowing. And its mouth was opened, I could see its teeth. It let out this squeal, like, really, really loud. I was terrified.”

“How big was it, would you say?” Kelsey asked.

“Oh…maybe, about like this big,” she said, holding her hands out past her shoulders. “About like this.”

“Three feet, then,” Frankie said, writing.

“I guess. Anyway, I didn’t know what to do. I was freaked out. It started clawing at the ground, and that’s when I decided I better do something. So I pressed the flash button.”

“What happened?”

"Nothing, for a second. Then it let out this blood curdling squeal. It clearly didn't like the bright light, so I did it again, and that's when it jumped. Right over the car, and on to the other side of the road, and then into the field."

Kelsey underlined the words *over the car* in her notepad.

"Any chance you got a picture when the flash went off?" Frankie asked.

"Not a good one. I was focused for distance. Remember, I was trying to get the sunset. The lens setting was all wrong. It's probably just a blur. But thank God the flash worked. And that's when I got a good look at him, when he was all lit up for just a second. He was one ugly creature, from his snout to his tag."

"His what?"

"His snout to his tag."

"What tag?"

"He had a tag taped around his back foot. There were some numbers on it, but I couldn't see what else."

"A tag? Are you sure?"

"Yeah, I told the police about it too. You know when you watch these wildlife shows. How these animals have tags? Same thing with this guy. Big ol' toe tag. I'm sure."

Kelsey and Frankie both looked at each other.

"Okay. Anything else?"

"No. that's it. Anyway, I have to get back to work. Patients are waiting. Good luck with the wedding," she said, and with that she was gone.

As soon as she closed the door, Kelsey and Frankie both shouted out the same thing, in unison: "A tag!"

Heading back to the diner, they tried to puzzle out what they just heard.

"She could have been mistaken," Frankie said.

"True," Kelsey added. "She was tired, she was scared, she thought she saw something that wasn't actually there."

"It could have been a piece of a barbed wire fence."

"Or some piece of aluminum foil it picked up while foraging through the garbage."

They both nodded, and Kelsey flipped through her notes. But then she put down the pad.

"If there really was a tag on that creature, do you get what that means, Frankie? Somebody is behind these weasel attacks. We've got to find out who."

Frankie pulled the car over and turned off the engine.

"Kelsey, we're not the police. I'm a journalist. I report stories. You're writing a dissertation. Let's not get carried away."

"Don't be such a weenie! Don't you want to know what's going on?"

He looked at her earnestly, smiled a little.

"I just want to write my story and go home." He started the car and pulled back on the road, Kelsey regretting that she ever agreed to be his pretend fiancé.

* * * *

Kelsey had been thinking a lot about what a tagged foot might mean, and who, exactly, might be doing the tagging. She spent the next few days contacting various state and national wildlife agencies to find out if there was any kind of study going on involving the genus Mustela. No one seemed to have any idea what she was talking about. She talked with a particularly devoted park ranger who told her that he'd been trying for years to do a census of the red fox population, but there wasn't any money available.

"You can't drive five miles in any direction without coming across some damn paving project tying up traffic for miles. There's always money for asphalt," he protested, "but not a dime for the little fox." Kelsey wasn't sure what the source of this ranger's attachment was to the red fox but she made a mental note to share his indignation with Frankie for a possible story idea.

Frankie would later laugh it off, telling her that the fox was such a common and unpopular menace in these parts—upsetting garbage cans and mauling chickens—that residents would only be willing to pay for a program "to count dead foxes, not red foxes."

Kelsey found Sheila Walter's account of her encounter with a wild, weasel-like creature credible. She'd begun to conclude that what was happening in Milton, Indiana was based in some way in reality, however bizarre or unlikely it might seem. Her hypothesis that these weasel sightings were the by-product of a fevered public imagination didn't seem to gibe with what she was uncovering. The dawning of this fact engendered a change in the way Kelsey viewed her time in Indiana. Having operated under the assumption that all she needed to do was poke a few weasel-sized holes in the accounts of some dubious eye-witnesses, Kelsey had never really prepared for the possibility that something might actually be out there.

Like any credible social scientist, she tried to interrogate her own prejudices. Was she starting to believe in the existence of the Indiana Corn Weasel because of the incident the other night in the barn? She'd never been able to discover any other reason for the hissing that woke her and Justin and echoed through their residence. So was she just giving in to her fear? Had the seeds of her shift in thinking been planted that night at Jesus the Redeemer church, when the collective mind of Milton closed ranks against the creature, when they "fortified" themselves against the very real threat it posed? Was it the story told by naïve Reggie Taylor, whose hayloft make-out session was interrupted by something suspiciously resembling "our friend," that planted the seeds of doubt in her theory? Sheila Waters might not have provided clear photographic evidence but her tale struck Kelsey as highly believable. What else was Kelsey to make of her story? Maybe the woman was exhausted after a long day of photographing people's internal organs? She said she wanted to take a picture of the sunset—was it a trick of the light, perhaps, or some sort of optical illusion caused by looking too long at the setting sun?

Even as she was becoming more convinced that something was out there, Kelsey still had trouble making the leap across the chasm of her skepticism. She simply wasn't ready to conclude that a being of almost supernatural ability and preternatural evil could really be roaming freely through the wheat fields and haystacks of Milton, Indiana. But she knew she could no longer pursue an investigation fueled solely by denial. Kelsey had to go to "Plan B"—a shift in strategy that would complicate her research and perhaps lengthen her stay in Indiana. Unable to write off these sightings as mass delusions, she'd have to dig deeper, get to the heart of the matter. This new commitment to confront, rather than debunk, her prey could threaten the integrity of her entire dissertation, she knew.

What she didn't know was that it could also threaten her safety and turn her and Justin's Indiana adventure into a most dangerous game.

Chapter 6

Kelsey spent Saturday helping Justin make a popsicle stick bird house for a class project, and later, taking him to a county-wide "harvest festival" to celebrate his eighth birthday. This being the Midwest, the festival was really just an excuse for over-consumption of home-made delectables and garden-variety carnival food: elephant ears hidden under a blizzard of powdered sugar, corn dogs on a stick, conefuls of unnaturally colored cotton candy, popcorn, pies of every imaginable variety—Justin's favorite was plum, as the laundry would later attest—homemade jams, cheese, honey sticks, muffins, fruit tarts, corn on the cob dipped in barrels of butter, sausage, ham rolls, éclairs, pumpkin soup, and deep-fried zucchini.

"Yum!" Justin said.

"Ugh," said Kelsey, after a lunch that consisted of a broiled bratwurst with sauerkraut, a caramel apple on a stick, homemade cider, and a cream puff.

* * * *

On Sunday Justin went on a field trip of sorts, a supervised nature hike through the local forest. The meeting point was, naturally, the church on Main Street. Since all of the kids in his class attended Sunday services anyway, it was the logical place to gather. Kelsey drove Justin there a few minutes before the morning service ended and they sat in the parking lot, waiting for the trickle of congregants that would signal that the service was nearing its end.

"Some people always sneak out early," Kelsey told him. "It happens at every church service no matter what the denomination."

"Why?"

"That's just how people are. They say they're Catholic, or Baptist, or whatever they are. But their real religion is leaving early. They leave work early, they leave football games in the third quarter, New Year's Eve parties at eleven p.m."

"That's weird."

"Yep."

Sure enough, a middle-aged couple in their Sunday clothes pushed open the doors, followed by a teenaged boy who was talking on a cell phone.

"Right on time, Mommy!"

When the trickle became a steady exodus, Kelsey and Justin got out of the car.

"Mr. Masterson said he'd be by the side door," said Justin, peering around and between the exiting parishioners. Kelsey was glad to see how excited he was about going on this excursion. She had the usual worries about him being away for the day. And today, she also had an unusual worry. She could barely believe it when she found herself worrying about a possible attack by the Indiana Corn Weasel. But Kelsey was assured that there would be several adult chaperones. Her own research into the recent spate of attacks revealed that they almost never happened during broad daylight. Weasels were generally nocturnal, and the plan was to get the kids back by sunset. Still she was a little worried. But also grateful—she had a little nature excursion of her own planned, and it would be easier for her if she was alone.

"There he is!" Justin waved to Mr. Masterson, who looked rather ridiculous in his scoutmaster uniform. But she was grateful Justin had been invited. Because Kelsey didn't expect to be in town very long, she didn't want Justin to begin the formal process of becoming a Scout, and then having to leave half-way through.

"When you begin something, you've got to finish it, Spinner," she'd explained to him. *"Otherwise, you just end up with a half-way life."*

But Mr. Masterson told her that Justin could come along on any outings as a "visiting scout"—a title in which Justin took unusual pride. She took her son over to him, made the obligatory small talk, and hugged Justin.

"Be careful, Spinner."

"I won't pet any weasels, Mommy. Scout's honor," he said, crossing his heart with his index finger.

* * * *

Now *her* field trip had begun. Over the past several days, Kelsey had been reading up on weasels, their habitat, their eating habits, their patterns of behavior. She learned that weasels don't drink a lot of water but that they do drink frequently, revisiting watering holes every few hours, lapping their tongues a couple of times, rewetting their salivary glands, and then it's back into the woods. Find the source of water and the lair won't be far away, she learned. In Milton, there were two large permanent sources of water. One was the drainage ditch running through town on the east side, and the other was the lake just northwest of town. The lake was located in a wooded grove, and when Kelsey plotted where the recent spate of attacks had occurred, most were within a mile or so of the lake. If there were any clues to be found, the lake seemed like a good place to explore.

Except…

Kelsey hated lakes. She'd known for years that what she felt went beyond a mere phobia, that it had latched onto her, that it was like a rival presence in her body. Kelsey had scrupulously avoided taking Justin to the Jersey Shore—no mean feat when everyone around them seemed to spend their summer weekdays counting down to "shore time." A few times over the past several years, Kelsey had been invited to join some graduate school friends at a small lake for an afternoon barbecue. She finally gave in, about a year ago, but that proved to be a mistake.

She'd made it through the cheese sandwich and potato salad portion of the afternoon, as she and her friends picnicked in a wooded area about a hundred yards from the lake, but when the whole crew headed down to the beach, Kelsey felt the first twinge. But Justin was there, and he wanted to play in the sand, and she didn't want to ruin his afternoon and besides she really wanted to be able to do this, thought she could finally do this. She remembered feeling a little woozy as she began the walk through the woods toward the water. Through the trees she spied the rental canoes and rowboats gently adrift on the water and as they approached the beach her heart raced and her palms began to sweat. By the time she actually felt the sand between her toes, it was too late. Nauseated, dizzy, her heart beating wildly, she knew she was going to be sick—or worse. She was right.

When she came to, she squinted up at the cadre of concerned friends who had moved her into the shade and were dabbing her forehead with dinner napkins dampened with lake water. It felt disfiguringly familiar. Kelsey lied and told them all she was on medication and she shouldn't have had that wine spritzer with lunch, and she should probably get out of the sun, and by the time she was back in the car with Justin, she felt better, at least physically. But she knew exactly what happened, and it frightened her. She also knew that unless she decided to get serious about dealing with her past and finally confronting her father's death and the torturous residue still clinging to her from that fateful morning, she'd always be a prisoner of that moment.

* * * *

And now here she was, alone, heading to a lake. But there were several factors she hoped would make this experience bearable—factors she continued to recite to herself in a litany of wishfulness. The lake she was going to was much smaller than the one still haunting her dreams. Also, there was no sandy beach. It was mostly marshland. This lake wasn't just recreational, it was naturally functional as well, a critically-important watering hole sustaining the raccoons and the golden squirrels and the great blue herons and yellow warblers and red-headed woodpeckers that the geologic survey claimed lived thereabouts.

"I have to do this. This is my work. My career depends on doing this right," she told herself. "I *have* to do this."

She turned on to the unpaved access road leading to the lake and drove another fifty yards before pulling over. She thought she could see the lake ahead in the distance. Breathing steadily, remembering why she was there, she took off her sneakers and laced up her hiking boots. She grabbed her notepad and her camera and stepped out of the car.

"I have to do this," she whispered to herself again. But before she even had a chance to get close enough to test her resolve, her attention was arrested by a rustling in the knee-length switchgrass she was walking through. She froze. Something was there, lurking, hidden, but close. After the first rush of adrenaline subsided, Kelsey reminded herself why she was there, and slowly reached down for the camera. She tried to focus on a patch of the yellow-green grass just a few feet in front of her where she thought the noise came from. She stood there, focused, waiting. But nothing happened, nothing moved or made a sound. Kelsey gradually relaxed and resumed her trek. After she'd taken her first step, a small, rust-colored furry creature with a pointed snout and speedy gate bolted from the protection of the high grass and dashed across her path.

Kelsey jerked back, breathless, but then saw it was only a baby red fox, much more startled by Kelsey's presence than she was by its.

"Well, that's *one*," she said, remembering the Park Ranger's desire for a census of red foxes.

Being able to focus on her work was a welcome distraction. She was so busy photographing and cataloging the flora and fauna and looking for animal tracks and signs of burrowing animals that she was surprised to see she'd gotten so close to the water. The fringes of the lake were algae-covered and the surface formed a kind of filmy patina over mud-colored water rippling gently in the chilly autumn wind. Kelsey was relieved to be feeling nothing but scientific interest in this locale. Adrift on the murky waters was a family of black ducks, unbothered by her interest. On the far side of the lake, a blanket of fading goldenrod caught the morning sun, milkweed genuflecting in the breeze. The lake was bordered by a small wood comprised mostly of cypress, yellow poplar, and persimmon trees, the ground mined here and there with wild mushrooms erupting under a blanket of bog grass, common oak sedge and phlox. A word Kelsey would never have thought to use to describe a lakeside scene came into her head, and she said it aloud: "Beautiful."

The setting appeared to be blissfully free from peril—psychological or mammalian. She walked about the fringes of the lake, making notes, taking pictures, taking it all in. She'd read extensive descriptions of weasel burrows, and she knew the tell-tale signs to look for: unnatural bumps ringed in mud arising in clearings or thinly forested swaths of land, shallow furrows in the ground, a faint acrid-smell, and small random piles of broken twigs and sticks that gave evidence of nocturnal gnawing. She didn't see any of these things—although Kelsey wasn't trained as a naturalist. What she knew of the habitats of crypto-zoological figures came almost exclusively from books. She was surprised to find how much she was enjoying her first plunge into field work.

Maybe Dr. Reeves is right. This could turn out to be a terrific opportunity.

Kelsey saw a steady stream of tiny air bubbles breaking on the surface of the lake at the water's edge. Small water-based creatures like crawfish and tadpoles could serve as a food source for any of the genus Mustela, so she wanted to get a picture of the bubbles. She took a couple of careful steps toward the water, gingerly traversing a mucky portion of ground that was more swamp than shore. She leaned forward so that she could point the camera directly down. She was hovering right over the bubbles, twisting the lens, the picture of professionalism.

As Kelsey depressed the shutter button, she felt herself being pulled down, sucked into the soft earth and ooze framing the murky lake. With no warning, the ground beneath her feet yielded with frightening speed, her lower body subsumed by the frothy muck and mire. In what seemed like seconds she was up to her waist in this swampy entrapment, stunned at how immobile her lower body had become.

It happened so rapidly she had no time to react, or even feel fear. But now, as she struggled to free herself, she felt the icy incursion of panic take over her body. Squirming, trying to kick herself free only seemed to make things worse, each contortion bringing more of her into the mud. She tried to feel for the bottom of whatever sort of sinkhole she was in, but her hiking boots simply squished back and forth, vainly seeking a foundation.

Kelsey tried to remain calm, she really tried, but something inside her resisted, some elemental force seemed to be pushing her towards panic and dissolution. She was trapped in mud and sinking slowly, her cell phone back in her car, her memories of other panics at other lakes revisiting her now with painful clarity. She knew what she *should* do—stay calm.

That's what they always say to people in this kind of situation, isn't it? That's the most important thing. "Try to relax, honey."

Kelsey reached down through the mud to feel through her jacket pockets for anything that might help her. Groping through the mud and slime, she discovered only her car keys and a small wooden pencil in her left pocket. With a great strain, she was able to pull her left arm free and hold it above the swampy sinkhole. The muck was now up to almost her chest—she was sinking faster now, and though she knew she should have been trying to figure out what to do next, instead she did what seemed more elemental and imperative at the time. She began to cry.

This couldn't be happening. She'd gone nowhere near the actual water. She stuck to the shore, where it was supposed to be safe. None of the books she consulted warned about this danger. The presence of such natural sinkholes was documented, and their dangers fully known, but only among experienced naturalists and Eagle Scouts, not weekend explorers and Ph.D. candidates in cryptozoology. Kelsey was wishing she'd been a scout.

Scouts. Justin. My God, what will happen to him if I can't get out of here? Oh God, please get me out of here, Kelsey the atheist begged.

She brought her hands together in prayer, briefly, though as she did, she felt herself slipping even further, so she immediately spread her arms back out, trying to support herself against the insubstantial ooze that threatened her with the encroachment of every additional inch.

Think, Kelsey. There's got to be a way.

She tried to turn her head to survey what was around her. She was limited in her range but she could clearly see that near where she'd been standing just minutes ago was a tree whose branches rose out and above the water. The autumn winds had removed most of its leaves, but there were still a few rusty ones hanging on, defiant, oblivious to the change of seasons. One of its branches jutted out, parallel to the murky lake, its reflection barely perceptible on the water's surface. The branch forked right above where Kelsey was struggling. She should have clung to that branch, she now realized, when she was taking the picture. She could have looked down right into the swamp from that branch, which was about the thickness of Kelsey's fist. Now, she was looking up at it, taunted by its closeness and its distance.

She put her palms flat against the muck and tried to push her body up but all that accomplished was caking her fingers in fresh mud and reaffirming her desperate situation. As she wiped her hands across her chest, her fingers tripped against the strap of her camera, which was still around her neck.

Her camera strap! She reached carefully down to her waist, now about a foot underneath the surface, and managed to wrangle the body of her 35mm Nikon, now fully bathed in mud and seaweed sinews, and she held it carefully above shoulder level, keeping her arms above the mud, which had risen another few inches, inching ever closer to her chin. She bowed her head and pulled the strap over her neck and hair, and holding the camera with her right hand, gripping it as tightly as she could given its nascent sliminess, she twirled the strap in the air like a lasso and threw it at the branch. She hit it, but the strap failed to catch on to anything, simply slapping it lightly before slipping away. There was a small knobby protrusion where the branch forked. If she could get the strap there, then maybe—

Kelsey's rational thoughts were hijacked by a noise, familiar and frightening, that filled her head. It was a hissing sound—the same hissing sound she'd heard with Justin in their barn in the middle of the night. It came out of nowhere, bursting into her head suddenly with a cruel and ferocious timbre. She looked around briefly, but could see little except the flora immediately in front of her and the branch over her head. The sound stopped, and Kelsey could hear only her heartbeat, pounding furiously, filling her head with the steady pulse of her own terror. She tried again to snag the branch but again failed to do more than graze the limb. And again, as if cued by her failure, the hissing returned, sounding louder and closer. Kelsey couldn't turn to see, but that didn't matter. Soon she'd be immersed, and there'd be no sound, only darkness and her own muffled screams, uttered vainly in the damp earth.

Amid the hissing and her heart pounding and the rising tide of slime she managed to hold the camera aloft and twirl once more its black nylon strap. Heaving with every ounce of strength left in her upper body, Kelsey aimed the loop of the strap at that gnarled knob sticking out from the branch and tried for what might well be the last time before she got sucked into the depths below.

"Please God Please God Please God..."

A perfect shot. It landed cleanly at the base of the knob and tightened up when Kelsey pulled on it. Before she could express relief or gratitude, she felt herself pulled lower, the sinkhole now dampening her chin. With both hands on the strap, she strained with every ounce of strength that her adrenaline-fueled muscles could muster and tried to pull herself up. At first, there was no movement, and Kelsey screamed out in fear and defeat. But then she felt something give way, a little. It was her boots. They were no longer on her feet. The slime and ooze had loosened them from her feet as she pulled forward, and buoyed by this small gift of movement, she strained again, and there was more movement, though just a little. She was now only in the muck up to her chest, so she heaved again, and a few more inches gave way, the tree branch bowing under the weight of its mud-soaked tenant.

After subsequent heavings, Kelsey had made her escape. Moving her hands up the strap, one over the other—*"Just like climbing rope in gym class,"* she would later tell Frankie—Kelsey was now able to grab on to the branch and swing her body, slowly, over to the trunk of the tree, from where she leaped back onto the solid shore, filthy, exhausted, and joyous.

Lying there on the damp ground, stretched out like some beached creature from the deep, Kelsey panted and rolled over, looking up at the sky. She could feel mud drying and caking all over her body. Her camera was ruined, she knew, without even inspecting it. And her boots were gone forever, a souvenir of the swamp's near-miss. She turned her head and studied the water. It was hard for her to believe that this placid lake and its decorative fauna lining the fringe of the water were the source of such anxiety and horror. Everything looked peaceful, sounded tranquil. Barely any wind, and only the isolated tweet of a sparrow to break the silence.

And no hissing.

Had she imagined it? Or was that sound that filled her head the echo of the anxiety she felt? She crawled up onto her knees and looked around, scanning for any evidence that might confirm the presence of a creature whose hiss could shatter the calm of this scene. The only trail she saw was her own, the damp remnant of her climb toward freedom. Everything else was as pristine as when she arrived.

She stood up and felt the spongy groundcover under her bare feet. She couldn't imagine what she must look like—probably like some creature from the annals of crypto-zoology. There was no place she could think of to go clean up or hose off so she simply trudged off toward her car. She paused as she got to the gravel path and turned back to look at the lake.

Later, recounting the story of her escape in her own head, she would reflect on how close she actually came to being swallowed by that sinkhole, her life literally hanging by a strap. And she'd feel the chill of narrow escape. But for now she just looked out across at the water and the surrounding trees and overgrowth. As she stood there studying the scene, shoeless, muddy, caked with slime and sore from using muscles she hadn't used since high school gym class, she uttered a vow that sounded almost like a dare, to herself and whatever might be listening: "Not going to stop until I *find* you."

Chapter 7

What caught Kelsey's eye as she drove past the military base's entrance was all that razor wire atop the fence, shining in the moonlight. Then there was the squat, formidable guard house. She couldn't tell if there was anyone inside, but there were lights on everywhere: inside the security kiosk just past the front gate, atop the guard house, and rows of flood lights lit up the entrance way like a perpetual noontime. She hoped she could get a glimpse of a shift change, or of some delivery truck, or any activity, but as she slowly cruised by the base it appeared to be what the military spokesperson she had talked to earlier in the day had said it was: a "non-operational facility being maintained by a skeleton crew until its disposition was finalized."

It might have appeared "non-operational" at the moment—there didn't seem to be any movement that she could see through the fence—but local legend had it that plenty was happening out at that base. Kelsey had been finding excuses to drive by the place throughout the past week, her imagination piqued by the stories she was hearing. Kelsey was far too skeptical of local lore and rumor to be taken in by the many wild tales and conspiracy theories she'd been hearing, but the last two reported sightings of the Indiana Corn Weasel had taken place on property adjacent to the base. It seemed unlikely to her that a nocturnal mammal would be attracted to a place so brightly lit and fortified as a military base, but perhaps this errant creature had found a home in one of the deserted barracks.

Kelsey's thoughts were subsumed by the intoxicating aroma coming from the passenger seat of her car: cheese and tomato and sausage and green pepper and onion seducing her senses, steaming the window and filling the car with a thoroughly appetizing scent. She liked her pizza with everything—Justin did too. That made ordering easier. "Load it up," they used to tell the waitress at Vinnie's Pizzeria back in Jersey. Kelsey had taken the long way back from the pizzeria so that she could get a good look at the base. Frankie was back at the barn keeping an eye on Justin. He'd invited her to dinner but she said she wanted to stay in, so he more or less invited himself over to her place. Kelsey promised him free pizza in exchange for a bit of babysitting, and he readily accepted—though he did try to discourage her from cruising by the base.

"If there isn't anything going on, it's a waste of time," he said. "And if there *is* something going on there, you think the military is going to actually tell you what it is? Trust me, you're better off leaving the speculation to the tin foil hat crowd."

Normally, Kelsey would be the one to take the skeptical line, but once she vowed to track the Indiana Corn Weasel to its lair, she committed to going wherever the trail led. Tonight, it led past the guard house of the military base on the edge of town. She'd hoped that Frankie—a reporter, for God's sake—would have been a bit more supportive. But she also realized where he was coming from. His publisher was apparently determined to squelch any story he might write about the base. Why spend time pursuing useless things?

Despite the rumblings of her stomach and the

intoxicating aroma of the pizza pie within arm's reach, she pulled her car over across the road from the base, turned off the engine, and watched. After a few minutes of squinting into the glare, Kelsey began to feel that she might indeed be wasting her time. "I'll come back later," she said to herself. She was about to restart the car when she noticed in the rear view mirror a figure standing behind her car. She couldn't make out who it was, or what his purpose might be. But she decided to find out.

As she started to climb out of the car, she heard a commanding voice from the direction of the guard house, booming through a loudspeaker.

"Do not exit the vehicle."

Kelsey was startled, and confused. She looked around. The figure at the rear of her car was dressed in army fatigues, and was copying down her license plate information in a small notepad. Kelsey turned toward where the voice had come from, and raised her hand to her brow, trying to see beyond the glare.

"Resume your position within the vehicle immediately," the voice commanded.

She was perplexed as to what she could have done, or why she was being ordered about by a disembodied voice in the night, but the tenor of the command left little doubt in her mind of the seriousness of the order.

"Okay," she shouted to no one in particular, and she gave a kind of half-wave toward the guard house. She climbed back behind the wheel, but when she checked her rear view mirror, the fatigue-clad figure was gone. Kelsey stuck her head out of the window and craned her neck to look behind her car, but there was no one there.

"Exit the premises immediately," boomed the voice in the night. Under different circumstances, Kelsey might have been inclined to investigate further—if it had been daytime, or if she had someone with her. But alone, at night, and a little rattled by the unexpectedness of it all, Kelsey complied. She started her car and slowly pulled

back on to the road, and though the aroma of the pizza still filled the car, Kelsey had lost her appetite.

When she told Frankie later that night what happened, she got the expected lecture. But she could tell he was surprised by the interest the military would take in an ordinary citizen idling a car outside the gate. The same question occurred to him that had occurred to her as she drove home. If they were being that vigilant, what were they afraid someone might discover? She could see that Frankie's reporter instincts were stirred by her story, but outwardly he maintained his posture of disapproval.

"So now you have another good reason to drop this silly investigation," Frankie told her between mouthfuls of pizza. "Not only do you have zero chance of finding out what's happening there but now you know they don't want you there." He jammed the rest of a slice into his mouth and chewed away, smugly. "And they have your license plate number."

"Yeah, they do. But what possible interest could they have in me? A harmless crypto-zoologist who pulled her car over to have a quick slice of pizza, that's all."

"Uh huh," Frankie said. "Until you go back there. Which you will do. Because you, Kelsey Kane, have this strange fascination with dangerous situations."

It's so odd that he thinks that.

She always felt the exact opposite was true, that she was drawn like a magnet to secure and safe situations. What Frankie mistook for courage was really just her New Jersey survival instinct at work. But she didn't correct him. If he wanted to think of her as the fearless explorer, she could deal with that. It was a kind of compliment she'd never imagined anyone paying her, and it felt pretty good. She reached out to pour another glass of wine, and refilled Frankie's glass. Justin had gone to sleep right after he ate, so they were alone, nibbling on leftovers. Frankie grabbed his glass and leaned back against the couch they were sitting on.

"The deeper you get in, the harder it is to get out," he

said, somewhat cryptically.

"What do you mean?"

"When I first talked to you on the phone, you said you'd be out here a couple of weeks, maybe a month. Well guess what, Dr. Kane?" He leaned forward and clinked his glass against hers. "Happy anniversary."

A month?

It hardly seemed possible.

"And I've got something for you—an anniversary present." He got up and walked over to his shoulder bag, took out a large manila envelope. He handed it to her.

"Happy anniversary."

Kelsey was amused and curious. She opened the envelope and removed its contents, a blurry, eight-by-ten black and white photo. It was dark and shadowy and formless, and she couldn't quite make out what it was.

"It's your little friend," Frankie said. "That's the picture Sheila Walters took when she was trying to scare off whatever it was she saw. I asked her for her film, and I had our photographer develop it in the paper's darkroom and blow it up."

Amid the shadows and the darkness she could see it now, a blurry but definite presence, the form of an animal. And there it was, attached to a hind foot, something appended, a piece of paper or metal with marks on it, faint but visible.

"The tag," she whispered to herself, somewhat in disbelief. There was no other object in the photo so it was impossible to gauge the size of the creature. But there it was, mostly—proof that something was out there.

"When I saw it, I thought of those blurry pictures you sometimes see of the Loch Ness monster, shrouded in fog, shot from a distance. I guess The Indiana Corn Weasel is your Nessie, huh?"

Kelsey just sat there, looking at the picture, stunned. All of the rumors, stories, and even eyewitness accounts she'd dutifully recorded since her time in Milton hadn't made the impression this grainy photo in her lap had made.

Tears began to well up in her eyes. She looked at Frankie.

Concern showed in his face. "Kelsey, what is it?"

"Don't you see? This picture proves I've gotten it all wrong. In my dissertation I argued that the corn weasel is just a phantom. It's my longest chapter, Frankie. I've got all this serious-sounding sociological research in there. But it's all a botch! All my clever theorizing—completely wrong! Here's the proof!" She threw the photo on the coffee table and put her head in her hands.

Frankie put his arm around her, tentatively. He felt responsible for her despair. But he also believed that Kelsey would come to see this as critical piece in the puzzle she was constructing. He leaned in close to her and said, confidently, "When we catch him, Kelsey, you can replace your merely clever chapter with one that will blow people's minds. Kelsey, this is a terrific opportunity!"

Letting go of her disappointment, she grabbed hold of Frankie and kissed him, reflexively. She was about to discover him a willing partner in her excursion into deep, dark places not on the map.

* * * *

In their brief time in Indiana, Kelsey congratulated herself on having been able to establish a routine with Justin. In an effort to achieve some sense of normalcy, she kept them both on a fairly rigid schedule on school days. Up early—well, "early" by New Jersey standards, though not the standards of Midwestern farm country—breakfast at their makeshift nook, and then off to school, Kelsey off to do her research, then back to pick up Justin, followed by dinner at home, and then homework for him and, depending on what she had gotten done that day, homework for her as well.

So it was a little unusual for Kelsey to stray from her routine. But as she lay in bed long past the first crowing of the rooster, her son Justin had to wake himself up. He got dressed and wandered into the area of the barn where Kelsey's bed was and he rubbed his eyes and, in the still dark shadows of the morning, looked again to see if he had things straight.

One bed. Two people.

He reached out and poked the person closest to him in proximity. It happened to be Frankie, who groaned and rolled over. So he poked again.

"What is it?" he mumbled. "Let me sleep."

He poked the person again.

"I need a ride to school."

A ride to school?

Frankie thought he was dreaming, and therefore he didn't move.

Kelsey heard those words and it took her only a fraction of a second to process them.

I overslept!

She bolted out of bed toward Justin but had forgotten that someone else was also still there, and she rolled over Frankie and landed on the floor, pulling down the blankets that were tangled about her legs. That left Frankie un-blanketed. As Kelsey's vision cleared up and her eyes adjusted to the semi-darkness, she let out a small shriek, throwing a pillow over Frankie's exposed bare bottom.

"Mommy, he's naked!"

Frankie opened his eyes. Uh Oh.

"Justin, get your backpack and your jacket."

"But Mommy, he's—"

"Backpack, Justin!"

As soon as he turned to get his books, Kelsey whispered loudly to Frankie, shaking him. "Put some clothes on and get going. We overslept."

Before Frankie knew what was happening, Kelsey had escorted Justin to the door and ducked into the bathroom to exchange a pajama top for her clothes, grabbed her coat and keys, and got her son on his way to school, somewhat tardy but with quite a story to puzzle out on his ride there.

When Frankie called Kelsey's cell phone only an hour later, she was expecting a strategy session about damage control. But he put something else on her plate.

"There was another attack last night," he said. "Pretty bad, from what I'm hearing. Thought I'd give you a heads up. Took place on the Trower farm, just west of the base. I'll call you when I know more."

"Thanks. 'Bye."

Any fears she had about lingering awkwardness from last night's impromptu tryst disappeared in the harsh glare of morning and the even harsher reality of another corn weasel attack. There wasn't a lot she could do at the moment, she figured, or at least until she heard more from Frankie. The police wouldn't even talk to her. She'd tried several times over the past few weeks to get copies of police reports, but they wouldn't let her past the reception desk.

Frankie once told her, "Sometimes, they won't even talk to me, even though the law says they have to." He said one of the few frustrations he had with his job was dealing with the paranoia and defensiveness of the local cops. "But when they want to show off a new, high-tech squad car to the taxpayers, or get some attention for one of 'Officer Friendly's' anti-drug lectures in the school, God forbid we don't put it on the front page."

Kelsey decided to stay the course this morning and go to the library as planned to do some additional digging on mammalian life in Northeast Indiana. She was headed to a branch of the county library in Conner's Field, a few towns over. According to a conversation she'd had with a local naturalist at the soil conservation corps office just beyond the county line, the library in Conner's Field had an extensive collection of samples and data about local wildlife, a tradeoff in its deal with a couple of local universities to catalogue and microfilm their collections for free. Most of Kelsey's research about the Indiana Corn Weasel had been focused on the creature as a fictional being. She'd done a lot of work in the field of folklore, oral history, and the growth and transmission of local legends. She knew how stories get born and passed along, from community to community, and she knew how religion helped fan the flames of belief in these kinds of beings. But what she didn't know much about was *actual* weasels, other than what she picked up incidentally from her research. She thought if she could find out a little more about their habits she might get an edge in her quest to actually track down whatever was wreaking such havoc among the cornfields of Milton.

Kelsey had made an appointment with Mrs. Martha Coffey, the library's director of special collections, for ten in the morning. She was early, so she got out her car and went into the building to wander around. Kelsey found libraries a comfort, and this was no exception. What it lacked in architectural style it made up for in accessibility. All of the stacks were open (she hated closed stacks—they seemed to go against the very idea of a library) and there were several large tables on which people could spread out their work. The children's library was a separate space, just off the entrance, and she could see that a good deal of imagination had gone into its assembly. There were gigantic hungry caterpillars made of paper maché, and a life-size statue of the Cat-in-the-Hat at the checkout desk. The wood shelves were festooned with vines and leaves, a jungle motif to promote its "Reading is a real ADVENTURE" theme. Kelsey mentally applauded whoever it was who spent the extra few hours trying to turn the staid shelves of a local public library into a theme park for the mind.

"Gotta love it," she said aloud, as she climbed the stairs to the second floor. Kelsey and Justin spent just about every rainy Saturday at their local library in New Jersey, having reading adventures of their own. As she reached the landing at the turn of the stairs there was a floor-to-ceiling glass cabinet with a display labeled "You CAN tell an animal by *its* cover," and featuring dozens of small samples of fur, feathers, quills and skin, each with a small, typed-out index card briefly describing the animal and its covering. There was a pelt of beaver fur, feathers from a blue jay, a length of discarded snake skin, a tortoise shell, porcupine quills, rabbit pelts, and a tuft of fur from a coyote. There wasn't anything from the weasel family. She hoped she would have better luck sifting through the formal collection.

Mrs. Coffey apparently had no trouble picking out Kelsey from the usual corps of elderly citizens who treated the library as a kind of unofficial senior center.

"Miss Kane, I presume?"

"Yes. Hi. Mrs. Coffey?"

"Just like the beverage," she said with the perkiness of someone who perhaps needed to cut back.

"Right. So, as I mentioned on the phone, I'd like to take a look at any materials you have pertaining to the genus Mustela."

"Of course. Follow me."

She took Kelsey through the main reference section of the library, back through the film and media department and then into a small, well-lit conference room with a laminate-finish reader's table surrounded by several wooden file cabinets.

"This is our naturalist research and reading area," she explained. "Behind you, in these drawers, is the mammalian collection, each specimen classified and catalogued in this book," she said, handing a massive, three-ring binder to Kelsey. "Local flora and fauna is here, on this shelf, cross-referenced in the main computer catalog and also here, in this journal of unpublished holdings," she said. "If you need anything, just let me know," she said.

"Thanks. This is amazing. I could get lost in all this stuff."

"You wouldn't be the first," Mrs. Coffey said. "Good luck."

Kelsey pulled a few books off the shelf and stacked them up on the table. She opened her notebook and took out a pen. She wasn't expecting to become an expert in a few hours but she was looking for something that might explain—in scientific terms—the phenomenon of the Indiana Corn Weasel. Its unprecedented size and its puzzling, ferocious behavior must be rooted, Kelsey felt, in rational science. Somewhere in that room could be the key to the mystery.

She took copious notes, even in areas she'd covered previously. She compiled a checklist of the basics, just to make sure she wasn't missing anything. Weasels are slender. Check. Weasels are carnivorous. Check. Weasels have curved, non-retractable claws. Check. Weasels emit a high-pitched screech when threatened. Check—there was nothing in the literature about a hissing sound. Weasels need to be near water as they are frequent drinkers. Check.

As she scoured the nature manuals and field guides nothing she found explained how a weasel could grow to more than three feet in length—more than three times the normal size—nor the lengthy airborne assaults it had allegedly been making. The other attributes she'd noted in her interviews with victims of recent attacks—glowing eyes, hissing, fearlessness, rapid ground speed—were simply inconsistent with what has been observed among the genus Mustela. The weasel generally has a zigzag sort of waddle as it runs, but from the account of eyewitnesses, the Indiana Corn Weasel has lightning speed and an Olympic-caliber vertical leap, none of which showed up in the literature.

Perhaps most inexplicable about the reported behavior of the Indiana Corn Weasel was its fearlessness. Weasel predation almost always involves attacks on smaller and more vulnerable animals, such as voles, or mice. Weasels won't even go after a rabbit, even though they usually have the advantage of size, unless driven by extreme hunger. One of the problems naturalists face in documenting weasel behavior is the reluctance of the animal to show itself in the presence of human observers. But to hear the frightened denizens of Milton tell it, human beings are the desired prey of the Indiana Corn Weasel. It just didn't add up.

Kelsey pored over the information, trying to reconcile what she was reading with what she was hearing. The more she read, the more her quarry seemed to stand out in relief from the general weasel population. While weasels ranged throughout the North American continent, the Indiana Corn Weasel was a true Hoosier phenomenon. Sightings dating back to the eighteenth century were largely limited to the northeast quadrant of the state, and mostly within the confines of traditional Amish communities. That's what made Kelsey so sure that the creature was somehow tied into religious belief. Her interview with Reverend Lonnie only reinforced this feeling. Whatever was out there, terrorizing the good, God-fearing people of Milton, wasn't a traditional weasel, Kelsey now felt certain. It was something else.

She spent the last hour of her afternoon looking through the drawers in the cabinets, randomly inspecting weasel teeth, fur, and skeletal remains. All of it seemed, to her untrained eye, rather unremarkable. On her way out of the library she stopped by Mrs. Coffey's office.

"I'm all done. Thanks."

"Did you find what you were looking for?"

"I don't think so. But I made some notes, and copied a few pages and some illustrations. I'll look through it at home tonight. Maybe I missed something."

As she reached out to shake Mrs. Coffey's hand she noticed a plaque on the wall with a gigantic ear of corn mounted on it, in much the same way some people mount a prized fish on the wall. The ear of corn was enormous—at least twice the size of any ear she had ever seen.

"Is that real?"

"Oh very much so. It was a gift."

"I didn't know corn could get so big."

"On its own, it can't. One of the universities nearby has a program where they do genetic engineering of plants. A student working on the project, who used to work here when he was in high school, gave that to me. Isn't it something?"

"It's like a small log, with kernels," Kelsey said in disbelief.

"Well, genetic engineering can do some pretty amazing things. The same fellow gave me a tomato last summer that was the size of a small soccer ball. Well, good luck, Miss Kane."

"Thanks."

When Kelsey got back to her car she turned on her cell phone and saw that Frankie had called—the library had a strict no-cell-phone-use policy, and Kelsey didn't want to run afoul of the librarians on her first visit there. She played his voice mail message: *"Kelsey, it's me. Thought you might want to know—that victim of last night's attack...she died this morning. Looks like your little friend is done with the appetizers and is now moving onto the entrées. See ya."*

Gallows humor—a normal response to repeated exposure to a distressing situation. And this situation was becoming quite distressing. The Indiana Corn Weasel was no longer a fiction but its reign of terror was starting to resemble a horror novel. Kelsey could only hope this one would have a happy ending.

* * * *

"Mommy, what happened today?"

"What do you mean, Spinner?"

"Well, something bad must have happened because they wouldn't let us play outside."

Wow, Kelsey thought. *This is really starting to get out of hand.*

She could tell Justin was bothered by something when she picked him up after school. In fact, even the teachers seemed to be much more subdued than usual. Word of last night's attack had no doubt reached the faculty, and they must have talked about it, though according to Justin nothing official was said—though recess was apparently cancelled.

"Well, something did happen, kiddo. Something pretty bad. Somebody died, and that's got people a little shook up."

Justin furrowed his brow and thought for a good long moment.

"But you said death was just a part of life, and that we shouldn't fear it."

You're a good listener, she thought.

"Well, yes, that's true. But in this case, it seems likely that the person might have been attacked. In which case, I'm sure they didn't want to die. When I said death is something not to be feared I meant that, well, it happens to everybody. But hopefully it happens after you've lived your life, a long life, where you did the things you wanted to do."

"Attacked by what?"

Kelsey couldn't believe she was about to say what she was about to say.

"Well, I'm not sure, but it sounds like it might have been the Indiana Corn Weasel."

Justin's eyes seemed to get as large as saucers.

"Really?"

Was he scared? Shocked? Did he think it was awesome that such a creature really existed? Was he surprised to hear his mother finally accept the weasel's existence? He didn't say. He just sat there with a rather stunned look on his face, all the way home, occasionally mouthing a silent "Wow" that Kelsey could see out of the corner of her eye.

"You okay?" she asked him when they reached their barn.

"Oh, I'm fine," he said, confidently. "It turns out, Otto was right! We have to call him!"

"Right? Right about what?" shouted Kelsey, running after him as he bolted toward the barn…

"Oh, Kelsey sweetie, your son has a great memory," said Otto during their phone conversation. Justin had dialed him up as soon as he got inside.

"Tell me about it. Anyway, what did he mean when he said 'Otto was right'?"

"The afternoon before you left, when I took Justin to Buster's for ice cream, he asked me why you two had to go all the way to Indiana to find something that didn't exist. He said—oh my God, it so cracked me up, Kelse—he said 'If it's not real, why not just stay here and look for it in New Jersey and save all the trouble?' He's precious."

"Agreed. But what did you say?"

"I told him even if you didn't believe it was real, that you would soon change your mind. He told me if it was real, you'd find it. We wagered an ice-cream sundae. You catch it, he wins."

"Otto, how in the world did you—"

"Kelsey, I've got to let you go, sweetie. I've got a call coming in that I simply must take."

"Mister Right?"

"Mister Right Now, anyway. Kiss Kiss."

And then he was gone, and Kelsey was left to puzzle over how something that just dawned on her could have been obvious to Otto a month and eight hundred miles ago.

Chapter 8

The thick plexiglass window that separated Kelsey from the police dispatcher had a small, circular, stainless steel grate located at chin-level, allowing sounds to penetrate the otherwise impenetrable barrier. Despite the thickness of the glass, Kelsey could see that the heavyset woman sitting behind the desk was growing impatient with Kelsey's repeated inquiries.

"Can you tell me how much longer before the chief is free?" Kelsey asked again, speaking through the grate. The dispatcher, one of three people hired to sit for eight-hour shifts behind the reception desk at Milton's tiny police station, relaying information to and from the patrol officers, looked up at Kelsey with annoyance written clearly across her furrowed brow.

"Ma'am, I told you, the chief is not available this afternoon."

"But he's in his office. I saw him come back from lunch. Can you just buzz him and tell him a citizen would like to speak with him."

She pushed back on the wheeled wooden office chair and glanced in to the chief's office.

"I'm sorry, but there's someone in the office right now."

"Can I make an appointment to see him next?"

"Ma'am, I'm sorry but his schedule is full."

"I'll wait."

Kelsey had been there for almost ninety minutes, and she was prepared to wait all day. Frankie had warned her that she wouldn't get anywhere, but she came anyway. As a purely professional matter of research, she needed to see the police reports from what were now almost a dozen reported encounters with the Indiana Corn Weasel in the last month. And from a purely personal perspective, Kelsey was determined to make her presence known and not be brushed off any longer. She might not possess press credentials but she felt entitled to see these reports. She had called, emailed, and even submitted formal "freedom of information" requests—Frankie showed her how to file the paperwork—all to no avail. So she decided she'd just camp out and make a nuisance of herself until the police agreed to show her the reports—or at least answer a few questions.

So there she sat, a fixture in the cramped waiting area just inside the doors to the station, when she heard the tail end of a conversation between the chief and a man exiting his office.

"And if there's any further need—"

"There won't be any further need," said the man talking to the chief. He was in his fifties, Kelsey guessed, based on the gray in his flattop haircut. He was dressed in a crisp military uniform, hat under one arm, a briefcase in the other. There was something oddly familiar about him, though Kelsey felt fairly certain they'd never met.

"Please, Major, give my regards to Mrs. Praeger," the police chief said as the two walked right past her, as if she didn't exist.

The military man put his hat on his head and pushed open the door. "Step away from that vehicle!" he bellowed to some teenager in the street who had dared to lean against the man's army jeep, skateboard in one hand, cigarette in another.

Very familiar, Kelsey thought.

She didn't have time to puzzle out just where or when that might have been, because the chief was returning to his office.

"Chief Eddings, I'm Kelsey Kane, and I was wondering—"

"I know who you are," he said, brushing past her, heading back, mole-like, into the safety of his inner sanctum. No "I'll talk with you later" or "Schedule an appointment." Nothing. Just a brush-off.

"Well, at least he knows who I am," said Kelsey in frustration, glaring at the dispatcher. "I guess I should feel flattered."

The dispatcher shot Kelsey a dirty look. But she was fairly sure the dispatcher couldn't have heard what she just said. Even so, she was definitely about to hear what Kelsey was going to say next.

"I'm not leaving until I get to talk to the chief!" she yelled through the grate. Now it was her turn to flash a dirty look, which she did before taking her familiar seat with its now-familiar view of the west end of Main Street.

It would be about two hours until Kelsey was informed, via the dispatcher's replacement, that the chief had left the building and would therefore not be able to see her today. Kelsey suspected this was merely a trick to get her to leave.

"I've been sitting here all afternoon and the chief never came out," she said smugly.

The dispatcher put down the stack of papers he was leafing through, walked up to the grate, and said simply: "Back door."

Later, when she told Frankie that story, and how foolish she felt at that moment, not even considering the possibility that the chief would sneak out through a rear entrance, he just shook his head and said, "Rookie mistake." But then he squeezed her hand and offered her an encouraging smile. "You really yelled at Mrs. Lawrence?"

"Who?"

"Mrs. Lawrence, the dispatcher."

"I just announced, loud enough for her to hear me through that pane of bullet-proof glass, that I wasn't leaving."

"When did you get so nervy?"

Kelsey thought for a moment.

"I think when I was up to my chin in mud and about to have my life snuffed out. At that point, I decided to be less polite to the jerks I meet in life."

"Well, you've obviously made an impression on him."

"Yeah, a lousy one. Maybe I need to wear a military uniform next time."

"What are you talking about?"

"Oh, the chief was all chatty with this army guy who was there while I was waiting. In fact, this gung ho G.I. had the chief on a pretty short leash, it looked like to me."

"Older guy, built like a hay baler?"

"I don't know what that is."

"Stocky, I mean. Solid."

"Yep. With a crewcut."

"Hmm. That's interesting."

Frankie's interest piqued her own. "What's going on?"

"That guy in the chief's office sounds like Major Praeger."

"I think that was his name. The chief said something about regards to Mrs. Praeger. So who is he?"

Frankie told her what he knew of Major Aldis Praeger, base commander of what was officially known as the Milton Supply and Re-armaments Depot. Or rather, what he had heard through "unofficial" channels. Like the military base itself, Major Praeger seemed to inspire a great deal of speculation.

"Some say that he used to work for the CIA, but that he got a little, well…soft in the head."

"What do you mean?"

"He started to lose his marbles. So they sent him out

here, like some sanitarium in the country, to recuperate. Others say he used to be involved in covert military operations—you know, like foreign assassinations—and that he ran afoul of the military brass, so they sent him out here as punishment. And then there's the story that he was being groomed for one of the top spots in the Pentagon, that he'd made it all the way to the rank of general but he got carried away. They say he was court martialed for committing war crimes during the Iraq war. He was busted down to the rank of Major and sent here as penance."

"War crimes? Jesus, that's a pretty serious charge."

"They say his brigade used tanks to flatten a village where some citizen insurgents were informing against the U.S. troops. From the story I heard, they flattened most of the people too. Men, women, and children—most of whom, it turned out, weren't insurgents after all. Praeger relied on faulty intelligence—though I hear he did offer to assist in the rebuilding of the village."

"So why isn't this stuff out there? Why haven't you written about it"

"Kelsey, we're not the *New York Times*. I write for the *Milton Forum*. I'm covering the county Pumpkin Fest this weekend. I can't take on the propaganda apparatus of the U.S. military. Besides," he said in a conspiratorial whisper, "I'm saving all these stories for my novel."

Kelsey didn't know whether to laugh or to curse him.

* * * *

As it turned out, Kelsey found herself at the county Pumpkin Fair as well. Justin really wanted to go and Kelsey was looking forward to a little mental time away from her quixotic pursuit of the Indiana Corn Weasel. So instead of a night spent contemplating real-life terror, Kelsey found herself and her son, and about twenty other people, sitting around a fire and telling stories during an event dubbed "Ghostly Encounters."

There wasn't a lot about Indiana that Kelsey found herself envying. The frenetic pace of life that New Jersey generally required had gotten into her, had become her normal and expected way of operating, and like many transplants from the Northeast, Kelsey was unaccustomed to the leisurely unfolding of life here. Justin was younger, less indoctrinated by the manic pace of their New Jersey life, and was having an easier time adjusting. Kelsey also felt self-conscious about her lack of religious faith, something new for her. In New Jersey she never really spent any time thinking about what she didn't believe in, but in Milton, there were perpetual reminders of the gulf between the sinners and the saved. She knew she'd never even be able to fake being part of the latter camp.

But here was one of the things she liked very much—sitting around an open fire with a group of strangers, bound together by their love of nature—and a good story. There was a "designated" story teller—a county park ranger—but he served as more of a moderator. Anyone was allowed to chime in, and in fact the ranger began by going around the ring of fire-lit faces, seeking volunteers to get the storytelling started. The sun had long set, it was Friday night—no school for Justin tomorrow—and a cool fall breeze fanned the flames teasingly. Kelsey felt a surge of warmth as she hugged Justin and they sat there, waiting for someone to begin.

"Don't know if y'all ever been down to the old Fulton swamp over the county line, but I was there about five years ago," began the man seated to Kelsey's left, a heavy-set man with a baby face belied by a knife-like scar just visible under his chin. "Ain't never going back there, I'll tell you that."

The man paused to spit, looked around at the faces of the others sitting around the fire, his eyes gleaming in the glow of the firelight.

"Don't advise any of y'all to go down there neither. Unless you think you can outrun the Devil."

Not the most subtle opening, but in this setting, pretty effective. He picked up a stick and, throughout most of his tale, he drew figures absent-mindedly in the dirt.

"It was July, five years ago. The summer of the drought. Y'all remember that? Blasted hot it was. That was the summer Jake Fulton sold his place—it's a swamp now, but it was mostly dirt-farm then, before the irrigation ditch reached his place—and then he just plum took off. For those of you who never met Jake, he was an odd sort. His father and grandfather before him owned the property. They were deeply religious people, but nobody ever seen Jake inside a church. Anyway, when the grandfather passed, he gave the place to Jake's father. When his father passed, it went to Jake. His mother had left long ago, took off when Jake weren't but a baby. Nobody knows where she went to, or why. Jake himself never married."

The storyteller pulled out a flask from his jacket pocket, took a swallow, put it back, without comment or apology.

"I used to do some work out at the Fulton place. He didn't have no help. Truth is, there wasn't a lot to do. Jake wasn't much of a farmer. Couldn't really grow nothin' in that field of his, all dirt and spider grass. But he kept a small stable with a handful of scraggly-looking plow horses and mules and such, and he needed help tendin' them. Some of y'all know how much I love horses, so I agreed to be sort of a hired hand.

"There was one particular animal he had. I barely know what to call it, even. It was like a horse, I s'pose. Jake kept it penned far away from t'others. Wouldn't let me brush it, or muck out its stall, or go anywhere near it. He told me that one was his "special" animal. I never did even get a good look at it, but I used to hear it make this weird sort of whinny noise, almost like it was a laughin' as much as whinnyin'. Used to give me the shivers. Jake told me if I ever tried to saddle, or shoe, or even groom that horse, it would be the last animal I ever worked on. Said it with a big ol' grin. 'Bout the only time I ever saw him smile. But it was a creepy smile. I'll never forget it," he said, looking off into the distance, shadows from the fire flickering across his baby face.

"Anyway, one night in July, I was up at the Frogger—y'all know the place, that dive and dancehall off Route 9 in Mason—and I was tellin' these guys at the bar about this weird horse, and we had a few drinks in us, so four of us pile into my van and head off to Fulton's place. I don't know what we was thinkin'."

He looked around, making eye contact with each of the listeners as he slowly shook his head, repeating "Just don't know what we was thinkin'." Justin was transfixed.

"So we drive up to his place and it's getting' on toward midnight, and there weren't any lights on in the house. So this guy named Smitty—don't know much about him, just met him that night at the Frogger for the first time—Smitty jumps out of the car and runs past the house and toward the stable. I tried to stop him, but we was all a little…well…" Mindful of his younger listeners, he changed "drunk" to "wound up" and continued, all eyes still fixed on him, all ears ready to hear more.

"So this fool Smitty runs right into the stall. And I was shoutin' at him, 'Get out of there, you dern fool!' but he didn't pay me no attention." The pace of the story slowed. He took the stick he'd been doodling with, raised it, and broke it in two. He threw the two halves into the fire. "I wish to heck he *had* listened to me."

The man sat there in stony silence, his eyes welling up with regret. He didn't say anything at all, barely moved. Everyone around the fire tensed up, wondering what he would say next, or if he'd say anything at all.

Justin broke the silence. "What happened then?" he asked bravely. The man looked at Justin, half-smiled, nodded.

"Okay, I'll tell you. We sat in that car as silent as you all are sitting around this fire. We waited, all of us afraid for Smitty. Afraid for ourselves, too. Finally, we heard Smitty yell out—a scream that echoed off the trees, setting off all the screech owls. And then the stall door slams, and we hear that terrible, demonic kind of laugh-whinny that carried across the fields. And then we seen it." He leaned forward, his stare fixed on the burning embers.

"There was a terrible flash of greenish-white light from the stall, like an explosion, but it didn't make no sound. I'll never forget it. It lit up the night like fireworks. And then right after the light, that whinny-laugh again, and this…this…horse-creature bursts out of the stall, wood planks and splinters flying everywhere. And this horse is glowing all fiery red! I mean, he was lit up like some damn bonfire, and he's bucking violently, and he takes off across the fields, and we see he's got a rope on one of his fetlocks and we look again and we see he's dragging something—and it's Smitty! We hear him screamin' and the horse whinnyin' and we didn't know what to do, so we start the car and I'm thinking of maybe going after him, trying to save him. But after the engine starts, this horse-creature, he hears it and he turns and stars galloping towards the car, and the other guys are yellin' at me to get out of there, so I floored it, and we got out of there as fast as I could, but in the rear view mirror I could still see that ghastly blood-red light gallopin' across the field and we could hear Smitty screamin'. It was awful!"

The climax generated the requisite gasps from the younger listeners, and even some genuine looks of concern from the parents in the circle. Kelsey looked down at Justin, who sat there open-mouthed, absolutely entranced. The storyteller continued the fireside tale of his ghostly encounter.

"Next day, 'bout noontime, I drove out to the Fulton place. There was no sign of Jake, but there was a big ol' 'For Sale' sign on the front of the farmhouse. The stall where that horse-creature had been kept was still there. I got close enough to see there weren't a scratch on it. No missing planks, no cracks, not so much as a splinter of wood. I walked around where Smitty got dragged and the dirt was smooth, the grass untrampled. Not a pebble disturbed. I was going to knock on Jake's door when I hear that horse-creature a laughin' again, and I jumped back in my car. I got out of there and never ever went back. And Smitty? He ain't been heard from since. And that's the blasted truth—God have mercy."

He spat again into the fire, leaned back, and looked up at the night sky.

"Well, that's quite a story," said the park ranger, heads all along the circle bobbing in affirmation. "So who's next?"

* * * *

It had turned chilly as the night progressed, and Kelsey and Justin were walking across a field, back to their car. It had been a long day for both, but despite the cold and the lateness of the hour, Justin was agitating to stay a little longer.

"Please, Mommy. There's no school tomorrow."

"Sorry, Spinner. I'm dead on my feet."

He looked disappointed but he didn't push back.

"Can we come back again?"

The Pumpkin Festival would last through the weekend, right up until the finale on Sunday, "the Sundown Hoedown," an outdoor country music jamboree. Kelsey hadn't thought about returning but she could tell it was a big deal to Justin.

"I guess we can come back. Why not?"

"Promise?"

"Promise."

"Thanks, Mommy," he said, hugging her. Kelsey was grateful for the warmth, however temporary. She hadn't really dressed for the cold, and the wind had whipped up in intensity. It was now zipping across the flatlands unimpeded, a brusque harbinger of winter—which the Old Farmer's Almanac said would be brutal this year.

"You can bring your boyfriend when we come back," Justin said, matter-of-factly. Kelsey stopped walking, unsure how to respond.

"I don't have a boyfriend," she said, half-heartedly.

"Oh yes you do," he said, defiantly, playfully. "I know who he is, Mommy."

"We'll you better tell me," she said, "so then we'll both know."

But instead of telling, he begin singing.

"Frankie and Mommy, sitting in a tree. K-I-S-S-I-N-G. First comes love, then comes marriage..."

Before he finished the first verse, she was already chasing him. She caught up to him and toppled him before he could sing another line.

"You vile munchkin!" she said, tackling him, tickling him on the cold hard grass of the county fairgrounds. "I shall make you eat those words."

Justin was unrepentant. Between squeals of laughter that almost left him breathless, he'd shout out "Frankie's your boyfriend! Frankie's your boyfriend!" She tried to muzzle him with her hand but he squirmed free and kept shouting Frankie's name as she chased him all the way back to the car.

"For the record," she said as she opened the back door of the car to let him in, "he's just an acquaintance."

Justin climbed into the car, still giggling. He seemed to sense he had her on this one. As she walked around the car to let herself in, she entertained the fleeting thought that just maybe, possibly, he was right.

"No more of that, Spinner, or I'll drop you off at the city dump tonight."

"Oh boy!" he said, in mock delight. "I can sleep with the corn weasel!"

Kelsey smiled to herself, proud of his resilience.

This trip to Indiana really has been good for him. Good for both of us. "That which does not destroy me makes me stronger."

"Do you think the man was right?"

"What man, Spinner?"

"The man who told about the horse that glowed. Do you believe it happened."

"I think that's what they call a 'tall tale', kiddo. Just a story. Don't let it scare you."

Justin was quiet for a second, thinking it over.

"That's what you said about the Indiana Corn Weasel, Mommy. That it wasn't real. But now you believe. So maybe this story about the glowing horse is true, too."

He didn't say it as a challenge, but just as an observation. He leaned his head against the window and looked out at the cold, barren fields illuminated by the full moon. His eyes were half moons now, the exhaustion of a day of being eight years old inexorably taking hold. But his comment had the opposite effect on his mother, snapping her into consciousness.

What's the difference between a demonic glowing-horse creature with a weird whinny-laugh that can't possibly exist and a demonic three-foot-long weasel with glowing eyes and a taste for human flesh?

Did she really now believe? Was the Heartland's apparent embrace of things unseen rubbing off on her? If that storyteller had told the tale of the Indiana Corn Weasel tonight, it would have sounded just as ludicrous as the story he *did* tell.

So why do I now believe? What's next—am I going to believe in ghosts, haunted houses, and evil spirits? Am I going to start attending seances to commune with the dead?

Justin saw no difference between the legend he heard tonight and the many stories she'd told him about the Indiana Corn Weasel. That connection hadn't even occurred to Kelsey, and now she was faulting herself for her lack of clear-headedness.

He was asleep now. They were almost home. As Kelsey turned onto the lonely road that would take them to their converted barn, a cloud passed over the moon. The only light now came from the headlights of the car. Kelsey slowed down, the nearly-bald tires spitting gravel as they churned up the long driveway. She stopped the car and, before getting out to hoist Justin into her arms, she stared deeply into the night. It was still and dark and featureless, and Kelsey sat there, uncertain what she really believed.

"What's out there?" she asked quietly, half hoping that she'd never find out.

* * * *

After breakfast, Kelsey started catching up on her emails. She was supposed to be sending dispatches regularly to Dr. Reeves, informing him of the progress of her research. But she'd gotten so caught up in her sleuthing that she hadn't sent him anything in the last couple of weeks. One of the other reasons she'd put off writing to him was she wasn't sure what to say. "Research going well"? Not really. She still had more questions than answers. "Expect to return soon"? Maybe. Maybe not. Kelsey recently began to feel that she was at the mercy of larger forces. Who knew when she and Spinner would return? "Grant money holding out"? She had done a pretty good job of stretching the dollars the University had given her, but the stipend wouldn't last forever. What would he say if she asked for more money? And if the university didn't cough up more dollars to sustain her in Indiana, where else could she turn? Frankie was barely getting by, and besides, she'd feel uncomfortable asking him for money. She flirted with the idea of trying to get a job, but then when would she get her research done?

So she stared at her laptop, unsure where to begin. Mercifully, the phone rang.

"Hey Kelsey. I'm working on a story that you wouldn't believe. Can you come to the paper?"

"Now?"

"Yeah. I've got the newsroom to myself. You can do some digging in the morgue."

She'd been wanting to go through the newspaper's files, searching for anything about the military base that might provide a clue about its purpose, or what's so secret that they keep a close eye on anybody who happens to drive by.

Benjamin Yoder's words rang in her ears. *"There's something going on out there, something not right."*

"Frankie, I'd love to. But I can't just leave Justin."

"Right. Okay, I think I can help you out. I'll call you right back."

After three years at the *Forum*, Frankie had met or spoken to pretty much everybody in Milton, so he was plugged in. He knew who to call if a water pipe burst in the middle of the night, or if his car got stuck in a ditch. He knew where to get the best homemade jam or the best price on a handmade rocking chair. And though he never needed one, he knew where to find a baby sitter. True to his words, in just a couple of minutes her phone rang.

"Found you a great sitter. Her name's Mrs. Simms. She's great with kids. She used to teach, now she's retired. Gives piano lessons, runs a day care during the week. She says she'd be happy to watch Justin. And he'll love it. Her living room is like a playground. I did a story on her about a year ago. Total fluff piece. She's still bringing me pies."

"Sounds good."

Kelsey hadn't put much thought into finding a good, long-term babysitter because she didn't expect to be in town long enough to need one. She took down the address and in ten minutes, she and Justin were headed into town.

"You'll like her, Spinner," Kelsey assured him on the ride to her house. "She makes pies."

"I like pie," he said.

It was just a two-minute drive from Mrs. Simms' house to the *Forum* office, which Kelsey found comforting. But that sense of comfort didn't last long, once she learned what Frankie was working on. He invited her to read the half-finished story on his computer screen, and after she read it, she looked at him, perplexed.

"I don't get it."

"I don't really get it myself. I'm sitting here yesterday afternoon, doing some mop-up work and setting up appointments for next week, when I get the call to come to the police department. That's pretty rare, Kelse. They never call me. Anyway, I go there, and the chief's waiting for me. He tells me there's been a change in the Audrey Wells case."

"The girl who was killed in the weasel attack this week?"

"Well, that's just it. The first reports we got were that she was attacked, and that she was in the hospital. Then I heard that she died. I confirmed that with the hospital right after I called you. I got the information about the attack from a County park ranger, who found the girl. She was out walking with her boyfriend in the woods near Boyd's Pond."

"Where's Boyd's Pond."

"You know those woods across from the military base? Well, just off the road, there's this place called Boyd's pond. It's a pretty popular make-out spot for high school kids. Anyway, it sounds like she was mauled by some sort of creature that resembles our little friend. But then the chief hands me a police report that says…well, here," he said, handing the report to Kelsey. "Take a look."

She scanned it for a minute, unsure exactly what to look for.

"Here," said Frankie, pointing. "This box."

"Cause of death…heart attack?"

"Heart attack. No mention of any wounds or bite marks. The ranger who found her told me she was bleeding pretty badly. I have a source at the hospital who told me the same thing. Said she needed three pints of blood when she came in. Three pints of blood—for a heart attack? Doesn't add up. So I called the Ranger station when I got back from the PD and guess what? The ranger told me he was 'mistaken,' and the girl wasn't bleeding, or wounded. He said he found her and tried to give her CPR. I called the boyfriend, but he wouldn't talk to me. And the girl's mother—she's divorced and it was just the two of them and a younger brother—has left town. Her neighbor tells me a moving van showed up last night, and she packed up all her stuff in the middle of the night. My publisher calls me this morning and tells me to come in and write a story. He even gives me the headline: 'Local girl suffers heart attack, dies unexpectedly'."

"Frankie, you can't write that story. It's a total lie! You know that. I don't care what your publisher says."

"He signs my checks, Kelse. Besides, what else have I got to go with? No witnesses, no verification of the attack. Just a police report."

"What about your source at the hospital?"

"Suddenly not talking. And medical records aren't public information. I can't get the info unless her mother signs a release. I'm boxed in here, Kelse. I've got to write this as a heart attack story. So that's what I'm doing."

Kelsey was a little overwhelmed by what she was hearing. She didn't know what was more alarming—another attack, this one fatal, occurring just across the road from the military base. Or the complete about-face the police and the witnesses were pulling after the event? And what about Frankie? Weren't journalists supposed to battle lying and corruption, not go along with it? The fact that she and Frankie were now sleeping together semi-regularly only enhanced her sense of confusion.

"I've got to get some air," Kelsey said, exiting the cramped and unkempt newsroom and stepping outside the building. She leaned against the wall, facing the parking lot and, a little further ahead, Main Street. She watched the inconstant stream of Milton's pedestrian life pass by, letting her mind drift back to New Jersey. She wondered what Otto was doing. Saturday morning—he was probably at the gym. Otto spent his mornings building up his body and his evenings destroying it. "Balance," he called it. Then she thought of Dr. Reeves, and how comfortable she felt in his office and how much she wanted to be a part of that lifestyle. It was hard to remember how close she truly was, the sense of finality tauntingly within reach. Now, when she thought of her future, everything was foggy, unformed. She didn't know what the endgame would be here, when it would start or what it might reveal.

"Mind if I smoke?"

She was so lost in thought that she hadn't heard Frankie sneak up next to her. He took out a pack of cigarettes, tapped it against his forefinger, drew out a cigarette and lit it. Kelsey, like everyone else of her generation, grew up indoctrinated against the dangers of smoking, but she didn't mind that Frankie smoked. She went through life silently applauding people who flaunted society's rules. That's why she was friends with Otto. And that's why she admired her son's independence and quirky way of looking at the world. She was always trying to be less obedient even though in the end she usually just went along with things, maintained the status quo. Rebels she admired, but she sensed that she was really a conformist at heart.

"What I do in this building, what they pay me to do, is their decision," he said, blowing a plume of white smoke into the clear Indiana air. "But what I do when I'm off the clock is my call."

"Oh yeah? And what have you decided to do when you're off the clock?"

"I'm going to play a game of 'sneak into the military base.' Problem is, the game requires two players." He turned his head and stared into her emerald eyes. "Know where I can find a partner?"

She squeezed his hand and smiled back at him, the lazy Saturday morning unfolding around her, its secrets as ungraspable as a plume of smoke.

* * * *

Frankie was right. There was not much information about the local military base in the archive of the *Milton Forum*. Except for the occasional head shot of some stolid-looking man or woman in uniform, announcing their promotion to a new and improved rank, it was almost like the base didn't even exist. She couldn't even find any mention of the base in any of the issues during the last couple of years. She did, however, discover that the base had an official name: The Clement Riley Research and Development Support Facility of the Third Army Non-Combat Special Operations Depot.

"Jesus," Kelsey said. "No wonder everybody just calls it 'the base.'"

The microfilms of the *Milton Forum* only went back to the 1960s. All the papers before that, Frankie explained, had been destroyed in a fire that started in the paper's darkroom. Legend had it that the paper's editor was having a dalliance with a local married woman and they were meeting for secret, candle-lit trysts in about the only private place in town free from gossipers or intruders. Apparently, the fire ignited the developing chemicals and ending up destroying the entire western wing of the building—which, much to the chagrin of local historians ever since, included the newspaper's "morgue," or archive of back issues.

"No help," she conceded, rubbing her eyes after scrolling through yet another spool of microfilm. "It looks like we're on our own here."

Kelsey meant that it would be up to her and Frankie to find out what was going on at the base, that the newspaper wouldn't be any help. But Frankie took her words a different way. Looking around the vacant newsroom, he arched an eyebrow.

"It does indeed appear we're on our own," he said, grabbing her hand gently and leading her away from her microfilm carrel and past the vacant desks and stacks of old issues that cluttered the newsroom.

"Where are we going?" she asked.

Still leading Kelsey by the hand, he turned back to look at her, smiled, and whispered the answer: "The darkroom."

Chapter 9

Justin didn't forget.

"Mommy, you promised!"

So there she was, driving her son back to the county pumpkin fair so he could experience his first hay ride. So Kelsey could experience *her* first hay ride. She was certainly racking up an impressive number of firsts over the past several weeks. She'd been so immersed in the research that brought her to Indiana she had little time to think about the other experiences she was having, and what effect they might be having on her. Justin was practically living another life here in Milton. She wondered if he'd grow up thinking about rural America differently than she did.

"Do you think you could live here?" she asked him as they pulled into the field doubling as a parking lot.

"We do live here, Mommy," he said.

That was the difference in how they saw it. For Kelsey, everything that happened in Indiana, every day they spent there, was an interruption in their lives. For Justin, it *was* their life. He didn't seem nagged by the constant tug of their erstwhile Jersey existence. For Kelsey, a hay ride was a sociological field trip. For him, it was just another fun thing to do on a Sunday. His enthusiasm, his utter lack of disdain for so many of the elements of small-town living that Kelsey felt, kept her going. But she also realized that he was probably going to be disappointed when they finally left Milton.

"HAY RIDES—THIS WAY!" the hand-painted cardboard sign nailed to the telephone pole said. They followed the crowd into the fairgrounds. It seemed to Kelsey that there were a lot more people here today than on Friday. Most of them had probably come for the free concert at sundown. She'd already assured Justin they could stay for the hoedown—another first.

"In for a penny, in for a pound," she told him when he asked if they could stay to the end.

"Pound of cotton candy," he replied, licking his lips.

So this is a hay ride? she thought as she climbed, along with a dozen other fairgoers, onto a large flat piece of wood on top of a trailer. The trailer was bordered by hay bales along the perimeter, and everybody took their place on these huge bundled straw blocks. The trailer was attached to a tractor, and when everybody was aboard, the tractor chugged noisily to life and then slowly, the whole contraption surged forward, rolling through the fields, en route to a pumpkin patch about a half mile ahead as the crow flies. On the ride, there was fresh apple cider, and talk of the weather, and some bird-watching.

"Hawks keeping close together," said a woman Kelsey took to be in her fifties, riding with her daughter, who was about Kelsey's age, as she scanned the horizon.

"Bad winter comin'," said her daughter, translating her mother's observation.

Justin wasn't paying any attention to the idle conversation. He was busy stuffing straw into his shirt.

"Hey, Mommy—look! I'm a scarecrow!" he said, grinning, straw protruding from his sleeves and between the buttons of his flannel shirt, tucked into the waistband of his jeans and the neck hole of his t-shirt.

"Stay away from any open flames," Kelsey cautioned.

The pumpkin patch was impressive, a huge field of

tangled vines mined with misshapen orbs gleaming in the afternoon sun. There was a stand nearby where kids could paint their pumpkins, and a rack filled with homemade jars of pumpkin butter and pie filling. Kelsey was used to picking up her Halloween pumpkins at the ShopRite, in a large cardboard box jammed into the produce aisle for two weeks every fall. This was a much better way to pick a pumpkin, she decided.

"Cool!" Justin said as he surveyed the landscape.

They all clambered down off the trailer and the man driving the tractor, an honest-to-goodness farmer in a straw hat and overalls, bellowed "fifteen minutes," and everyone scattered throughout the field, running and tripping and hoisting potential candidates. Justin was excited, too. Kelsey could barely keep up as he hopped over the vines and leaped through the field, determined to come home with the perfect souvenir. Kelsey let him run on his own, slowing down herself to examine a few smaller pumpkins at her feet.

She'd been crouching for a couple of minutes, weighing a few small specimens, thinking about picking up a pumpkin to give to Frankie for his desk when the woman in her fifties who was on the hay ride with them came up to Kelsey rather frantically.

"Ma'am, there's somethin' wrong with your boy."

A surge of momentary panic possessed her. Immediately she reached for the inhaler in her purse and discovered to her horror that she'd left her purse in the car back in the parking lot.

"Oh shit!" she said, following the woman, who was leading her to Justin. "I'm going to need some help!" she cried out to no one in particular as she ran. Several of the adults who were there sifting for pumpkins with their kids stopped what they were doing and immediately followed Kelsey. As she raced toward Justin, she calculated in her mind how long it would take to get back to her car on that tractor. The answer sent another wave of fear through her body, paining her.

"Justin, I'm coming! Hang in there, kiddo!"

He was in pretty bad shape. Something in the field, maybe his running, or the dirt and dust on the pumpkins, or the hay he'd stuffed into his shirt, had triggered a sudden, severe asthma attack. He was doubled over on the ground, wheezing loudly.

Kelsey was afraid, but she tried to keep calm. The other parents had begun to huddle around, and she heard several voices speaking urgently into cell phones. Justin lay on the ground, shoulders rising and falling rapidly as he tried to get air into his constricted bronchial passages.

"Kiddo, let's remember what to do here," she said, tears filling her eyes as she struggled to think clearly. "Try to breathe."

That was a mother's instinct talking, not a clinician's sound advice. Kelsey put her hand on her son's back and could feel him battling the constriction. "Does anybody have an inhaler?" she shouted, sounding desperate. Then she turned to the woman who had alerted her and asked in a quavering voice, "Can we get an ambulance way out here?" The woman looked confused, and mumbled, "I think somebody just called—"

"There's no time to wait for an ambulance."

Kelsey didn't recognize the voice at first. But when he turned to her and said, "I can help him. May I?" she thought she was having a hallucination.

"Um. Yes. Of course. But—"

"I might need to put my hands on him. Is that okay?"

Kelsey nodded. She had no time to ask the other questions that were occurring to her, like what was Reverend Lonnie doing in the middle of this pumpkin patch? Later, when she learned that the free pumpkin give-aways were being sponsored by Jesus the Redeemer church, and that Reverend Lonnie had been seated just a few yards away at the pumpkin painting booth all afternoon, it would make a kind of sense to her logically-inclined mind—whereas the Reverend would maintain that it was an example of "Providence."

"What's his name?"

"Justin."

"Okay, Justin. I want you to listen to me and do exactly what I say, okay?"

Justin half-nodded.

"All right. I want you to hold your breath. Pinch your nose if you have to, but don't breathe out at all."

Kelsey was confused and fearful.

"But he can't get any air. How can he—"

"Trust me," he said, turning briefly to her but then focusing back on Justin.

What little air Justin had in his lungs he tried to hold, though not too successfully. When he blew it out, and inhaled again, Reverend Lonnie told him to blow the air out more slowly this time, as slowly as he could, until every drop of oxygen was out of his lungs.

To Kelsey this seemed like a kind of a torture, but Justin did exactly as he was told, blowing slowly until his face seemed to turn a pale blue-white.

"Excellent, Justin. Breathe in and hold it. Now this time, after you exhale, I want you to wait ten seconds to take a breath, okay? I'll show you."

And together, in a pumpkin patch in Northeast Indiana on a late Sunday afternoon in the autumn, a scene that seemed right out of a movie unfolded in front of Kelsey's eyes, as her son and a minister exhaled in sync, Reverend Lonnie looking at his watch, waiting for ten seconds to pass. And then they both inhaled, held their breath, and exhaled again. But then he did something that terrified and angered his mother. He placed his hand across Justin's mouth and pinched his nose so he couldn't take a breath. Justin struggled and Kelsey screamed, "What are you doing?" It looked like the Reverend Lonnie was smothering him, not allowing him to inhale. But when Justin appeared almost ready to pass out, he released his hand and forcefully commanded him to "Suck in as much air as you can as fast as you can right now! More! Breathe in, Justin! More! Come on!"

He did it. A rich stream of air filled his lungs, and Justin looked at his mother in shock that he was able to take any kind of breath, let alone such a deep one.

"Now, this is important, Justin. I want you to blow this air out as slowly as you possibly can. Do this," he said, as the Reverend demonstrated how he should purse his lips. "Like you're blowing out a candle, but nice and slow."

Justin's eyes were locked on Reverend Lonnie. He pursed his lips and blew out slowly.

"As slow as you can go, Justin. Until all the air is out of your lungs. Every bit, okay? And when you think you can't blow any more, then hum."

Kelsey shot him a quizzical look.

"It gets rid of any residual air," he explained.

Kelsey closed her eyes, but soon she heard Justin hum.

"Now, a fast deep breath. Fast as you can."

Justin inhaled with ferocity, devouring the available air.

"Now exhale as you normally would."

He did, with great relief to all. He was breathing again, fully, without any noticeable tightness or wheezing.

"It's a miracle," whispered the woman next to Kelsey, who was too grateful and stunned to argue with her.

She reached over and hugged Justin. Miracle or not, she realized as she sat there embracing on a floor of vines that this story could have had a much worse ending.

"Cancel the ambulance," the Reverend said softly to one of the parents who had been standing around. When Justin got to his feet, and when his mother had a chance to look him over, she hugged him again and then she turned to Reverend Lonnie.

"Thank you so much."

"I'm glad I was here to help."

"What you did—that seemed a little…well, I wasn't sure you knew what you were doing."

"I used to have asthma. I'd get attacks all the time," he explained. "I couldn't even be in a field like this. And then when I was in seminary, I met an older priest who did breathing exercises every day of his life. He was in his nineties, and he was as healthy as any of us young bucks. He swore by those exercises. When he found out I was asthmatic, he taught me how to breathe. That sounds funny, I know, but most people really don't know how. It's okay. They can get by without proper technique. Asthmatics can't."

"But it seemed like you were *keeping* him from breathing. Pinching his nose…"

"I'm sorry. That must have been difficult to watch. There wasn't time to explain. You see, during an asthma attack, the problem isn't that you can't draw enough air in. The real problem is that you can't exhale. The bronchial muscles you need to push the air out are in spasm. You can suck all the air in that you want, but there's nowhere for it to go. Your passageways are swollen and you just can't push enough air out to make room for inhalation."

He stared at her. "I can see that you're skeptical—I recognize the look. The key is to force air out of the lungs. When the lungs are empty, the swelling of the breathing passages recedes. Remember, bronchial passages constrict because of some airborne trigger. Dust, pollen, grass, whatever. Eliminate the tainted air from the lungs, the swelling decreases and the passages open up. It's like dislodging food from a choking victim. People who are choking are desperately trying to inhale, but what they need to do is exhale. But it's hard to think of exhaling when all you want to do is breathe."

As Kelsey tried to process this bit of counter-intuitive medical advice, the farmer who drove them all out to the pumpkin patch hollered "Time to go, folks." Kelsey pulled Justin closer, kissed him, and said "We better get back,

Spinner." He started to walk toward the trailer when Reverend Lonnie called out to him.

"Justin!"

He turned and stood facing the minister, who was now framed with the backlight of the setting sun.

"I think you forgot something." He reached down and grabbed a basketball-sized pumpkin, a little oblong, but more than serviceable. He twisted the vine, severing it from the groundcover, and he handed it to the boy.

"Here you go."

Justin looked at his mom to see if it was okay. Kelsey nodded.

"Thanks!" he said. "Look at it, Mommy!"

"It's great," she said, turning back to the Reverend. "Best one in the patch."

If they had only been looking in a slightly different direction when they climbed back on to the trailer, they would have noticed an ambulance about fifty yards away, emergency lights turned off, driving away from the patch. As Jason wrapped his arms around his pumpkin, the ambulance disappeared in the twilight, unneeded.

* * * *

The colorful tempera-painted banner hanging across the front entrance of the school welcoming parents to "Career Day" contained a grammar error, Kelsey noticed. "Its nice to have you here!" was missing an apostrophe after the "It" and before the "s." But she had colleagues in graduate school who still didn't know how to use the apostrophe, so she couldn't hold it against a bunch of elementary school students. And she was just happy to be invited, considering she—unlike most of the other parents who were also there—didn't really have a career. Not yet, anyway. But she knew Justin would have been disappointed if she'd declined the chance to participate.

So there she was, sitting in the faculty lounge, awaiting her turn, from ten-fifteen to ten-thirty, to speak to Justin's class about her "career." There were a half-dozen other parents assembled there, some looking through notes, and one man, in a powder-blue polyester suit, was looking over several typed pages, moving his lips as he read along with the typescript. But Kelsey was just going to wing it. She felt pretty sure she'd be able to talk about crypto-zoology without notes to a group of second graders.

"Mrs. Kane, if you'll just follow me," said the school secretary, whom she had told at least fifty times that it was "Ms." Kane, not "Mrs." Apparently, the idea of single motherhood was so unusual—or so aberrant—that the secretary simply couldn't lower herself to use that courtesy title. Kelsey didn't bother correcting her. She merely followed her down the hallway and stood patiently outside Justin's classroom, waiting for the current speaker to finish up.

"If there are no more questions for Norman's daddy, let us give him a big round of applause," said Mrs. Biederman, Justin's teacher. "We certainly did learn a lot about septic tanks. Thank you for coming."

"No prob," said Norman's daddy, who reached for a cigarette the minute he crossed the threshold, brushing by Kelsey without so much as a nod or a "good luck." As he lit up in violation of the health department's clearly posted prohibition on smoking on school grounds, Kelsey took a deep breath and waited for her turn.

"Now boys and girls, we're going to hear from Justin's Mommy. She's hear to talk about—cyto… um,…crytic…let's see here…this card is kind of smudged," said Mrs. Biederman, looking furtively at the index card in her hand through her reading glasses.

"Crypto-zoology," volunteered Kelsey from just outside the door.

"Yes. Well, I see we'll *all* be learning a little something this morning. Won't you come in please?"

Kelsey walked in and scanned the faces to find Justin. There he was—third row, next to the window. The light was streaming in. He was smiling broadly. She gave him a little wave, and then she leaned against the teacher's desk, informally, and began.

"My name is Kelsey Kane, and I'm Justin's mom. Thank you for inviting me here this morning. I'm here to tell you about what I do. But first, let me ask you a question. How many of you have ever seen a monster?"

Giggles and gasps, with a smattering of hands shooting up.

"Really? That many? Wow. You've got a very brave class, Mrs. Biederman," Kelsey said.

The next fifteen minutes flew by. Kelsey told them all about crypto-zoology. The kids seemed fascinated that someone could actually make a career out of chasing unusual, monstrous creatures.

Probably following the septic tank guy didn't hurt.

She told them about Bigfoot—"although he seems to prefer being called by his native name, Sasquatch"—and she told them about the Loch Ness Monster and the Jersey Devil and Mothman and the Nandi Bear of Africa and the North American Thunderbird and they sat there absolutely fascinated. Even Mrs. Biederman seemed entranced. When it became clear that the ten-thirty speaker was late, or not coming at all, Mrs. Biederman asked Kelsey to stay an additional fifteen minutes.

The kids had lots of questions, of course. Kids and monsters. It could have gone on all day. But it was just a matter of time until someone brought up the topic Kelsey was hoping to avoid.

"What about the Indiana Corn Weasel?" a little boy with red hair in the front row lisped. "My Pa tells me he seen him."

"Mine too!" said the little girl next to him. "He knows somebody that got bit."

There was general nodding and a lot of chatter. Clearly, this was a crowd of believers. Kelsey wasn't exactly sure what to say so she decided just to be honest.

"He's one of the reasons Justin and I came here from

New Jersey. We wanted to meet him."

"Did you see him?" a boy in the back row shouted out.

"Well, not yet. We're still looking. We go looking for him all the time—don't we, Justin?"

Justin nodded, and there was a general gasp of admiration.

"Cool! I wish my dad had your job," said a girl sitting near the door.

"Oh, I'm sure he's got a very interesting job," Kelsey said. "What does he do?"

"Mortician."

"I see."

It seemed Mrs. Biederman's many years of experience suggested to her that this would be a good time to stop.

"Well, that certainly was interesting, and we all want to thank you for coming. Don't we, boys and girls?"

Kelsey was fairly certain their applause went on much longer than it did for the septic tank guy.

* * * *

Mrs. Simms had turned out to be a great find—a babysitter who worked nights and weekends, all for a fairly cheap rate. Best of all, Justin seemed to enjoy hanging out at her house. Kelsey felt comfortable leaving him there, which she needed to do tonight. So she packed up his books and his notepaper and pens and threw a couple of Twinkies into his backpack and they headed off to Mrs. Simms.

"Got plans, my dear?" she asked when Kelsey swung by after dinner to drop Justin off.

Indeed she did. She was planning to commit a felony by breaking into a U.S. Military installation, take notes and photos, and then sneak out—hopefully with enough evidence to clear up the mystery of its existence and, in the process, help her finish her dissertation and get her Ph.D.

Could be a big night—a life changer.

"Nothing special," she said, kissing Justin on the head as he walked into Mrs. Simm's house. "Have fun, kiddo."

"'Bye Mommy!" he said, dashing into her playroom.

"Thanks again, Mrs. Simms. I really appreciate it. I might be late getting back."

"Not to worry," she said. "We'll be fine."

Her evening promised a great deal more risk than she was usually comfortable taking. This was a big leap, she knew, from sitting on the sidelines and waiting for more evidence to land in her lap. But with each passing day she became more convinced that something was going on at that base, something mysterious, something dangerous. All of the recent weasel attacks were close to the base. Benjamin Yoder's words were becoming prophetic—There's something going on out there, something not right. Ever since the stern warning that night outside the base to leave the area—and the unsettling incident of the mysterious man taking down her license plate number—Kelsey had gotten a shiver every time she drove by the place. She was grateful Frankie was coming along with her. She was happy to swing by the newspaper office and park her car there, letting Frankie drive his car.

"They know your plates. You're probably on some sort of list by now. That makes it much harder for us to be inconspicuous. Plus, if we get into any trouble, I can tell them I'm working on a story and you're helping me."

"You'd lie for me? That's sweet," she said, kissing him on the cheek. "A federal crime, but sweet."

"This is no time to joke," he said as they climbed into his car. "These military types have no sense of humor. If we get caught, things could get—"

"We're not going to get caught," Kelsey said, sounding more confident than she actually felt. "Anyway, if they do catch us, we'll just tell them we're two lovers who went for a stroll in the moonlight and wandered onto the base by mistake."

"Yeah, I'm sure that'll work. 'Sorry, Major. We were so caught up in the mood that we didn't notice all those tanks… We were just heading to the guard tower for a quickie.'"

"You're such a romantic," Kelsey said, slapping his shoulder gently with the back of her hand. He smiled, but then he reverted to his game face: all business. Kelsey probably should have been more afraid, but that would come later. For now, they were more like two kids who were planning to steal apples from a local orchard on a dare.

They drove by the base a couple of times, hoping to see something that might make their unauthorized entry less likely to arouse suspicion. They had already decided that going through the heavily-fortified front entrance was an impossibility. There was no way they could talk their way past security. Fortunately for them both, Frankie knew the area surrounding the base pretty well. He'd spent several hours prowling the perimeter of the base on various assignments, from tagging along with Eagle Scouts trying to earn a merit badge to the annual "Turkey Shoot" every Thanksgiving. From what he told Kelsey, there were a couple of places along the wooded border of the base, opposite the road that passes by the entrance, where the fencing had loosened up over the years. He told her he thought they could probably crawl under. He remembered helping to free a kid who got stuck underneath the fence during a nature walk sponsored by the local branch of the Optimists' Club.

"He was pretty fat, and he almost made it under," Frankie said. "That was a couple of years ago. With natural erosion, and a couple years' worth of institutional neglect, that gap should definitely be big enough for us to get under."

If Dr. Reeves could only see me now, she thought. *You're going to have a real adventure!*

It was impossible to park anywhere near the place where Frankie thought the breach in the fence was. They'd have about a half a mile hike to get there. Kelsey was feeling nervous and thought a brisk walk might help calm her down. Frankie, made soft by three years of desk work, cigarettes, and rhubarb pie, was less thrilled by the prospect of a long hike. But he found a place to park his car where it was unlikely anyone would notice, and they got out. He had a flashlight, and Kelsey had a notepad and her camera.

"I feel like I'm in a Hardy Boys novel," Frankie said.

"Nancy Drew, if you don't mind," Kelsey retorted.

Frankie lit up a cigarette and they began their long trek to find a breach in a fence that might or might not be there. A light rain had begun to fall.

"This rain might help us," Frankie said.

"Why is that?"

"If they run patrols, maybe the guard will feel less like leaving his cozy little guard shack to go walking in the woods if its raining."

"If they run patrols? You don't know?"

"Gee, Kelsey, I'm just a crusading newspaper reporter," he said, stepping across the road and into the thick underbrush they'd be marching through for the next half-mile. "I'm not actually part of the evil military-industrial complex."

They walked on, mostly in silence, punctuated only by Frankie's panting and the occasional "Oh Shit!" when one of them stumbled in the dark or tripped over the tangled overgrowth of the woods. Finally, after about twenty minutes, they could see in the distance the floodlights that illuminated the rear of the base. They couldn't see the fence, but Frankie knew that if they just continued straight ahead, they'd run into it.

"Head toward the light," he said.

"You sound like Reverend Lonnie," she said.

He raised his arms and began shaking his hands in a mock-evangelical posture.

"Praise the Lord, brothers and sisters! I see the light! Can I get an A-Men!"

Kelsey laughed, and they kept walking toward the light, toward a fence they couldn't see and a mysterious creature they hoped they could. Thoughts of the corn weasel caused Kelsey to temporarily freeze.

"What's wrong?" Frankie asked.

"What if we find him? What if he really exists and he attacks us? What would we do?"

Frankie surprised her. It was almost as if he was waiting for her to ask that question.

"I've got a greeting for your little friend, if he chooses to introduce himself to us," he said, pulling out a hunting knife, its serrated edge gleaming in the glow of the flashlight.

Kelsey was a little stunned. Frankie didn't seem like the kind of a guy who would own a knife, let alone brandish it with such zeal.

"Where did you get that?"

"Kelsey, in rural Indiana you have to own a hunting knife. Didn't you get yours yet?"

"I'm a pacifist," she said.

"Explain that to the Indiana Corn Weasel," he said. He was really taking this thing seriously. Maybe too seriously. Kelsey was having second thoughts about the whole operation. What was she doing, a girl from New Jersey, a mother, an almost-doctor-of-philosophy, trampling through the woods at night in the rain with a companion brandishing a hunting knife as they made their way to a secret military facility to find a mythical bloodthirsty weasel?

Really, what the hell am I doing?

Concluding that this wasn't the right time for such introspection, she brushed aside the wet strands of hair hanging in front of her face, lifted her boots off the muddy earth and followed Frankie, the man with the knife. Almost as soon as they resumed their walk, Frankie raised his arm. He whispered to her now, which meant he saw or knew something she didn't.

"The fence is up ahead, about fifty feet. See it? We just have to find the spot where we can get under. Then, we stick to the perimeter until we get to that Quonset hut. No lights. It's probably abandoned, hasn't been used for years, I'd guess. It looks like it's in pretty bad shape, so if they're not keeping it up, that means they don't need it. From there, we can watch for the shift change. If there's any time to move, it would be then. Gates will be down, and the guards will be busy checking in the new detail."

She was glad Frankie had thought this through because she certainly hadn't—not to this extent. Mrs. Simms, I'm going to be a little late, she thought to herself.

Their progress was slow. It took Frankie a while to find the place where he thought they could slide under. For the most part, the fencing seemed to go right down to the ground, with little give underneath. Above was all razor wire, so they weren't going over. There was nothing to do but keep foraging for a crawl space. Finally, Frankie found an opening.

"Here, look at this," he said, shining the flashlight on a kind of smoothed out ravine under a portion of the fence about a hundred feet from where they had started looking. Kelsey studied the gap.

"No fat kid did that two years ago," she said. "That looks pretty fresh. Someone—or something—has gone under there recently."

"Never mind. It's an opening. That's all we need," he said, getting down on all fours, preparing to slide on his belly through the opening. "I'll go first," he announced.

"Fine by me. Just don't get stuck. I don't think I could pull you out."

"Is that a crack at my weight?" he asked. "And to think, I was about to kiss you for good luck. Lost your chance."

"When we crawl out," Kelsey said, "you'll get a congratulatory smooch."

He decided to try to go through on his belly, and then when his head cleared the fence prongs at the bottom of the fencing, he'd flip over and slide through on his back. The spot was tighter than it looked like from his standing position. He'd expected the ground to be a little softer. He didn't seem to be able to displace much of the hard earth beneath him. Regardless, he pushed ahead, bracing the bottom of his feet against the ground and trying to push his body through.

"Here goes nothing," he said, and then he grunted and shoved himself partially under the fence. His head cleared, but just barely. His shoulders were right under the fencing, He lay face down.

"You okay?"

"Swallowed some dirt," he grumbled, trying to regenerate some momentum by pushing himself forward, arching his feet and digging his toes in to get some traction. He grunted some more, but didn't really seem to move. After a little more scuffling of his boots against the ground and a couple of profanity-laced utterances, he asked Kelsey to grab the flashlight and see what was wrong, why he couldn't move.

"Not sure," she said, shining the light up and down the length of his body. "I think you're just too big to get through. There's not enough room for the rest of you. If you can make it past your shoulders, I think you might be able to scoot through."

"I can't really move forward. The ground slopes upward on this side of the fence. I didn't notice that. If it was level I could maybe do it."

Kelsey shone the light just beyond where he lay and saw that he was right. There was a gentle upward slope, but enough to make simply pushing him through impossible. He'd have to be able to arch his body upward. She had an idea.

"If you were on your back, you could probably get up that slope. Can you turn over?"

"I'll try," he said. But almost as soon as she said it she realized that was a mistake. Kelsey could see in the flashlight that the fence terminated with the pointed ends of the metal strands that made up the fencing, and when

Frankie turned to flip over, his jacket and sweatshirt immediately got snagged by several of the wiry prongs.

"Oh shit," he said, feeling his ability to move suddenly arrested.

"Don't move," Kelsey shouted, dropping to her knees.

"Very funny," he said.

"No, really. Don't move. I'm going to try to un-snag you." It was no use. The torque of his twisting, the weight of his body, and the angle of the fence made freedom impossible.

"You're going to have to get a new jacket," Kelsey said.

"At this point, I just want to get the hell out of here." Kelsey didn't know if he meant simply that he wanted out from under the fence, or whether he wanted to be away from the base completely. He sounded a little desperate. She realized they were in a bit of a pickle. He was quite stuck. As long as they stayed calm, she was sure they'd be able to find a way to get him loose.

"Okay, Frankie. I'm going to grab your legs and pull. Relax your shoulders. If this works, you'll probably slide out of your jacket, but then we can unhook it from the fence after you're free. Okay?"

"Whatever. Just get me out."

After digging in with her boot heels to get something to push against, she grabbed both of his ankles and yanked his legs as hard as she could. She heard Frankie let out a hiss of pain.

"You okay?" she asked, dropping his legs immediately.

"Yeah, I'm fine. Why'd you stop?"

"I heard you hissing. I thought maybe you were hurt."

"I didn't hiss."

"You didn't?"

"No."

"Oh. Maybe it was the rustling of the leaves. Let me try again."

She brought his ankles together and grabbed his lower legs. Just as she was getting ready to pull him out, she heard the hissing again. They both heard it.

"What was that?" Frankie asked. Kelsey knew better than to tell him. Instead, she pulled his legs as hard as she could. All that did was drive the fence edges more deeply into the fabric of his coat. He was starting to resemble a human shish-kabob.

The hissing returned, this time a little louder.

"Kelsey, take the light and shine it around. See what the hell is making that noise."

Her hand trembled as she picked up the muddy flashlight from the ground and pointed it into the woods. The light flickered dimly for a brief moment, and then suddenly went out. They were in the dark.

"Quick—I need your knife."

"What are you talking about?"

"Don't argue. I need the knife!"

"It's on my belt. You'll have to grab it."

More hissing. Definitely louder, definitely closer. Kelsey reached under the hem of his jacket and sweatshirt and felt her way along the waistband of his jeans until she felt the handle of the knife.

"Hold on," she said, pulling the knife out parallel to his body. Once she had it firmly in hand, she told him to hold his breath.

"Hold my breath? What in the world are you—"

"Holding your breath immobilizes you—keeps you from moving. I don't want to cut you. It's important you don't move."

"But Kelsey, I—"

"DO IT!"

The hissing filled their ears, filled that portion of the woods where they were trapped, stuck, pinned in the dark, helpless. With a couple of efficiently vicious slashes, Frankie's outerwear gave way, and she yelled at him to twist onto his back. It was raining now. Kelsey grabbed his ankles and pulled but she slipped and ended up on her back. She got up as the hissing continued, close enough she felt that she could reach out and find the source. Frantically, she grabbed one of Frankie's legs and pulled as hard as she could. Between his twisting in the mud and her yanking, he was finally able to wriggle free from under the fence, his face scratched and his legs and back sore. But he was free.

"Now scream."

"Kelsey, are you crazy? The guards will hear us."

"Exactly!" And with that, Kelsey screamed as loud as she could.

"Whooo-hoo! We're in the woods! Trying to sneak in! Guards! Guards!"

The hissing continued. She felt something scurrying through the groundcover. She leaped up and grabbed part of the fence, hanging on to it, still screaming. Now Frankie was finally screaming too.

"Hey! Hey there!! Here we are! Hell-oooo!"

"Guard!" screamed Kelsey. "Guard!" She couldn't tell how loud she was screaming. The hissing in her ears was drowning out her own voice. She was banging on the fence with one of her hands, barely hanging on with cramped fingers of her other hand, supported by her mud-crusted boots, jammed against the wire mesh. She was about to lose her grip and fall back to earth and into the clutches of whatever was creating that hideous, unceasing hissing, when a searchlight from the guard tower swung around and flashed brilliantly on the fence.

"Who-hooo! You found us! Come get us!" Kelsey heard an alarm sound, and the familiar voice bellow at her *"This is restricted property. You are ordered to stand down."*

The light was blinding. Kelsey couldn't even see where Frankie was. But she reached out to where she thought he was and grabbed a handful of sweatshirt.

"Run!" she cried.

Run they did, as fast as they could, through the wet and uncertain terrain, darkness assisting their escape. They could hear a motor revving in the distance—probably a jeep sent out to discover the source of the commotion. It wouldn't be able to get through the fence, Kelsey suspected, but they didn't slow down until they had traversed almost the entire half mile they had to walk to get there in the first place. By the time they stopped to catch their breath, the sounds of the military base had long since faded into the distance. The hissing too had stopped, though Kelsey couldn't say when, exactly. Where they stood now, exhausted, scratched, and soaked, the only sound they heard was the rain falling all around.

"Jesus Christ," Frankie said. "What just happened?"

"Not here. In the car," she said, tugging at Frankie to keep walking. "You'll get pneumonia."

They were both relieved to find the car exactly where they left it. As soon as they were inside, Frankie started the engine and pulled out of his sheltered spot along the side of the road, violating the posted speed limits all the way back home.

"That was him," she said. "The hissing. It was definitely him," she said, trying to dry her hair with the tail of her jacket. "That's the same sound I heard at the lake. I knew the only chance we had to escape was to shine a light in its eyes. Remember Sheila Walters? This thing hates direct light."

"The search light. That's why you screamed."

"You did much better screaming than I did," she said, bringing a smile to his scratched and muddy face. "Anyway, it worked. I figured it was better to take our chances with the guards then with, well, whatever it was that's out there."

Frankie nodded. He was a mess. Still trying to catch his breath, he sat behind the wheel of his car with dirt in his hair and scratches on his face and neck. Kelsey fared a little better. The damage done to her was less physical, more psychological. Another encounter with her little friend—and another narrow escape.

"You want to go somewhere? Get cleaned up? Go grab something to eat?"

"I think I've had my fun tonight," Frankie said. "I better get back. I'll need some time to come up with a story to explain these scratches at work tomorrow."

"Just tell the truth. They'll never believe you anyway," Kelsey said.

"You're probably right," said Frankie, wincing as he inspected himself in the rear view mirror. "I'm not sure *I* even believe it."

They drove back to the newspaper office, mostly in silence, Frankie clearly preoccupied with the scarred face he'd seen in the mirror, Kelsey brooding on what she had yet to actually see.

* * * *

After the emotional and physical tumult of the previous night, Kelsey needed a day at home to unwind and catch her breath. After taking Justin to school, she returned to the barn and made herself a cup of tea. She told herself she wasn't going to even think about the Indiana Corn Weasel, or whatever it might have been that she thought she heard last night. But, of course, she ended up thinking very much about the Indiana Corn Weasel.

She'd intended to keep a journal of her experiences in Indiana. She even bought a separate notebook to write down her thoughts, a marbled composition notebook that she bought at the 99-cent store just before leaving. As she sat there drinking her tea, she noticed it in the stack of books on the floor near the reading chair. It was on the bottom.

It's not like I haven't been writing.

And she had, in fact, done a great deal of writing, filling several smaller, pocket-sized notebooks with information gleaned from interviews with eyewitnesses, casual talks with local residents, or cribbed from the pages of nature guides or back issues of the *Milton Forum*. She'd written a lot of stuff, but all of it was about him, about it, about her "little friend." None of it was about her. She wished she'd done a better job of setting down her own thoughts on paper because she had the clear sense now that she was being affected by what was happening. She wasn't sure how, exactly, except she knew she would now put herself in the category of "believer." She would have loved to record that process more closely. If she never got a look at the Indiana Corn Weasel herself, if he remained a noise in the night, or simply the retold terror of someone else's encounter, she knew she'd start to slide back toward skepticism. She wanted a record of her movement toward belief.

Hoping to recapture something of that interior journey, she reached down and pulled the composition notebook from the stack and put it on her lap. She flipped open the cover and stared at the lined white page blankly. She took a sip of tea, looked out the window, and decided she'd work backwards, writing what was freshest in her memory and then, she hoped, triggering memories of what had come before. She was halfway through her first sentence when her cell phone rang. She didn't recognize the number, and was tempted to let it go, but she knew she'd spend the next few minutes trying to puzzle out who it was, so she picked up. The connection wasn't great, but she recognized the voice immediately.

"Kelsey, I'm glad I was able to reach you. I got your number from Doris, the department secretary. I hope you don't mind my calling you."

"Dr. Reeves? No, of course not. It's good to hear from you. What's going on?"

"I was hoping you could tell me. I've been trying to piece together a narrative from your rather brief and irregular emails. I thought I'd call to see if there was more to the story."

Kelsey's emails had been deliberately vague, and only

frequent enough to satisfy the terms of her research grant. It's not that she didn't want to communicate with Dr. Reeves. She genuinely missed talking to him. She just wasn't sure that she could adequately condense everything that was happening to her, everything she was feeling, her uncertain tiptoeing along the tightrope of doubt, in an email message.

"Well, as you can imagine, there have been a lot of adjustments. I feel a little bit like an alien on a strange planet," she told him. "Midwestern life is a little different."

"Yes, yes, but what about your research? Have you found any answers to the mystery you went out there to solve?"

He made it seem so cut-and-dried, so logical, like everything you find in life can be put in boxes marked "For" or "Against." She wanted to tell him that it wasn't that way at all, at least not here, and that she had found lots of answers but they were all to slightly different questions, and that she still didn't know, after all this time, what it was she had, what the puzzle picture was supposed to look like.

"Well, I think so. Some answers, yes," she said, weakly. "Still digging."

"Good for you," he said buoyantly, not really picking up on the subtext of desperation in her voice. Maybe it was the connection that caused him to hear only confidence. Or maybe it was that he imagined himself where Kelsey was, back in the hunt, doing the field work that he loved so much. There was one issue she needed to talk to him about, a question that had been bothering her for a while.

"If I don't actually get any proof...that is, if I come back and I'm still not sure—"

"Oh, you'll find what you need," he said, cutting her off. "There's nothing like being out in the field, eh? How I envy you, Kelsey!"

He had his narrative worked out, and he was sticking to it. She might as well just play along.

"I'm sure you're right."

"I imagine you've got important work to do, so I won't interrupt you any further. Good luck, Kelsey. And let me know if you need anything. Goodbye."

"Goodbye, Dr. Reeves."

She put down her phone and stared at the still almost-blank page in the notebook on her lap. She crossed out the unfinished half-sentence and with Dr. Reeves' words still ringing in her ears, she wrote across the page: *There's nothing to say until I find him.*

She closed the book, picked up her cup of tea and took a sip. Better get back to work.

Chapter 10

It was almost noon. She knew Frankie ate lunch every day at the diner—though she didn't know he always ordered the same thing: a tuna melt on wheat toast, a side order of mashed sweet potatoes, and a Mountain Dew—but she called anyway, hoping to catch him before he left.

"I'd love to join you tonight, Kelsey, but it's Wednesday."

"What's so special about Wednesday?" Kelsey asked him.

"Town Council meeting. Gotta cover it."

"You'd rather cover a council meeting than risk your life in the woods with me? Are you getting soft?"

"Nah, I've always been soft. But to answer your question, I'd rather shave my pubic hair off with a rusty cheese grater than spend three hours sitting around with the geriatric citizen representatives of the Milton Town Council, discussing zoning ordinances and sewer contract bids. The last meeting was so boring I had an out of body experience."

"So?"

"So it's my job. It's the weekly price I pay to be able to live a life of glamour and riches."

"But if I can't endanger someone else's life, what fun is that for me?" she asked, trying to make light of what she knew was still a lingering and scary memory for both of them.

"You're really going back there tonight?" he asked, with genuine concern.

"Actually, I'm just going to drive around the base. Maybe I'll see or hear something."

"Okay—but do me a favor and stay in the car. I really do have to cover this meeting. It's where I get like ninety percent of my news leads. Anyway, I can go with you this weekend if you want, but just not tonight."

He was clearly worried about her, about what might happen if she decided to revisit the scene of their almost-crime.

"You really care. That's sweet."

"Of course I care. If anything ever happens, you won't be able to replace my jacket that you destroyed."

"Oh, you mean the jacket that got destroyed while I was saving your life?"

"I paid almost forty dollars for that jacket, Kelsey. Do you know how many council meetings I have to sit through to make that kind of money?"

Kelsey laughed, and then promised him she'd stay in the car. She really had no desire to go chasing corn weasels through the woods on her own.

"Call me when you get back tonight. If I'm still conscious after the council meeting, we can talk. And if you feel like dropping by, that would be cool too."

Kelsey knew what he was suggesting. She had been "dropping by" quite a lot lately. They both seemed to need what the other provided. Frankie desperately needed a little excitement and passion in his daily life, and also material for his novel. Kelsey needed to feel connected, secure, not completely adrift in this still-foreign land. She wasn't sure what they really had with each other. She often thought about asking Frankie how he felt, if their relationship was just a convenient excuse for some afternoon sex between story assignments.

"Aren't you supposed to be working?" she once asked him during one of their mid-day trysts.

"I told my editor I was going to do some undercover work," he said. "So technically, I wasn't lying."

But Kelsey put a damper on any plans he might have had for later that evening.

"I probably won't be able to make it. I'll have to pick up Justin from Mrs. Simms and get him home at a decent hour. Sorry."

"That's cool. But call me anyway."

"All right. Have a fun meeting. And be careful. I hear senior citizens can get pretty cranky when they stay up past their bedtime."

"I'll take my knife," he said before hanging up.

She loved that Frankie was always able to make her laugh. She also loved that he understood that her role as mother came before anything else. He never made her feel like Justin was an impediment, or even an inconvenience. He was a great baby sitter, and he often ended up picking Justin up from school and letting him hang out at the newspaper office until Kelsey could extricate herself from wherever her research had taken her that day. Her limited experience with other single men had suggested that usually wasn't the case.

She caught herself thinking warmly about Frankie, but then the social scientist part of her interrupted. *"Do not get too involved with this guy,"* she warned herself. *"He's not going to leave Milton, and you're not going to stay. There's no future in this relationship. Focus on your work. Get what you need, and then get out. Pretty soon, you're never going to see this guy again."*

That thought echoed in her head as she re-dialed his number.

"Your place. Ten minutes," she said, hanging up the phone and heading out the door.

* * * *

That night, as she cruised along the road that wound

by the military base, she was thinking about something Frankie had said during their brief "undercover" lunch-time meeting. Kelsey was telling him that she hoped the weasel would still be hanging around the base and that the guards hadn't scared him away. That could make him harder to find. At least now she knew where to look.

"Kelsey, if that really was him that night we were there, that means somebody at that base wants him there. They could get rid of him fifty different ways: traps, poison gas, small-arms gunfire, flame thrower. The fact that they haven't gotten rid of him means they don't want to get rid of him."

Why would they want such a creature around? It obviously posed a threat to humans. That much was clear. So why put up with it? If Frankie was right, there was no shortage of ways to rid Milton of such a malicious creature. So why don't they? If the presence of a young woman from New Jersey merely parked in her car was enough to set off alarm bells, why allow a flesh-eating mammal of gargantuan size and ferocious temperament free reign over your property? It didn't make sense.

Frankie might have been right, but there was no sign of the Indiana Corn Weasel that Kelsey could discover. At least, not from the safe vantage point of her car. As she followed the road that traced, roughly, the base's perimeter, she kept her windows rolled down and her ear attuned to any unusual noises. Several times she pulled over and turned off her engine and lights, waiting and listening. Occasionally, she would flick the lights on, illuminating the foliage in the distance and frightening the occasional night-feeding squirrel or opossum. But she didn't see or hear anything remotely resembling her old friend. After about an hour of her rolling stakeout, she decided to call it a night and head back to town to pick up Justin at Mrs. Simms' house.

As she drove through the night, wondering if Frankie was having a more productive evening than she was, she noticed something in the distance. There was a strange glow coming from one of the cornfields on the edge of town. The field had long been stripped of its stalks, and was now just a barren stretch of earth, but for some reason there seemed to be something aglow there. As she got closer, she saw not just one light but dozens of lights, maybe more. They looked like flashlights, with the beams criss-crossing randomly in the night sky.

She pulled her car over and got out. Was this some sort of search party at work? What were they looking for? And what was it they seemed to be chanting in unison? She climbed up the gently sloping hill to reach the field and as she stood on the edge of the field, she could see there must be almost a hundred people standing there, flashlights turned every which way, making a crazy-quilt of light against the dark and distant horizon. Someone was speaking. She thought she recognized the voice.

"Brothers and sisters, we come together as a community of believers, strengthened by faith and determined to rid our town of evil."

Scattered "Amens!" echoed across the dark plain. She could see they had organized themselves into a circle, with the man speaking standing directly in the center, holding his flashlight parallel to the ground, shining it in the faces of his flock.

"When they came for Jesus, he didn't run. He welcomed them, as a host welcomes an uninspected guest. My good people, we have an unexpected guest, and I shall not run! I shall not flee! I shall not turn my back in denial, or fear! I shall seek him out! Our Christian duty demands it!"

The flashlight beams filtered through the evening air in jerky waves of affirmation. The man in the middle of it all, she could see now, as random lights swept through the center of the gathering, was Reverend Lonnie. He had taken his troubled flock outside the safety of their brick and mortar citadel to encounter first-hand "the demon in disguise," staging a dramatic night-time religious revival on the enemy's own territory, the shadowy province of his recent maulings.

"Be not afraid of him who comes in guises of deception. Be afraid of him who stands next to you in deceit, professing to be a believer but harboring in his heart the cold-blooded predator of doubt!"

This was the same language, the same kind of fervid and hypnotic patter that she remembered from her first night in town when she and Justin stumbled across the service at Jesus the Redeemer church. She remembered feeling vulnerable back then, a slightly frightened sheep in the larger flock, connected in a way to her fellow gatherers that surprised her. But here, she felt no connection whatsoever. The starkness and venom of this cornfield tableau was off-putting to her, like a scene from a movie where the local villagers grab pitchforks and torches and head out in a frenzy to destroy the creature.

Reverend Lonnie seemed to be playing directly to those fears, and it was working on most of them.

"Now is not the time to bar the door! Now is the time to pick up your sword and challenge the demon! Pick it up, I say, and like St. George, slay the beast that gorges on your fear and desperation! Defeat it with the full weight of your faith!"

"Amen!" and "Here! Here!" and "Hallelujah!" and "Praise God!" resounded through the cold and dark as those gathered in that field tried to summon their courage—or at least mask their anxiety—through this show of lamplit Christian fealty. Kelsey kept her distance from the gathering, hovering just on the fringes of this undulating circle of faith. But she could see that the good Reverend's words were having an effect. Fists were pumping, lights flickered on and off, and the general level of courage seemed to be rising. They were fortifying themselves against the enemy.

"I tell thee, be not afeard of thou that tormenteth the

righteous, for there can be no torment in the temple of God's love, in the sacred soil of God's only field, the heart of the righteous!" He was working them into a frenzy. If there was a local windmill or lonely farmhouse that contained the creature, she had no doubt that they would have stormed it by flashlight this very moment. But the beast they professed to seek was not to be found this night.

"It shall come like a thief in the night, so you must stay awake," he said, launching a refrain of the last two words, turning the phrase into a holy mantra.

"Stay awake! Stay awake! Stay awake!!!"

And then, all was silent. Reverend Lonnie turned off the flashlight he had brandished and he walked through the crowd, down the gently sloping hill, and toward the church, a quarter of a mile away. Thereafter followed the parishioners who had followed him there, their flashlights also turned off, trudging silently behind, enfolded in wake of the Reverend's peroration and braced by the fortifying winds of faith. They marched off one by one, like Pharoah's army, blindly pushing forward in the darkness. As Reverend Lonnie walked past Kelsey he offered no gesture of recognition, no acknowledgement of her presence. He strode toward the road, with the fearless and the fearful right behind, mingling inextricably, all of them seeking a foothold against whatever perils were hidden in the darkness ahead.

Kelsey stood by as the parade of pilgrims marched past her. She stayed there as they trod off into the night, their footfalls fading as they moved closer to the church and further from the reality of the creature's existence. Kelsey wondered if their revived sense of Christian empowerment would help them sleep better tonight. She marveled that a few Biblical phrases spoken by flashlight could change their whole mindset. Most surprising to her, however, was the man at the center of it all, Reverend Lonnie. Just a few days ago, in the pumpkin patch at the fair, he seemed so reasonable, so logical, so scientific. But here he was tonight, presiding over this pageant of paranoia, stirring up emotions and seeming to believe what he was saying. How could someone seem so level-headed one moment and so superstitious the next? Kelsey had yet to reconcile the gulf between faith and reason, the same gulf that separated her from the Indiana Corn Weasel. She wondered if she would ever reach a point in her life when she could accept as true those things she couldn't see, put her hands on, catalog in her notebook.

Her musings were interrupted by her cell phone's ring tone. It was Frankie.

"Meeting over already?" she asked.

"Yeah. Slow news night. At least, it was until I got back to the office. Something was waiting for me. Something you'd be very interested in seeing."

"It's pretty late," she reminded him, pre-empting any thought he had of getting together later. "Tomorrow okay?"

"I've got to go over to Jessup tomorrow to cover a barn raising. We could meet for dinner?"

"Sure."

"Okay. Let's say Mabel's. Six o'clock. Don't be late, Kelse. What I have to show you is pretty astounding."

Frankie has probably been in rural Indiana too long. I can't imagine anything being truly astounding in this place. But at this point, I'll take anything that might help solve this puzzle. Besides, the pie at Mabel's is out of this world.

* * * *

"How was your barn raising?" she asked him, sliding into the faux red leather booth near the window looking out at the parking lot. Mabel's was located just past the county line, in a backwater called Sawyersville. It was part truck stop, part cafeteria, and—if the rumors were to be believed—part whorehouse. And they were famous for their huckleberry pie, which Kelsey had never had—or even heard of—before coming to Indiana. Now, she was addicted.

"No matter how many times I've seen them do it, it still impresses me," Frankie said. "Can you imagine putting up a barn from scratch in one day? A whole barn? You know how long it would take me to do that?"

Frankie wasn't the most industrious soul in the world. And from what she saw of his apartment, he didn't even own a tool box. He could never build a barn. Not in fifty years. He'd learn to like sleeping outside before he'd even finish the foundation.

"Oh, I don't know. A handy guy like you? I'm sure you'd get it done quicker than you think."

Frankie shrugged off her lie. "Maybe," he said, repressing a slight smile, flattered by her embellishment.

They both ordered the buffet.

"Do you think they have the usual selections?" Kelsey asked.

"They haven't changed the buffet in three years," Frankie said. "It's always the same. And it's always great."

Frankie was as much gourmet as he was handyman. But Kelsey had to admit that the buffet at Mabel's was, at the very least, filling. And cheap. And for a slice of their addictive huckleberry pie, she'd chew through rope. They filled their plates and returned to the booth.

"So what's this amazing thing you want to show me?"

"Not yet. Let's eat first."

So their dinner table conversation consisted of the usual end-of-the-workday chatter. Frankie talked about a couple of assignments he had gone on this week. Kelsey told him about a school project Justin had made for science class, a model of the solar system made up of picture wire, marshmallows, and a casaba melon.

"Sounds delicious,' Frankie said, cleaning his plate.

"He was supposed to use a grapefruit for the sun, but they're out of season. So we improvised."

"That's probably how Newton got started."

"I think you mean Galileo."

"Whatever," he said. "Are you going back for more?"

"No. Just pie."

"Oh, right. I forgot I was dining with Huckleberry Hound."

"Did you just call me a dog?"

"Huckleberry Hound. You know—the cartoon character?"

Kelsey shrugged.

"You know Galileo but not Huckleberry Hound? How is that possible?" he asked, shaking his head as he headed off for seconds.

After Frankie's multiple platefuls had at last been dispatched and Kelsey's pie fix temporarily satisfied, Frankie lit up a cigarette and they sat there, groaning contentedly.

"I'm never going to be able to get out of this booth," Kelsey said.

"I think I have something to show you that's going to get you pretty riled up," Frankie said, reaching into his canvas shoulder bag with the "Mercy 5k Run For Your Life" logo printed on the side and pulling out a business-sized envelope. "This was delivered to the office yesterday. Look at the return address."

Kelsey squinted at the handwriting and the lone name in the return address spot.

"Wells," she said aloud. "Is that supposed to mean something."

"It didn't mean anything to me either. At first. Then I remembered where I'd heard that name before: the girl who was attacked last week, the one who died, Audrey Wells, remember?"

"You mean the girl who had the heart attack?"

"Yeah, heart attack. You better read this."

The handwriting on the lined paper was just as bad as the handwriting on the outside of the envelope, but Kelsey was able to decipher most of it. She started to read the letter aloud, but Frankie stopped her.

"To yourself," he cautioned. Intrigued, she silently read on:

"My name is David Wells. My older step-sister was Audrey. She was killed last week by an animal. The police said it was a heart attack. That's a lie. The police delivered money to my mama, enough to fill a suitcase, all bundled up. They told her to take the money and shut up about the attack. We're poor, so we took it. But my conchince bothers me since, and I needed to tell somebody. Anyway, it wasn't a heart attack. We've moved and when you get this, I don't know where we'll be. Sincere, David."

Kelsey looked at Frankie for some sort of confirmation about just how astonished to feel.

"Some sort of hoax?" she asked.

"I thought about that. But what would be the point? A private letter that's not asking for anything? If it's a hoax, what's the motive?"

"Maybe they want you to write a story about it."

"Oh sure—here's a reliable source," he said, waving the letter at her. "A handwritten letter from some kid, with no address or phone number, that contradicts everything the police and medical staff have said. My standards might be low, Kelsey, but they're not that low. I can't possibly run with this. There's nothing there."

"You said he's a kid. How do you know that?"

"Look," he said, putting the letter down on the sticky tabletop. "He calls her his 'older' step sister. She was only sixteen. So he's fifteen, at the oldest. Maybe younger. Plus, he's not the best speller. Look," he said, pointing to the word "conchince."

Kelsey studied the letter.

"I believe him," she said.

Frankie extinguished his cigarette and lit another one.

"What he's saying is pretty remarkable. Are we supposed to believe the Milton police are now paying off the families of victims of the Indiana Corn Weasel?

What's the point—why try to cover it up? Everybody in town knows about these attacks."

"True," Kelsey said, "but this was the first fatal attack. Maybe if word got out, there'd be a lot of media people sniffing around."

"Why should the Milton police care?" Frankie asked. "They're not capable of orchestrating a conspiracy. That's light years beyond them."

"You're probably right. They seem pretty small time."

"I've seen the budget," Frankie said, "and believe me, there's no way the town could ever even get a suitcase full of money. Without the taxes from the military base, they couldn't even meet their payroll."

The military base. Of course.

"Frankie—that's it. The military base!" She was shouting, and Frankie put his hand over her mouth.

"Shhh!"

"Frankie, think about it," she said, ignoring him. "The military has the money to make this happen. They're the ones who are paranoid. We know that. Remember how they wrote down my license plate number? How they told me to move along when I was just sitting in my car?"

"But this kid said the police delivered the money, not somebody in the military."

"Maybe the police are working with them. Maybe they—"

And then it came back to her, vividly, in a moment of disarming clarity.

"Oh my God! Frankie, remember that afternoon I spent at the police station? When they wouldn't let me in to see the chief? While I was there, remember I told you, I saw this military guy. What's his name?"

"Praeger?" said Frankie. "Major Praeger, base commander? Oh shit, Kelsey, do you know what you're saying?"

"You bet 'oh shit.' Praeger was walking out of the chief's office—I saw him—and he had this huge briefcase with him. Frankie—that must have been filed with cash! He gives the cash—in bundles—to the chief, leaves, and the chief sneaks out of his office and goes to the victim's house. He pays off the mother. The step-brother sees the whole thing go down. Next thing, the family's gone. Attack victim? What attack victim? And so the only two people sniffing around that base are you and me, not the camera crews from CNN."

Frankie blew a plume of smoke, shaking his head.

"You should be writing a novel instead of me," he said. "That's a pretty amazing story."

"Tell me," she said, elbows on the table, leaning across, staring directly at him. "Tell me you don't believe it."

Frankie broke out into a nervous laugh.

"I feel like you're interrogating me on one of those crime shows."

"Frankie, this isn't TV. This is reality. We can't ignore this now. We've got to go back to the base. They're tied in to these attacks. Something's going on in one of those buildings. If we can get inside, I think we'll get our answer."

She looked at him pleadingly.

"We've got to do this," she said. "You know that."

He leaned back, exhaled another column of smoke, and snuffed out his cigarette.

"I guess it wouldn't hurt to go out and look around."

She squeezed his hand, certain that things were finally about to break her way.

Chapter 11

The trick was how to get in. Kelsey and Frankie discussed the direct approach: flashing a quick set of press credentials—he would grab a press pass from the drawer for her—and just walk through the gate. They might be able to hoodwink some grunt on the graveyard shift, but what kind of story could they say they were working on at two in the morning? Also, if there was any activity in those abandoned-looking cinder-block buildings that used to be research labs, it probably took place during daylight hours, Kelsey concluded. So they needed to be there during the day.

"We could walk in carrying a tool box and a ladder, tell them we're contractors there to hang a loudspeaker or fix a bank of security monitors," Kelsey said. "We can tell them 'headquarters' sent us. We'll get right in."

"Look at us, Kelsey," Frankie said. "Do we look like we even know how to open a toolbox? I mean, realistically, no one's going to buy that we're part of the building trade. We look more like a couple of lost tourists, backpacking through the Midwest on our way to the Appalachian Trail."

"Do you think that might work?" Kelsey asked him, considering for a moment whether the idea had any merit. Frankie shook his head.

"It seems pretty clear that we're going to have to sneak in. We know where the fence breach is. If we can get there during the shift change, the guards might not pay any attention, and if it's morning time, our little friend may be loathe to show his whiskered face. That means we have to get there around six-thirty a.m. The first shift goes on duty at seven a.m. We get to the fence, but this time, we dress appropriately. No clothes that can get caught on the fence."

"So what do we do, go naked?"

Frankie appeared to be thinking about it. "Only during rehearsal in my apartment. But when we go live at the base, I know just what we'll wear."

Kelsey arranged for an early-drop off for Justin. She would take him to a classmate's house at around six a.m., and then she'd rendezvous with Frankie at the newspaper parking lot, and they'd once again drive up there together in his car, going over the details of their latest scheme.

"Precision is everything," Frankie said. "This has to go like clockwork. We'll beat the military at their own game."

It didn't seem like much of a game as they drove to the base that morning, the punishing glare of the rising sun practically blinding them as Kelsey tried to process in her caffeine-starved brain all the detailed information Frankie was throwing at her.

"From what I've been able to learn, the shift changes take a total of about twenty minutes to accomplish. During that time, the outgoing personnel have to fill out some sort of checklist and the incoming personnel have to sign in with the base commander. That means they all have to pass through this building right here," he said, handing her an aerial photo of the entire compound.

"Wow. Where'd you get this?" Kelsey asked.

"We had it in our morgue. It's from the time when we used to run stories about the place, but I think it's pretty much up to date."

So Frankie had done his homework. He had maps, tools, and a plan. All Kelsey had was her desire to get into the place and her certainty that somehow the base was connected to the weasel attacks. Hopefully, that would be enough.

"If we enter at the rear perimeter just before the shift change, we should be able to make it into the research facility by the time the new patrols are dispatched, which is every half hour. It'll be daylight, so there won't be anyone in this tower, here," he said, pointing to the map.

"Keep your eyes on the road," she said.

"Kelse, I could drive this road in my sleep. Look here. See this building? That's where the searchlight is. That's where the light came from when we tried to break in. This is the closest building to the perimeter, but there's no one there during the day shifts because there's no need for a searchlight when the sun's out, obviously."

"How'd you find all this stuff out?"

He gave her an indignant look.

"Give me a little credit," he snapped. "I've been working as a reporter here for three years. So I talked to a couple of people—don't worry, nothing that would arouse suspicion. I told them the paper was thinking of doing some sort of feature story about the base's upcoming anniversary year."

"What anniversary year?"

"How the hell should I know? It was just an excuse to get 'em talking."

Kelsey looked at the map, and at Frankie, and at the stretch of road ahead, and she understood now that they really were doing this. She had to get focused.

"All right. So we can get in. How do we get out?"

"Same way we got in. Under the fence and out through the woods. Only problem is our window to get back out is a little smaller. At ten a.m., the base has a daily 'Call to Arms.' It's kind of a pledge of allegiance ceremony. There's a flag raising, some guy blows a bugle, all very spit-and-polish. All the non-essential personnel turn out for it. That takes place here," he said, pointing to a concrete parcel just behind the motor pool. "At that time, everybody is either there, or working in the lab, which is here," he said, indicating the largest of the base's buildings. "Those guys don't have to show up to play soldier boy. They're exempt. It's mostly civilians who work there anyway."

"How many?"

"I couldn't find out. Even people who have been on that base for years aren't exactly sure. Anyway, during this flag raising, the soldiers who patrol the perimeter have to serve as the color guard. They take the old flag, fold it up, and unfurl the new flag. So there are no guards at all anywhere near the perimeter. But the whole thing takes less than ten minutes, so we'll have to be ready. If not, we're stuck until the next guard change, which takes place at lunchtime. High noon."

Kelsey nodded, trying to take it all in.

"I think we should split up after we go under the fence," he said, "and meet back at the research lab. I'll go along the western perimeter and try to get into the C.O.'s office. He doesn't come in until about nine, and his secretary will be at the guard kiosk until then, checking ID's. The office is basically unguarded. I thought if I could get in there and pull a couple of files, it might be helpful. You should go east, past the old Quonset hut that used to be a barracks. It's supposed to be deserted. Maybe you can take a peek inside. Then, we'll meet up behind the research facility. There's a berm—a sort of grassy wall—and we can meet there. If I'm late, you go ahead without me. Vice versa. If we don't meet up there, for whatever reason, we'll meet back at the fence during the call to arms. Okay?"

Kelsey nodded, but it still didn't seem real to her. As the car approached the spot where they were going to pull off the road, she wondered again if they were doing the right thing. That small but insistent voice that would regularly torment her—the one that would say *"I just want to finish my dissertation!"*—spoke up again. Was it really necessary—or even sane—to run around northeastern Indiana playing spy? *"I'm a crypto-zoologist,"* she said to herself, *"not a cat burglar."* But then she looked over at Frankie and he was, somewhat inexplicably, the picture of resolve. He was in this, all the way. Maybe it was his reporter's instincts kicking into high gear. Or maybe it was his indignation at being told he had to stay away from the base, three years' worth of prohibition about to be annihilated with one dramatic blow.

Or maybe, she thought warmly, *he's doing this for me.*

Whatever the reasons, there they were, getting out of Frankie's car and going after a quarry that might not even exist.

"Here, put this on," Frankie said, handing her a poncho.

"It smells funny," she said. "And it's hideously unattractive."

"The funny smell's gun oil. I rubbed it down. It'll be nice and slick when we go under that fence. I can't speak to its aesthetic qualities."

Making a face, she slipped hers on.

"Where in the world did you get these?"

"They're mine. I wear them when I go duck hunting."

"You hunt ducks?"

"Kelse, if you want to fit in with the locals, you've got to do more than develop a taste for huckleberry pie."

"Very funny," she said. "Aren't you going to put yours on?"

"I have to pee," he said. "I'll be right back."

He trudged off about twenty feet and positioned himself behind a mid-sized sycamore tree.

Kelsey tried to get a glimpse of herself in the side-view mirror of Frankie's car. She hadn't had a chance to brush her hair or put makeup on. She noticed dark circles under her eyes—which she attributed to the unkind morning light. She pulled the hood of her poncho over her head. She looked like some sort of garden gnome unexpectedly sprung to life.

"Otto, if you could only see me now," she said quietly, shaking her head.

Frankie had returned, and was wearing his poncho. Somehow on him it looked good.

"Okay, we've got about half an hour until the shift change begins. We can get to the fence breach in about twenty minutes. Once there, we can go over the plans again."

"Roger," said Kelsey, saluting.

So off they went into the woods, the reporter and the graduate student. They talked very little on their march to the fence. Kelsey could sense that Frankie was focused, locked in. She noted a kind of macho swagger in the way he had taken command of their mission, and wondered if he was as confident on the inside as he appeared. Nonetheless, she was glad he'd adopted a take-charge attitude. Although she was the one who had to talk him into coming, it was *her* resolve that she felt waning. His determination was helping her muster the courage to keep from calling this whole thing off.

When they got to the fence neither of them recognized the place, and might have missed it except for the bits of cloth from Frankie's jacket still clinging to the prongs of fencing near the ground.

"It looks different in the daylight," Kelsey said.

"If I had known that was such a tight squeeze, I probably wouldn't have tried to get through. But we've got about ten minutes. Stay back, in the woods. I'm going to loosen up some of that soil and dig out a little more of a trench."

He got onto his knees, took out his hunting knife and began chopping at the hard clay and groundcover under the fence. Kelsey watched him go at it, bits of earth flying here and there, Frankie panting but undaunted in his mechanical assault on the terrain. From where she stood, about twenty-five feet back, in a small grove of sugar maples, she couldn't really tell if he was making progress, but when she approached after he stopped digging, she was surprised to see how much he had widened and deepened the gap under the fence. He was sweating and looked exhausted.

"Quite a workout," he said, getting to his feet and lighting up a cigarette.

"Nice job," she said. "You're pretty good with that knife."

"Three years of porterhouse steak night every Friday at Mabel's," he said, drawing the smoke deeply into his lungs and then exhaling lovingly.

"What's next?"

He peered into the distance, squinting.

"I don't see any movement yet. Should be just a couple of minutes. When they go, we go."

"Got it. And after?"

"We meet at the lab, just like we discussed. You remember which building?"

"I remember," Kelsey said.

"Here, take this," he said, handing her a swatch of flannel fabric.

"What's this for?"

"Use it to wipe off any fingerprints you'd otherwise leave behind."

"Good thing you like spy movies," Kelsey said, tucking the rag inside the poncho. "And thanks again for coming along, Frankie. I couldn't do this without you." She sidled up next to him and kissed him, pressing her lips against his for much longer than seemed appropriate for a couple of would-be felons in ponchos standing outside a military base at daybreak. But he didn't seem to mind, his hands smoothing the folds of her well-oiled outerwear.

"Look!" he said. "There they go."

Kelsey stared through the fence and across the compound and she saw the dust kicking up from a jeep rolling from the central guard tower toward the base's entrance. Before she could even ask him what was next, he was on the ground, on his back, going head first under the fence. His eyes were closed, but his teeth were gritted and he got through with unexpected quickness.

"Okay, now you," he said. Kelsey got down on the ground and stared up at the cloudless blue sky and had a kind of surreal moment, imagining herself in a movie, the director having just yelled "Action" and actress Kelsey snapping to and bravely re-enacting this daring day-time assault. But then she opened her eyes and looked from the sky to Frankie. She must have had a worried look on her face.

"You can do this, Kelse," he said. "If a fat ass like me can make it under there, you'll have no problem. Lean your head back and push with your heels. Once you get a little bit under, I can pull you from this side."

But she was able to manage it herself, and before she knew it, she too was standing on the other side of the fence. There was no director to shout "Cut," however—she'd have to play out the whole scene, apparently.

"All right, we've got to get going. If you see anybody coming, just crouch behind the berm and wait 'til they pass. If disaster strikes just wait for the flag-raising and make your way back here, and we'll meet outside the fence."

"What could possibly go wrong?" Kelsey asked. For the first time all morning, Frankie smiled. And then he was gone.

"Focus," she told herself. *"Remember why you're here."* She felt in her pocket for her camera and her notepad. What she needed to do was simple, really. Get inside a building, take a look around, maybe snap a few pictures, then back out and back home. Simple. She was right: what could possibly go wrong?

Thanks to Frankie's advance planning, the base, or at least what she could see of it, seemed deserted. She moved along the fence quickly until she got to what looked like an obstacle course, with punching bags hanging on ropes, and a makeshift wall composed of rough-hewn logs stacked on top of each other and tied in place with a stiff nylon rope. In her mind she could imagine the scene of grunts in fatigues humping over the wall while some sergeant screamed obscenities at them, disparaging their parentage.

Just like the movies.

Emboldened by the fact that she'd made it this far so easily, and that there still appeared to be no one around that she could see, she moved closer to the old Quonset hut Frankie told her was abandoned. She could see from where she was that the corrugated tin that arched over the barracks like a covered bridge had rusted and, in a few places, cracked completely. If she could get a little closer, she was sure one of those cracks was big enough to allow her to peek inside. She looked around—still no one within her sight. She imagined Frankie, who could move pretty fast for a slightly-overweight chain-smoking newspaper reporter when he had to, was getting close to the research facility.

* * * *

What Kelsey had no way of knowing was that Frankie had run into a slight problem. A handful of personnel assigned to the motor pool didn't change shifts, and he had to duck behind an old Humvee parked outside one of the maintenance garages to avoid being seen by them. What Frankie's pre-assault intelligence had failed to reveal is that many of the personnel at the base often worked a double-shift, since the military paid triple-time for any overtime hours. It was a way for many of the patronage workers to turn a modest paycheck into a bonanza.

* * * *

Kelsey looked around just to be sure, took a breath,

and bolted for the Quonset hut. She imagined she was quite a sight, dashing across the dusty compound in her duck-hunting poncho. But she made it and was able to get to the rear entrance, which was unfortunately padlocked. Her suspicions were correct, however. There were several breaches in the exterior covering, and just a few feet away from where she was, there was a gash where a piece of the tin had been folded back and she was able to almost stick her whole head into the opening. There wasn't much to see. There were no bunks inside, no crates, no desks, no people. It was dark and empty. If people were sleeping on the base at night, it wasn't here.

Kelsey leaned back against the arching wall of the Quonset hut and, step by step, made her way closer to her next destination, the research lab. If her luck held, there'd be no one near the entrance to that building until the shift change ended. She calculated that she had fewer than five minutes to get inside. There was a lighted entranceway that she could see, and the top of a stairwell. Once again, Frankie's intelligence proved to be correct. A downward stairwell meant that whatever was going on in that building was going on below ground, out of site.

She reached the other entrance to the Quonset hut and from there she was only about a hundred feet from the research building.

No guards. This is almost too easy.

She looked around for Frankie but there was no sign of him. She knew she couldn't afford to wait for him, that she had to make her move now, before she lost her chance. She'd be completely exposed as she scurried from her hidden vantage point to the entrance of the research lab, but there was no other way. And so she went.

* * * *

Frankie, meanwhile, had run into more bad luck. In his attempt to avoid the personnel at the motor pool—who appeared to be deeply involved in a card game—he took the long way around, which meant getting back out to the fence, and following the tree line around to almost the front of the base, where there was a small supply warehouse that would hide him from view until he could meet up with Kelsey at the lab. Unfortunately, the building he currently found himself leaning against was the base's mess hall, and it appeared to be buzzing at this hour. Shortly after the changing of the shifts, most of the newly-arrived personnel reported to the mess hall for a quick breakfast. There was no way to go past there without being seen. Frankie's reporter instincts took over. He took off his poncho and ditched it in the weeds, stuck his notepad in his back pocket, and simply strolled in to the mess hall. There were always some civilians on the base, and with an air of belonging there, he just walked in to the mess hall like he'd been there a hundred times before. In a further effort to blend in, he picked up a tray and got in the chow line.

"What's for breakfast today?" he asked the young man in fatigues who was standing in line in front of him.

"Grits," the soldier said. "It's our lucky day."

I hope you're right, Frankie thought, clutching his cafeteria tray and moving through the line.

* * * *

While Frankie was enjoying his free breakfast, Kelsey had somehow managed to get herself into the research laboratory. The stairwell leading down was unguarded, so she hit the first flight of stairs running, and down she went. At the bottom of that flight, the stairs kept going. So she took the next set. Then, another flight down. Then still another. "This is incredible," she said to herself.

Six flights later, she came to a metal door with a small slit of plate glass at eye level. She pulled on the door, but it was locked. She looked through the tiny rectangular window but all she could see was a fluorescent light and a long hallway. Her brief moment of triumph had turned to potential tragedy as she realized she was now trapped. She couldn't move forward, and if she were to climb the six stories back to the ground floor entranceway, she'd most likely be discovered. She looked again through the window and saw two people in protective clothing—hair nets, goggles, surgical masks and medical scrubs—coming directly toward her. She only had a moment to think.

As they pushed open the door, they saw a hooded figure in a duck-hunting poncho on her knees, wiping a large flannel rag across the floor.

"Watch your step, folks," she said, authoritatively. "Chemical spill. Non-toxic, but it'll stain your clothing. That's why I'm wearing this poncho. Wouldn't want you to get any on yourself."

They nodded and then continued on their way. Before the door latched, Kelsey was safely inside the hallway, plotting her next move.

* * * *

Frankie, meanwhile, was in line for a second helping of grits. He figured he might as well linger as long as possible until the mess hall emptied out, and if he was eating, his presence might seem less conspicuous. Plus the grits were really tasty. He tried to appear deeply interested in his breakfast so as not to get drawn in to any casual conversation that might reveal his unauthorized status. After a few more minutes, he looked around and noticed he was the only one still eating, so he put his tray on the conveyer belt and walked toward the door.

There were now two guards at the entrance to the research building, both armed, both looking alert. There was no chance Frankie was going to get in. He'd have to resort to Plan B—retreat to the berm, wait for the flag raising, and then race back to the fence, where he'd meet Kelsey. There's no way, he knew, that she'd try to make it past those two guards. It was obvious no one was getting in or out without being seen by them. No way at all.

* * * *

Six floors underground, Kelsey tried to act like she belonged there, though she was sure that if anyone saw her they'd know immediately she was an interloper. Fortunately for her, the floor was empty of any other personnel. She had no idea what she was looking for, but she kept alert and just kept moving. At the end of the hallway, on her right, there was a large set of double doors. As she got closer, she heard a buzzing sound coming from that room, which she assumed housed some sort of generator or furnace. As she got closer, the buzzing turned into kind of a whistling sound, something you'd expect from a gigantic teapot. A steam room, maybe? By the time she reached the doors, she knew what the sound was. She'd heard it that night in the barn with Justin, and again when she was at the lake. She heard it that night when Frankie got stuck under the fence, and here it was again, that horrible hissing sound. Only this time, it wasn't a single hissing sound but rather there appeared to be multiple sources of the noise, overlapping, contrasting. It was disorienting. And it was coming from behind those double doors. Kelsey pulled on them but they didn't budge. Next to the doors was a small black plate with a flashing red light on it, some type of security scanner, she figured. These doors also had a small, thick glass slit, and when she stood on her tiptoes to look through, she couldn't believe what she was looking at: the entire room was filed with large wire cages. Each cage had a metal plate in front, so she couldn't see what was behind them all, but the hissing was now unmistakable, almost unbearable. She reached into the pocket of her poncho to grab her camera when she felt the metal handcuff snap onto her wrist.

* * * *

"Hello? Anybody out there? Hello? Hey, I really need to pee! We're going to have a situation pretty soon here. Hello?"

Among the many difficulties facing Kelsey—her hands were handcuffed behind her back, she was sitting on a wooden bench in a cinder block room with a naked light bulb hanging from the ceiling, and all of her personal belongings had been confiscated, plus she was still wearing that stupid-looking duck hunting poncho—she really did need to pee.

"That's not just some ploy to get out of here. I really have to go," she shouted out, not sure if anyone was listening. She didn't know where she was, or even who had brought her here. After she was handcuffed, she was blindfolded, and then marched down a hallway to an elevator. Through the whole ordeal she tried to remain calm but the levers of panic had already been pulled. She had the presence of mind to ask "Who are you?" and "Where are you taking me?" but the two people who escorted her—she sensed that there were two of them—refused to answer any of her questions, forcefully handling her and then depositing her in the cell. She was told to stand with her face to the wall, and one of her abductors roughly pulled the blindfold off. By the time she turned around to see who was there, the door had been slammed and she found herself in this desolate room.

"Hello! Isn't there supposed to at least be a sink and a toilet in here? Don't you guys watch prison movies?"

Okay, so she still had her sense of humor. But that was about all she had left. Her dignity, her hope of a quick reconciliation with Frankie, her freedom were all gone now. She sat on the bench, studying the room she was in. There were no markings on the wall, no signs anywhere of what might have once happened here. There was no intercom, no window, no grate in the door through which to shout her protests. And yet she had the uneasy feeling that her every move was somehow being watched.

She closed her eyes and tried to clear her mind.

What's the worst that can happen to me? It's not like they can execute me. They can't, can they?

As this troubling question crawled through her mind, she heard the lock being turned. She looked up and saw two young men in military fatigues. They came over to her and lifted her off the bench.

"What are you—"

"Come with us."

Each of her escorts grabbed her under her arm and pulled her along forcefully.

"You must be the guys who threw me in here, right?" she asked her stone-faced companions. "I recognize your hospitable manner." They were unmoved by her sarcasm, leading her along a short corridor that led to a larger room that they all now entered. The room was filled with 1950s-era upholstered chairs, coffee tables and floor lamps. Her military escorts stopped in front of a door marked "Ladies," and they stood there, crossing their arms, expressionless.

"May I?" she asked.

"Two minutes," one of them said, unlocking her handcuffs.

"How very gracious," Kelsey said, rubbing her wrists.

She wasn't eager to test their resolve, however, so she made sure she was back out in two minutes. They resumed their unnecessarily harsh grip of her as they moved through the room to an ornate, polished wooden door marked "Private." One of the grunts knocked authoritatively, and then before waiting for an answer, they opened the door and took Kelsey in.

Sitting behind a huge black-lacquer desk was a vaguely familiar figure. He nodded to the escorts, they saluted crisply, and then they disappeared.

"Sit down," he commanded.

I see where those guys get their manners.

She sat down. He picked up a file folder from the desk, opened it, and began reading.

"Miss Kelsey Kane. Twenty-seven years old. Born in Connecticut. Currently a legal resident of New Jersey. Graduate student in Cryp-to-zo-ol-o-gy," he said, enunciating each syllable slowly, separately. "Mother to Justin Kane, eight years old. Temporary resident of Milton, Indiana, supported by a study stipend approved by

Dr. Eugene Reeves, distinguished professor of Anthropology and Sociology." He glanced up at Kelsey. "Do I have my facts straight?"

She wanted to say a lot of things to him, like how he left out the fact that she was currently being held by a bunch of rude jerks playing soldier boy. And he left out the part of paying off the mother of a dead girl to avoid bad publicity. And also how easy it was for Frankie and Kelsey to break into their super-secret compound. She wanted to mention that there were all these mysterious caged animals in the research lab.

There's a lot of facts you left out.

But at the mention of Justin, she got a shiver. Right now, more than anything, she just wanted to get out of there, get to her son and hold him tightly. Her sarcasm and anger were defense mechanisms, functioning at full throttle to keep her from having a meltdown, from emotionally flying apart right there in Major Praeger's office.

"All true," she said, flatly.

He scrunched his nose as he leafed through her file, looking perplexed.

"There seems to be something missing here. I see nothing in this dossier that explains why someone with so much going for her would throw it all away by committing the federal offense of breaking into a restricted military base. Nothing at all. Perhaps you can supply those facts for me?"

She looked down at the floor, shaking her head slightly.

"I see. Well, perhaps that mystery will have to remain unsolved. At least for now." He put the file down and walked around to face her, leaning on the desk.

"It would be a shame for such a promising future to come to an end so...abruptly."

Kelsey looked into his steely gray eyes and saw that he was enjoying this. Suddenly aware of her utter powerlessness, and beginning to think she'd really gone too far, too fast, into this whole adventure, her façade of defiance crumbled and she started to cry. She was afraid she would lose all control. Her tears became choking sobs as she dabbed at her cheeks with her oily parka sleeves. Why was he treating her like a criminal? All she wanted to do was finish her dissertation. She was crying harder now, so hard now that she was shaking. She was embarrassed and frightened and pissed off and unsure what was happening to her, or what was going to happen to her. She tried to stop crying, but she couldn't. Sadness and confusion tore through her, and through her tears, she thought she caught Major Praeger fighting to repress a grin.

"Yes, that would be a real shame," he said. He pressed a button on his phone, and the two guards who had just left reappeared. They picked up their tearful charge and led her out of the office, through the corridor, and into an elevator, where they all wordlessly rose several floors. When the doors opened, she was back on the ground floor, at an exit near the guard tower at the base's entrance. No sooner did the three of them appear than a buzzer sounded loudly, and the front gate began to pull back. Once it was wide enough for a person to step through, the two guards propelled her forward and pitched her with unnecessary force through the opening, out onto the road, and then they turned away and disappeared back into the building they'd just come from. The gate now began to close, and seconds later it was almost like none of it had ever happened.

Alone and cold and tearful and shaking, she gathered herself and walked slowly along the path toward the back of the base, where she hoped to discover both her ride and some portion of her dignity. It was a long walk, but a long walk was what she needed. There were so many conflicting emotions she was trying to sort out. She felt humiliated by her show of tears. The last thing she wanted to do was make Major Praeger feel even more powerful. To feed his arrogance and ego with her own vulnerability gnawed at her. But as she walked along the dirt shoulder of the circuitous path that would take her back to Frankie's car, she gradually talked herself down. "It *was* a pretty stressful morning," she reminded herself. And even the most steel-nerved individual would find handcuffing, blindfolding, and a military escort to an interrogation unnerving. As her anger and embarrassment yielded to reason, she remembered what she saw just before she was apprehended.

I know what's in those cages!

Kicking along that lonely stretch of road, hungry and wrung out, she was buoyed by the realization that her mission had been partly accomplished. The tumult of her capture had eclipsed the very real success she had chasing the Indiana Corn Weasel to its lair. Maybe. Probably. That hissing sound was unmistakable. But if those really were the legendary weasels, confined, angry, what were they doing there? Had the military trapped them? Were they studying them? And how many were there? Was the countryside being over-run by an army of wild corn weasels? Where did they come from? What was going on in that lab? Behavioral studies? Blood tests? And what was causing all that hissing?

So she wasn't wrong to connect the attacks to the base, she realized. And she still believed that Praeger was connected to the sudden windfall that allowed the mother of the dead girl Audrey Wells to start a new life in parts unknown.

He obviously plays a key role in all of this or he wouldn't be so protective of that lab. And to think Frankie thought this was all some over-heated conspiracy I dreamed up…

Frankie!

Kelsey was so busy reassembling the puzzle pieces of her own fragmented morning that she'd completely forgotten about Frankie. Had he made it out of there—or was he now being interrogated?

Maybe they let me go because they were more

interested in what he had to say. A Ph.D. candidate from New Jersey isn't much of a threat. But Frankie is a journalist. The Milton Forum *might not be required reading for society's movers and shakers, but one damning article about a top secret operation at a military base could be enough to ruin careers—starting with Frankie's.*

She picked up her pace, eager to get back to his car. After another few minutes, she was back to where they started their trip.

"This is the place, I'm sure of it," Kelsey said aloud. "But where the hell's the car?"

* * * *

If Kelsey didn't make it to Justin's school by three o'clock, he'd automatically go to after-care. They would probably try to reach her on her cell phone to find out when she was coming for him—the same cell phone that was now in the possession of the U.S. Army. She looked at her watch. Plenty of time. Though it had been a while since she had to hike five miles in a single afternoon, she kept a pretty good pace, partly out of concern for Frankie's wellbeing and partly because she wanted to focus on something physical. It felt good to fixate on the pain in her legs and her labored breathing rather than revisit the stew of jumbled thoughts in her head.

She made it to the newspaper office by four p.m. If Frankie wasn't there, she figured she'd have to tell his boss what happened. There was ample cause to be concerned about his safety, she felt. Even though it might get him in trouble, she would have to reveal what they had done.

"Is Frankie Auden here?" she asked the receptionist, who was busy clipping the current issue into neatly-cut individual stories that would be inserted into various envelopes marked "Schools," "Town Council," "Weddings" and "Obituaries."

"Frankie Auden to the front desk," she announced

into the intercom. Kelsey sat down in the small waiting area and looked out at Milton's Main Street, the sharp sound of scissoring slicing through the afternoon quiet.

"Hey Kelse. How you doin?" Frankie said, totally surprising her. He had a half-eaten cheeseburger in one hand and a can of soda in the other. Seeing him standing there, unmarked, unconcerned, given what she had just been through, left her speechless. But her expression spoke volumes. He apparently sensed she was about to erupt so he grabbed her by the arm and escorted her to the parking lot.

"What the hell are you doing here? Why did you abandon me? Do you have any idea what I've been through today?"

"Let's talk in my car," he said.

She got in, still fuming, and slammed the door. And then she told him everything that happened—the sneaking into the lab, the cages, the hissing, her capture, interrogation, her unceremonious expulsion from the base and her arduous hike back here.

"Why the hell weren't you there waiting for me?"

"Kelsey, I had no choice," he said. "After I retreated to the fence, I made it back to the car—only to find an M.P. waiting for me."

"M.P.?"

"Military police. They were getting ready to tow my car. He gave me exactly thirty seconds to get out of there. Said if he ever saw my vehicle there again, he'd impound it for good."

Kelsey thought about this. It sounded reasonable.

"But why did you retreat? We were supposed to meet at the lab."

"I know. I tried to meet you. But by the time I finished breakfast, it was—"

"Breakfast? You mean while I was risking my life, you were eating breakfast?"

"Had no choice," he said. "Circumstances compelled

me to blend in. I blend in best when I'm eating," he said, finishing off the cheeseburger he'd been working on since her arrival.

Kelsey shook her head.

"I can't believe this."

"I was waiting all afternoon for you to call me to come pick you up. I called your cell phone like twenty times. I was really worried about you."

"You were worried about me?"

"Of course. When you didn't make it back, I knew you probably made it into the lab. But by that time, the new guard detail was posted. There was no way to get in."

It all made sense—except the breakfast part.

"Major Praeger knew all about me," she said. "He had a file."

"Me too," he said. "He called my boss. When I got back, as soon I walked into the office, my publisher was waiting for me. Told me if I ever set foot on base property again, I'd be fired. It was a very short conversation."

Kelsey shook her head.

"So what do we do now?"

"What do you mean? That's it, Kelse. We've gone as far as we can go. Game over."

"Yeah—game over, they win."

"Fine. They win."

"Frankie, there's something really strange—and dangerous—going on out there. And we're this close to figuring it out. How can we just quit now?"

"It's quit or be fired," he said.

"I can't believe you're just going to cave," she said, not trying to hide her anger at what she viewed in the heat of the moment as a betrayal. "You're a journalist, for Christ's sake! Don't you want to know what's going on out there?"

"I agreed to help you, and this is the thanks I get?" he said. "I put my job on the line today for you. But that's as far as it goes. You want to do something stupid, go right ahead. But count me out."

He got out of the car and she followed, slamming the door.

"Then you can count me out too," she said. "Completely out—as in out of your life."

He stared at her and saw the depth of her anger in her eyes. His answer surprised them both.

"Fine by me."

He walked into the newspaper office without looking back.

Chapter 12

The argument with Frankie had bothered her all night, but she felt her frustration burn off with the morning sun. Slowly, a change had taken place that Kelsey was only barely aware of. Amid the countless adjustments that her move from New Jersey required, and all of the work she was doing to document the Indiana Corn Weasel so she could finish her dissertation and go home, something had happened on the periphery that she would never have expected. She was becoming a nature lover.

And no one was more surprised than she was. Growing up and living in an urban environment where wildlife meant gang bangers cruising the streets after midnight looking for buyers, rival gang members, or sex, she never gave any thought to the natural world, except for the occasional basic cable nature channel she'd watch with Justin. Nature was always "out there," something to be gawked at while driving through it. In New Jersey, "back to nature" usually meant back to the beach, and Kelsey didn't do beaches. But for the past couple of months, she'd come to really love those moments when she caught herself marveling at a sunset over a stretch of wheat field, or a flock of crows standing sentry on harvested stalks of corn, or the playfulness of a family of red foxes as they raced around the barn, tumbling over the earth and each other.

Her morning routine had become pleasantly fixed: after driving Justin to school, she'd come back to the barn, make a cup of tea, and then go outside to watch daybreak consume her particular slice of Midwestern landscape. This morning found her standing with her steaming tea, "World's Greatest Mom!" emblazoned on the side of the mug—a Mother's Day gift Justin picked out for her during on one of their Saturdays at the mall, watching with great interest as a bird she recognized as a downy woodpecker clacked away madly at the bark of a white birch tree. She'd become interested in ornithology, and had even taken out a couple of books on the subject from the county library. She liked to check out the birds flying around the barn and then look them up in the book, trying to cram a few non-weasel facts into her brain. She learned, for example, that the woodpecker taps trees with its beak for two primary reasons: to find crevices that might be hiding insects, and to communicate with fellow woodpeckers. The downy woodpecker, the smallest of the woodpecker family, knocks its beak against a tree up to twelve thousand times a day. Maybe that's why Kelsey liked watching woodpeckers so much—she felt a kinship with them. She often felt like she was banging her head against a wall all day. Standing there, watching the bird hack away, she had the nagging feeling that she'd missed a chance yesterday, an opportunity that might be lost forever. She was thinking about how close she came to getting to the bottom of the weasel-military base connection. She was also thinking about Frankie.

Her train of thought was derailed by the blaring of the phone inside the barn.

"Hello?"

"Sister, you've got to say more in your emails than 'Call me on my landline.' You've been there two months and all I get is five words?"

"Hey, Otto."

"Don't you 'Hey Otto' me. You've got a lot of

explaining to do. Why didn't you return the message I left on your voice mail last night?"

"I sort of lost my cell phone. Sorry."

"You've got to be more careful. I had a few drinks in me when I called. If that message falls into the wrong hands, it could tarnish my reputation. Don't be so selfish!"

Kelsey laughed, and then, because it was Otto and because she was still upset, she started to cry. Otto picked up on the transition.

"Oh, girlfriend. Something is rotten in the state of Indiana. It's man trouble, isn't it?"

Kelsey nodded.

"I can't hear you nod," he said, intuitively. "Tell me all about it."

So she told him the story about how she and Frankie risked life and limb together, and how she felt they were getting really close, but then how he suddenly seemed to care more about his job than he did about Kelsey, and how confused and angry she was.

"Kelsey, you can't really blame him," Otto said. "Pretty soon you'll be gone, and he'll still be there. He sounds like a lifer. What's he going to do if he loses his newspaper job? Work at the local dude ranch rustling cattle?"

"Otto, you know nothing about Indiana, do you? Rustling cattle? That's not even a job, for heaven's sake. You've watched too many bad westerns."

"I might not know cattle, but I do know men—though they're not as different as you might think. Anyway, you're asking him to give up the most secure thing in his life for what? A police record and a weekly appointment with Grace, the clerk at the local bureau of unemployment. You've got nothing to lose on this quest of yours. Why not go all the way? But he's got nothing to gain."

"He could have gained me."

"Oh, please," Otto said, dismissively. "Kelsey, you're a rental, not a purchase. He knows that. I think you know that, too. Right?" After a pause, he added "I still can't hear you when you nod."

Kelsey half-laughed, half-cried. Otto had a certain wisdom about matters of the heart. Maybe she was asking Frankie to go too far. But she didn't want to be the merely convenient option. If he wasn't willing to make her his top priority, she was better off knowing that now, she reasoned.

"I guess it had to happen eventually," she said.

"Welcome to my zip code," Otto said. "You're going to be okay. Just stay focused on your work. Now go find that rabid furball that's causing all these problems and get back home."

With the click of Otto hanging up, something clicked inside Kelsey.

He's absolutely right. Why am I allowing myself to get distracted?

She picked up her cup of tea and walked outside. The woodpecker was gone, flown off to batter some other, more promising timber. Birds fly away, seasons change, relationships fizzle. "Cycle of life," she said, aloud, concluding that one way or another, it was time to bring things to a close.

* * * *

Kelsey spent the afternoon thinking about her options. There were only two. She and Justin could pack up their belongings and head back to New Jersey. Some mysteries simply weren't meant to be solved, and perhaps this was one of them. She'd tell Dr. Reeves she had done all she could to find the source of the legend and she felt pretty sure she could make him understand that there just wasn't anything more to be gleaned from her time in Indiana. Maybe in a year or two, after she defended her dissertation and took a steady teaching job, she and Justin could came back, maybe on summer vacation, and she could pick up the thread. But in her heart she knew there would be no coming back. Once she left, Milton would forever be an interesting adventure, a part of her past, catalogued like a beaver pelt or a finch feather, stored away, a fossil of another time.

Or she could stay, even if that meant risking her safety and her unsullied police record. She wouldn't have Frankie's help. And despite her continuing efforts, she might not end up with anything more than she had now, two ends of a rope that refused to be knotted in any binding way. If she stayed and forged ahead, would it truly be scholarly resolve driving her quest? Or was it personal stubbornness, an Ahab-like mania that placed personal pride before everything else? She wanted to show Dr. Reeves she could be a real crypto-zoologist and she wanted to show Major Praeger that she couldn't be intimidated and she wanted to show Frankie Auden what a real researcher did when the going got tough.

Was it personal vanity? Or was it professional resolve?

The questions lingered throughout the afternoon until it was time to pick up Justin after school.

"Spinner, I've got a problem," she said as they pulled out of the school's driveway.

"Big problem or little problem?"

"Big enough to require ice cream therapy. Are you game?"

"Let's go!"

The ice cream at the Milton diner was not only delicious but it was served in ornate pewter bowls that were kept in the freezer to help keep the ice cream cold. Justin loved to wrap his fingers around the bowl, chilling them. He went for his usual, butter pecan, while Kelsey opted for the rum raisin. When she got near the bottom of her bowl, she broached with him what had been on her mind all day, telling him how it might be time to close the book on the Indiana Corn Weasel and go back to New Jersey.

"We had a pretty good adventure, didn't we,

Spinner?" she asked him. He ignored her, licking the rim of his bowl.

"I mean, it was worth it, wouldn't you say?" Again, he ignored her, staring at his own reflection in the spoon.

"Spinner, what's going on? Why won't you answer me?"

He got up from his seat, facing his mother in the booth, and squeezed in next to her. He hugged her and then put his face close to hers.

"I don't win the bet until you catch him."

"What are you talking about?"

"The bet I made with Otto. If you don't catch him, I don't win. So we can't leave until you catch him," he said, matter-of-factly, climbing down. "Which means we have to stay. Come on, Mom." He grabbed her hand and led her out of the diner. As she walked to their car, she realized that there was never any doubt in her son's mind, that the questions that had been torturing her never even occurred to him.

He expects me to catch him. He believes in me. He thinks I really can catch the Indiana Corn Weasel. So, I guess, I'll have to catch him.

* * * *

She spent the next couple of days huddled in her barn, reviewing her research and making a list on a yellow legal pad of everyone she'd talked to about the Indiana Corn Weasel since she got to Milton. She wanted to make sure she wasn't overlooking any piece of information that might help her going forward. She had several notebooks filled with interviews and research and she methodically went through them, page by page, sifting for clues. As Kelsey sat cross-legged on the floor of her make-shift living room, surrounded by the flotsam of her research, she felt a renewed sense of vigor.

Look at all the work I've done, she thought. *I was a fool to think of walking away from it.*

She held out some hope that she might be able to

figure out what was going on at the military base without having to risk a return visit. She remembered reading all those Sherlock Holmes stories where he was able to solve the mystery without ever leaving his cozy Baker Street apartment. Maybe she could do the same. But there were still pieces missing. That's why she was reviewing what she had, hoping to find something she overlooked the first time through. The longest interview she'd conducted was with Reverend Lonnie. That was probably an occupational hazard with him—he was used to sermonizing. But throughout their interview Kelsey had the sense he knew more than he was saying, that he was shrouding his real meaning in parables—another occupational hazard. She decided to fish in those waters again.

She called up the church, but no one picked up and she was routed to the church secretary's email.

"Hi. This is Kelsey Kane. I'd like to speak with Reverend Lonnie. I'll be in town later today, around one p.m. I'll drop by then."

She felt pretty strongly he would talk with her. She hadn't seen him since that weird outdoor candlelight vigil, but she knew he'd be eager to talk to her. During their first meeting, she dangled her disbelief before him like bait, and he bit. He wouldn't face too many spiritual challenges in Milton. Everyone in his parish came ready-made, theologically speaking. They were devout believers, right out of the gate. But Kelsey, in her doubt and disdain for religion, presented a challenge to him. She knew that he wanted another crack at her disbelief. At the very least, she figured he'd be willing to grant her a follow-up interview, if for no other reason than to sow a few more seeds.

She made the short drive to Milton's downtown, figuring she'd grab lunch at the diner and then walk over to the church. There were no parking spots outside the diner—it was the noon rush and all four spots were taken—so she parked in front of the bank a block away. Walking to the diner, she passed a newspaper box and saw the latest issue of the *Milton Forum*.

"What the hell," she said, dropping two quarters into the slot.

The diner was crowded but she found an open stool at the counter. She ordered a BLT and a black coffee and then leafed through the newspaper, learning all about the Rotary Club's winter coat drive, the Ladies' Auxiliary scholarship winner, and Mrs. Windebourne's recent trip to Egypt, complete with grainy tourist photo of Mrs. Windebourne herself in front of the sphinx. But buried deeper inside the paper was a short article that leapt out at her, causing her to spill her coffee.

> *Weasel sightings "The UFOs of This Generation"*
>
> *By Frankie Auden*
>
> *The recent spate of sightings of the mythical "Indiana Corn Weasel" is probably due to a phenomenon called "public suggestibility," one expert is claiming.*
>
> *"When everyone around you is seeing something, you want to see it too," said Dr. Evan Cullen, a professor of psychology at Indiana University-South Bend. "Instead of seeing the emperor's new clothes, people are seeing the Indiana Corn Weasel."*
>
> *Dr. Cullen made his remarks at the Monday night dinner meeting of the Milton Lions' Club at Gracie's Lounge in Syracuse Township.*
>
> *"From time to time, UFOs become all the rage in places, and people start calling up their local police departments, claiming to have seen a flying saucer," Dr. Cullen explained. "There's nothing to it at all. It's a phenomenon of the imagination, not an alien invasion."*
>
> *Dr. Cullen dismissed the claims of people who say they've had encounters with the creature*

as "more corn liquor than corn weasel," and he added that reported physical attacks by the creature are easily explained.

"Most of these attacks take place at night, out in the woods or the fields," he said. "Guess what? There's all sorts of predators out there in the wild: beavers, possums, foxes. But there's no romance in saying you were bitten by a common fox. It's much more dramatic to say it was the corn weasel. That will get your name and picture in the newspaper."

He said he expected the sightings to diminish with time.

"Fads come and go. Next year, people will be seeing the Bayville Prairie Ghost, or the Phantom Truck Driver of Jackson," he said, alluding to other well-known local legends. "And the Indiana Corn Weasel will retreat into the storybooks where he belongs."

The Lions club meets monthly and is always looking for new members. Interested persons should call Roger Hartwell, membership drive chairman, at 993-339-2296.

Kelsey's jaw dropped.

"What a complete snow job," she said aloud. A fad? A storybook legend? How could Frankie ever write that after what he knew—knew—to be true?

She pulled a pen from her canvas bag and flattened the newspaper out on the counter in front of her. In large block letters across the text of the story Kelsey wrote "SELLOUT." The she folded it up and stuck it in her bag. She'd drop it off at the newspaper office on the way to her interview with Reverend Lonnie. Putting a five dollar bill on the counter and gulping down a last sip of coffee, she turned to leave.

"What the hell did I ever see in him anyway?" she

muttered to herself as her fellow Milton residents gorged happily on their noontime meal. Out the door, onto the sidewalk, and heading toward Jesus the Redeemer church, Kelsey tried to organize her thoughts. She couldn't let her anger at Frankie's dismissive story distract her. She needed to find out what Reverend Lonnie knew.

By the time she reached the church's walkway she was focused and ready to cross swords with Reverend Lonnie. She remembered the ease, and power, he exuded sitting behind his large desk, so she was genuinely surprised to see him on his hands and knees down in the dirt.

"Reverend Lonnie?"

He nodded to her, and returned to his earthly labors, churning the soil in his hand, letting it trickle between his sullied fingers.

"What are you doing?"

"I'm looking for slugs," he said without looking up at her. "The vegetation along this patch didn't thrive this past summer. It might have been the result of parasites. So I'm looking for slugs. They tend to burrow in the fall. That's when they're easiest to find. Usually, they like rocks to hide under. So I'm lifting up rocks, looking for them."

Theologian. Firebrand. Slug hunter.

"I'm looking for something too," Kelsey said. "I thought maybe you could help me in my search."

He scooted along the ground for a foot or two on his bended knees and resumed his search.

"Your problem, Ms. Kane, is that you're looking for something that isn't, and you've stopped looking for something that is."

Another riddle. But she was prepared to be patient, to wait out his parables to see if they added up to something she might actually be able to use.

"Pardon my bluntness, but the Bible gives me license to be so frank," he said. "When I think of all the anguish your search is causing you, and the misplaced energy you are putting into it, I can't help but feel a great sadness. If you would only direct your focus toward more substantive matters, I believe you'd find a real reward for your efforts."

He dug slowly with his fingers in the soft, loamy soil along the patch of grass in front of the church.

"Well, right now I'm trying to focus on just one thing: finding and capturing the Indiana Corn Weasel."

He looked at her and shook his head, more in amusement than in anger.

"Capture it? You can't capture it," he said, laughing slightly. "Ms. Kane, the creature you're looking to capture has been slipping through people's fingers since the beginning of time, all the way back to the Garden of Eden, our first parents. You don't 'capture' evil. You recognize it. You defeat it. But evil is slippery, persistent, crafty. It reinvents itself. One day serpent, one day temptress, one day weasel."

"You're saying it's a shape shifter."

He paused from his rooting around and looked up at her.

"Oh, that's right. You're a student of medieval legends," he said, nodding appreciatively. "Tell me. Do you know anything of the hydrus?"

Kelsey shook her head.

"It was a mythical beast of the middle ages. It was a kind of water snake said to live in the Nile River. It didn't harm humans. What it did was swim into the open mouths of crocodiles. Once inside, it would eat its way through the stomach and the innards, bursting through the side of the crocodile. For medieval Christians, the Hydrus came to be a symbol of the power of sin."

"I don't get it."

"To these believers, the Hydrus was the original serpent reborn. A harmless-looking creature taking down a much-larger, more formidable host, a potent reminder of the power of evil to insinuate itself in our lives."

"So you think the Indiana Corn Weasel is related to the hydrus?"

"It's all related, don't you see?" he said to her. "It's the serpent, and the Golden Ram, and the Whore of Babylon, and then the Hydrus, and later on the Banshee. Now it's the Corn Weasel. One day, it will be something else, perhaps something beautiful. 'The Devil hath power to assume a pleasing shape.'"

"Hamlet."

"Very good. A scholar of Shakespeare as well. My oh my, Ms. Kane. When I think of what a person with your formidable mind could do if you would only give your heart to Jesus, it jolts me."

She knew he meant it as a compliment of sorts, but she also felt a little insulted. As theologically interesting as all of this was, Kelsey felt like her quest for the corn weasel was being hijacked by a wild goose.

"About the other night," she said, trying to get the conversation back on some useful track. "That meeting out in the field, with people standing around in a circle. Can I ask what that was about?"

"Same thing my search for slugs is about," he said, fingering through the soil and then lifting a small, slimy, dirt-covered slug from the ground and holding it aloft. "Learning to see in the darkness by the light of faith." He dropped the slug into an empty coffee can and brushed the dirt off his hands, standing up.

"You have something against science?"

A slight smirk crossed Reverend Lonnie's face, as if he was being interrogated by an impertinent child.

"Do you remember that man I told you about, the old priest who taught me how to breathe?"

"Yes."

"How's your son, by the way?"

"Oh, he's fine."

"Good. That's good. Anyway, this older priest who became my mentor used to tell us 'Faith, not reason, keeps a bumblebee aflight.'"

"Oh, I get it," Kelsey said, nodding knowingly.

"Because scientifically, a bumblebee isn't supposed to be able to fly. His body is too heavy for those little wings."

"Fortunately, the bumblebee never took a science class, so it doesn't seem to bother him."

They stood there on the lawn for a moment, wordlessly. Reverend Lonnie finally broke the silence.

"I would invite you in, but I have a parish council meeting, and, as you can see, I need to get cleaned up."

"Right. Thanks for your time."

"My pleasure, Ms. Kane. I'm available to you anytime. Best days are Sunday, around ten," he said, gesturing toward the sign on the lawn that listed the time of Sunday services: ten a.m.

"I'm a night owl," Kelsey said. "On Sunday mornings, I'm usually asleep."

"I'd advise a new routine," he said. "An awakening can change your life."

Maybe so, Kelsey thought as she headed back to her car. But at this point she'd settle for something less lofty. Like another clue. If Reverend Lonnie truly knew something tangible about the Indiana Corn Weasel, he wasn't letting on. Maybe he really did think it was the devil.

She spent the next ninety minutes driving somewhat randomly through the roads that criss-crossed the county, eyes and ears open, windows rolled down, thinking about her next move, turning over in her mind what she already knew, wondering if there was another way.

But there wasn't another way, she knew. There was only one way—she had to get back into the military base, back into the research lab building, back into the room with the cages and the hissing. She had no idea how she was going to do it, but she knew she had to. Driving across the terrain that had once seemed so foreign to her, staring across the now-barren fields, a chalk gray sky pressing down on the land, she began to feel a predatory impulse. "Gonna get you," she said softly but confidently, a bracing wind cutting through the front seat of her car. Her hands tightened on the steering wheel and she nodded, surveying the landscape like a warden scanning for runaway prisoners. "Gonna get you," she said again, louder this time. She was driving across the flatlands and the prairies that had tested the courage of ten generations and she was tapping into that courage, feeling confident, even ruthless. "Gonna get you!" she screamed to the empty pastures and lonely farmhouses dotting the horizon. It was no now longer a matter of resolve, but of time. She felt like she wasn't even driving the car, that she was instead being pulled through the maze of cornfields by some force, powerless to turn back, forced to trust her instincts like Reverend Lonnie's night-time pilgrims, plunging ahead, the road ahead lit only up by faith.

Fortify yourself!

Shc was ready. The only question was how she would actually get in to the base. But she knew, rolling through the Indiana afternoon that cool gray autumn afternoon, she knew without the slightest shred of doubt that it was going to happen, that she would find a way to get what she came here to get and to make her son proud, and Otto proud, and Doctor Reeves proud, and—

"Oh Jesus!"

Jerking the wheel violently, she swerved to try to avoid ramming an Amish wagon that was ambling across the road. Kelsey had been lost in thought when the slower, horse-drawn vehicle lurched from a side road, turning right in front of her. Braking and turning the steering wheel, she raised a tremendous cloud of dust as she skidded to an abrupt stop. Frightened, the horse reared up and whinnied loudly, and Kelsey bolted from her car to see if everyone was okay.

She hadn't actually struck the wagon, but when the horse bucked, a number of pumpkins spilled out of the back. Kelsey began profusely apologizing to the young Amish couple, a man and his wife, who were seated up front. Both were dressed in the traditional Amish clothing and both went about silently restocking their lost cargo in the back of the wagon.

"I'm so sorry. I wasn't paying attention," she said.

The Amish man waved her off, saying nothing. Kelsey bent down to pick up an errant pumpkin that had rolled away.

"Here," she said, handing it to the man. "This one seems okay."

He inspected it, nodded, and put in on the stack with the others. His wife continued to pick up pumpkins on the other side of the cart, and after a few more moments of Kelsey continuing to apologize and the man and his wife saying nothing, all was as it had been just before the mishap.

"I'm really sorry. I just didn't notice you!" she shouted to them as they drove off, her heart still racing. And that's when the idea came to her.

* * * *

She couldn't help but wonder if he would open the door this time. With no appointment and no real reason for a return visit, she half-expected to be ignored. Before she knocked she peeked through the windows at the cavernous interior and thought she could see the movement of a couple people inside. Outside, there was no one on the land around the house that she could see, though the barn and the distant fields were hidden from her view. It was a crazy idea, truly crazy, she acknowledged. But she was running out of rational ideas, and something told her she had a shot here, though probably a long shot.

She knocked on the door and stood there, trying to look respectable. No response. She knocked again.

Be patient, Kelsey. You know how these people are, she reminded herself. *Maybe there's something I can do to convince them to let me in.*

What she came up with, standing there, desperate to get inside and feeling now totally impulsive, would have made anyone who knew her well giggle, or scratch their heads. But Kelsey thought it was worth a try.

"The Lord is my shepherd. I shall not want," she said in a kind of sing-song chant. "The Lord is my shepherd. I shall not want!" she said again, closer to a shout this time. It was the only line from the Bible that Kelsey could remember, maybe the only one she ever knew. Trying to project the image of a righteous, God-fearing woman, she stood there, repeating it like a mantra, hoping she might be mistaken for just another pilgrim.

"Hello? The Lord is my shepherd! I shall not want!" she yelled at the closed door. "The Lord is my shepherd! Yes indeed! I'm not wanting, standing here. I shall not want, except I'd like you to open the door. Oh, the Lord is My Shepherd!"

It was kind of pathetic. Kelsey, the atheist, trying to appear holy by mindlessly repeating a line from the Bible. Standing there she resembled a mental patient as much as a pilgrim. But she wouldn't leave, and she wouldn't stop chanting.

They can't turn me away if they think I'm a believer. You can't turn away one of the flock.

"The Lord is SO my shepherd, I can't even tell you," she said, freelancing a bit. "Totally my shepherd. Which explains my lack of want. Hello? Anybody there?" As she made a mental note to learn at least one more line from the Bible, should she ever find herself in a similar situation again, the door opened.

"Are you here to convert me, young lady? But I'm already a believer, you see," he said, smiling broadly. "Or maybe were you testifying to the chickens and the pigs?"

"Mr. Yoder, thanks for opening the door. It's me, Kelsey Kane."

"Oh. I'm glad you told me. I thought perhaps you were a missionary with a head injury."

Kelsey laughed as Benjamin Yoder, elder member of the Amish community of the endangered Milton

Mennonite faith, stepped aside to allow her entry.

"Thanks. I've really got to talk to you."

With his trademark vocabulary of wordless gestures honed through a lifetime of laconic distrust, he indicated she should walk through the house, back to the room where their first interview had taken place. As she passed through, she saw a couple of Amish women working in the kitchen, and a young Amish boy in the "community room," standing and holding a simple wooden cross at arms length, fidgeting.

"Praying?" whispered Kelsey as they walked by.

"Punishment," Benjamin Yoder said aloud. "He needs to learn to be patient. We are helping him."

Kelsey nodded, though she felt sorry for the boy. He really should be out playing, running around, chasing the other kids and climbing on hay bales in the barn, she thought, instead of being sequestered and silenced.

"Patience is the great gift," said Benjamin Yoder, as if he were aware of her thoughts.

They reached the last room. Benjamin Yoder indicated she should sit as he once again took his place in a handmade wooden rocking chair. He looked above her, beyond her, out the window facing his fields.

"Nice day," Kelsey said.

"Rain coming," the elder Yoder said.

Better get right to it, Kelsey thought, *before I lose my nerve.*

"Mr. Yoder, when I was here before, we talked a little bit about the military base. I got the impression you weren't all that crazy about their operations."

"Evil place," he said.

"Right. I sort of agree. I was able to get inside the base and look around for myself. And I think there's something wrong going on out there. Evil, maybe. But before I could find out what it was, exactly, I was interrupted by a couple of military police officers who need a course in basic manners."

Kelsey saw she had Ben Yoder's attention.

"You got into that place?"

"Yes. Me and a friend."

"How?"

"We snuck in, under a fence."

He leaned back in his rocker. For the longest time, he said nothing. Kelsey was afraid that maybe he was bothered by the illegal nature of her activities and that he was about to ask such a blatant scofflaw as herself to leave at once. But he only said two words: "Go on."

"Well, I made it into the research lab. There are all these rooms, most of them underground. In one of the rooms, there were a bunch of cages, and I heard all this hissing, and anyway I think all these weasel attacks have something to do with that room. But before I could get in—"

"You were caught!"

"Yes, I was caught," she admitted. He broke into a grin, though she wasn't sure why, a lifetime of keeping his thoughts to himself paying off. He was opaque.

"You have a vibrant spirit," he said.

"Thanks," she said. "Anyway, I want to get back in there and find out what's happening. Given how you feel about the military, I thought maybe you could help me."

"In what manner?"

"Well, when I was on the base, just before they threw me out, I vaguely remember seeing a couple of Amish women there. I think they were in the guard house. Could that be? Or was I imagining that?"

"There are few opportunities to make money here, Ms. Kane. We don't approve of the military. We abhor it. But certain sacrifices have to be made to sustain our way of life. It's one of the few places that our community can find employment. The Amish you saw are modest women from our community who clean and cook. Their hearts are heavy that they must work there, but in a small town such as this, one has to face reality."

"Oh, believe me, I'm not criticizing. I'm a mother. I

get it. You have to do what you have to do. But the reason I'm asking is I was thinking that it would be a lot easier to get back into the base if I wasn't so, um, noticeable."

Benjamin Yoder's eyebrows practically vacated his forehead.

"You want to pretend to be Amish?"

She nodded.

"If I were in Amish clothes, and if an Amish person took me there, I'm sure they wouldn't look twice at me. No one notices the Amish out here. You're practically invisible. I almost drove my car into one of you."

He seemed a bit confused by this bit of intelligence, and in fact Kelsey's whole proposal seemed to have unsettled him.

"You would require clothing. And transportation," he said thoughtfully.

"If I could pull up to that guard house, seated next to you in one of those pumpkin wagons you guys drive, I could waltz in to that place."

"We don't dance," he said, soberly.

"Just an expression," she said meekly.

Benjamin Yoder was a God-fearing man. When faced with a difficult problem, he placed it in the hands of Providence.

"Let us see what the Good Book has to say," he said, lifting his bony frame from the rocker and walking over to a shelf, reaching for a Bible. He returned to Kelsey and put the book in her lap. He sat back down in the rocker.

"We believe the Lord provides guidance for his people, Ms. Kane. We have learned to discern signs of the Almighty in what you call the 'real' world. I believe we need his guidance now. I would like you to leaf through that Bible and stop at any page. Open it, and without looking, put your finger on a verse. That will tell us how to proceed."

Kelsey couldn't believe that his decision, her plan, maybe her future, depended on this Biblical game of Magic 8-Ball.

"Seriously?"

"Trust the Lord to guide you to the appropriate verse. I have no doubt he shall."

She nodded and took the Bible in her hand. Really, this was no more irrational than a lot of things she had found herself doing since she came to Indiana.

Maybe there really is a greater power guiding my quest, she thought. *Anyway, if it will get me in to that base, why not give it a try?*

She started to flip through the Bible when he stopped her.

"Not yet."

He reached out, grabbed her hand and closed his eyes. He was praying silently, his lips moving almost imperceptibly. Kelsey felt awkward. What should she do? Pray along with him? Close her eyes? She looked down at his hands and saw the calloused and aged flesh of a man who'd lived his life close to the earth. The scars and scratches and veins on his hand formed a kind of life map, a record in flesh of his quest to discover truth through hard work. Hands that had raised countless barns, tilled miles of rocky soil, rocked crying babies to sleep on bitterly cold nights, clasped the sides of pine boxes, lowering them back into the earth, dust to dust.

"Dust to dust," she said aloud.

Ben Yoder opened one eye, startled by her curious oration, amused at the effort she was making. He released her hand.

"Let us trust in the Lord," he said. "After all, someone told me recently he is my shepherd, and I shall not want."

I can't tell if he's mocking me. These Amish people are impossible to read.

But caught up in the moment, she picked up the Bible, let the cover fall open and held its spine in her left hand. She gathered all the pages between her right thumb and forefinger, arched the pages and began running her thumb down the balance of pages, thousands of verses racing through her hand. She stopped, opened, pointed, all without looking at the page. She appeared to have picked a spot near the middle of the book.

"Now read," he said, gently but confidently.

"Okay," she said. "The print is pretty small. Let me see. Psalm 119, Verse 78."

"Read it!" he repeated urgently, but he was smiling now, almost as if he knew what the book said and he couldn't wait for her to hear it too.

"Okay. 'Let the proud be ashamed; for they dealt perversely with me without a cause: but I will meditate in the precepts.' That's the end of it."

His eyes were closed now but he continued to smile. Kelsey re-read the verse. "Let the proud be ashamed," she said, and immediately an image popped into her head: Major Praeger. She looked up and saw Ben Yoder looking back at her.

"So what does this mean?" she asked him.

"It means you'll be needing some clothes, Ms. Kane," he said, excitedly lifting himself out of his chair. "I'll get one of the womenfolk in here to help you. Praise God, I have a wagon to hitch!"

Chapter 13

They agreed to meet the next morning, early. The plan was to sneak Kelsey into the base along with Benjamin Yoder's niece, Sarah, who actually worked there as a cleaning woman in one of the office buildings. Kelsey was to remain mute, garbed in the traditional dress of the Amish. Once inside, she would shadow Sarah until the morning flag raising, when she would once again make her way into the research lab. Sarah would show Kelsey where the cleaning supplies were kept and point out where the guards were stationed. But once Kelsey had her bucket and scrub brush in hand, she'd be on her own. She'd have to finish her investigations by the end of the half-shift, which gave her about two and a half hours to get in and get out, reuniting with Sarah at the base's personnel office and then meeting Benjamin Yoder at the front gate for a ride back home. In, out, no problem.

"Well, what do you think, Spinner?" She twirled about once, showing off the long dress, smock, and bonnet worn by Amish women. She'd tried on the outfit while still at Ben Yoder's house, and one of his daughters helped hem it here and pull it up there until it looked like it was made for Kelsey. She was trying it on again, just to get comfortable in it. Her son was transfixed.

"You look funny, Mommy!"

"Funny, huh? I'll show you funny!" She took off her bonnet and tied it around Justin, who vainly fought off her efforts to turn him into an Amish woman.

"Let's see who looks funny now!" Kelsey pulled him into the bathroom and when he saw himself, they both erupted in laughter. When they quieted down, she turned to her son.

"Do you think I'll get away with it, kiddo?"

Justin hugged his mother, still wearing the lacey blue covering.

"Mommy, don't be afraid. Maybe because you're dressed like a religious person, God will protect you."

Justin's theological observation gave Kelsey pause. With no formal guidance from her, he was developing his own views on religion. He wasn't nearly as cynical as she was—not surprising for an eight-year-old. He had a trusting heart and a genuine desire to believe.

It might be his youth, Kelsey thought, *or it might just be he's more open to these sorts of things. I wanted to believe at that age, too, but when you lose your father....*

She glanced at herself in the mirror, feeling less like a researcher and more like an imposter. She couldn't believe how far she'd gone in her quest to come face to face with the Indiana Corn Weasel. Once upon a time, she knew the Amish only through stories she'd come across in her research or pictures in books. Now here she was, in full Amish clothing: Kelsey the atheist, all dressed up for a God she didn't believe in and a mythical beast she increasingly did believe in. And she used to think Otto was mixed up.

But by the next morning, when her alarm clock roused her to consciousness, Kelsey's head was clear and her thoughts focused. The time to wrestle with doubts had passed. She had to get Justin to Mrs. Simms' because school wouldn't be open for another hour and a half and she had to hurry out to Ben Yoder's place. She made him a quick breakfast and drove into town, dropping him off at the imperturbable Mrs. Simms. Then she checked, yet again, to make sure she had her change of clothes, her camera and her notepad. As she drove past Jesus the Redeemer, she noticed a trickle of parishioners queuing up for morning mass. "Wish me luck, Jesus," Kelsey said.

The sun had just begun to inflame the eastern sky. Hundreds of stars still shone defiantly against the encroaching dawn, shimmering, refusing to yield. The air was cold but still. The morning seemed poised on the brink of a decision, to break one way or the other, but still it lingered, unsure. Kelsey betrayed no such uncertainty. She hit the gas and tooled along Milton's narrow roads, fired with expectation. Before she knew it, she was at the Yoder place, where her escort was awaiting her arrival, already seated on the pumpkin wagon next to Sarah. Kelsey exited her car excitedly, but her partners were the picture of solemnity. Ben Yoder looked like a man of stone. Sarah had her head bowed, perhaps in prayer, and barely acknowledged Kelsey as she climbed aboard. No sooner had she mounted the bench behind Ben Yoder than he lashed the horse and they were off, an Amish assault vehicle, David galloping toward Goliath.

Kelsey had frequently found herself stuck behind these pumpkin wagons as she drove around town. She liked the romance, the whiff of history, and the picturesque quality of those encounters. What she never realized is how thoroughly uncomfortable they were. The Amish built everything solidly but they didn't seem to believe in shock absorbers. The winding, pastoral byways of Milton, Indiana were much bumpier than she had imagined, and right about now she was feeling every bump. But her companions registered no obvious agitation. She glanced over at Sarah, a woman of indeterminate age but probably not too far from Kelsey's own. She wondered if Sarah had ever even been in a car. Kelsey often thought that she'd faced hardship in her own life but in her time around the Amish, she'd begun to understand what real hardship was, and that she might not quite be the brave warrior she had once thought she was. Anyway, her butt hurt, and she was eager to get to the base as soon as possible.

She got her wish. The brisk and steady clop-clop of the horse's hooves against the frosty pavement began to slow as Kelsey saw the compound come into sight. From where she sat she couldn't tell if there was any activity, and she couldn't see how many guards were at the gatehouse. She'd find out soon enough, she figured. She settled back and endured a few more bumps as they approached the front gate.

"Speak not," Benjamin Yoder said without turning his head. Sarah had not spoken since they began the ride so Kelsey presumed that was directed at her. She nodded, unseen, and looked down at herself, arrayed in the centuries-old traditional dress of the Amish. The dress felt like a costume in some drama she was acting out. It didn't seem like she was leading anything remotely resembling real life this morning: A horse-and-buggy ride on her way to sneak onto a military base dressed in her best seventeenth-century outfit to find a mythical weasel.

"State your business," said a guard, flatly, holding a clipboard.

"Cleaning detail, morning shift. Yoder. Dropping off two," he said, gesturing slightly with his head toward Sarah and Kelsey.

The guard nodded and waved them in, looking at his watch and making a notation on his clipboard. The pumpkin wagon pulled into the base with a jerk and then, after a short ride, stopped just as abruptly. Kelsey was grateful for the opportunity to climb down and stretch her legs, which were starting to cramp up. After both Sarah and Kelsey decamped, Benjamin Yoder turned his horse around and passed by the same guard who had just waved them in. And there they stood, in the middle of a stream of military personnel passing by, though no one so much as gave them a glance. Even though she was being ignored,

Kelsey had never felt so conspicuous.

Sarah and Kelsey each held onto a bucket filled with cleaning supplies and cloth rags and then headed toward the base's personnel office to check in. The woman who worked there was a civilian, which was good, but a bit chatty, which was not.

"Good morning, Sarah," she said when the two entered the office. "How have you been?" Sarah smiled meekly and whispered, "Fine, thank you."

"And who's this?" the woman asked much too enthusiastically, inspecting Kelsey, who was sure there was something in her appearance that screamed "Displaced New Jersey Girl."

"Cousin," Sarah said quietly. "From the hill country."

"Oh!" said the woman, so starved for any gossip that she giggled at this piece of intelligence. "How exciting it must be for you to be in our town," she said. "I hope the pace isn't too much for you," she confided to her with a wink.

Kelsey remembered Ben Yoder's words. She spoke not.

"Shy one," said the woman, nodding sympathetically. "Got it. I'm kind of shy myself."

She looked down at a stack of paper on her desk and lifted the first one, reading aloud: "Cleaning detail, Area A, half-shift. No laundry, just spot cleaning," she said, handing Sarah a key. "Nice to meet you," she said to Kelsey, extending her hand. Kelsey impulsively started to reach toward her but Sarah put her arm around Kelsey and turned her toward the door.

I almost blew it.

Kelsey remembered that Amish women generally don't shake hands with people outside their order.

Then they were back outside, walking across the base. As they proceeded, Sarah reached down and took the bucket out of Kelsey's hand and replaced it with the bucket she was carrying. Then she stopped, faced Kelsey, and embraced her tightly around the neck before heading off toward the recreation building while Kelsey walked toward the research lab. The doors were open but there was a guard posted there, behind a small steel desk just behind the entrance. He looked up at her and then back down at his newspaper. It was almost as if he didn't see her at all. She felt insignificant and powerful at the same time. She brushed by him and started walking downstairs, bucket in hand. Everything was going as planned.

Just a few more flights and I'll be back where I was before. Now think about what you're doing. Think about the mission. Get in that room, take pictures, look for any files that might be of use, and then get the hell out of there.

She was going over that checklist in her head, not really paying attention to her surroundings, her bonnet pulled down to the bridge of her nose, shrouding her. So she couldn't be blamed for what happened next.

When she reached underground level four, the door opening onto that floor was hurriedly flung open and a man came running out, almost knocking her down as he headed up the stairs.

"Pardon me," he said, his momentum already carrying him several steps above her. He looked back at her.

Kelsey peered up at him from under her bonnet and nodded, turning away quickly, biting her lip, unseen. It was Major Praeger. He looked at her, just for a second, then continued on his way, taking the steps two at a time.

Oh shit, is there any way he could have recognized me?

Kelsey wished she could see herself in a mirror.

He only saw me for a second, she thought, trying to calm herself. The Amish were practically invisible to the military personnel, she knew.

But I'm not Amish.

There was no time to wonder whether Major Praeger took the slightest notice of her. She was now on underground level five. She reached into the bucket and removed the master key that Sarah had gotten and opened the door.

There's irony. The most trustworthy people in the world have just broken into your super-secret facility.

She knew what she had to do. She walked slowly toward the end of the hallway. As she approached, she thought for a moment that she might be on the wrong floor. The layout was the same as she remembered, but there was no hissing, no sound of any sort. She reached the room and took out the key. Placing it in the lock, she turned it slowly as her hand shook slightly. She looked left and right, saw no one.

She opened the door, and with the practiced quickness of a spy, stepped inside.

* * * *

The staff of the Milton Diner had little to do but gossip among themselves once the morning rush subsided. From nine a.m. to noon was usually a dead time. There wasn't much pedestrian traffic on Main Street at this hour, so the talk turned to local intrigue, as it invariably did, usually involving second-hand reports of bank managers taking two-hour lunches, their cars reportedly seen parked behind the houses of secretaries who'd called in sick for the day. The talk at the bait and tackle shop was far less salacious. The only nibbles they were concerned about came from the mouths of river carp and walleye, shad and bluegill. The hot news was about the likely kill limit for the coming elk season.

Not much news at all, Frankie would soon realize, bored, sitting at his desk as he sifted through his Rotary Club calendar, looking for potential feature story ideas, thinking about taking a smoke break, and listening to the local police scanner, which was also blaring at the police station where the chief pored over last night's shift reports noting nothing but minor transgressions. The major transgressions of the day were reserved for Reverend Lonnie, who was out on call, ministering to a troubled soul who confessed to thoughts of suicide, which he knew to be a most serious sin.

Reverend Lonnie listened in silence, nodded, prayed with the man, prayed for peace, just as Mrs. Simms was doing that very moment, her playhouse shaken by the tug and tumult of unrestrained youth hopped up on sugared cereal. One particularly raucous child seemed destined to have many a date with principal Hochstetler in her office at the elementary school, where Justin's science class was currently outside doing bark tracings—a gaggle of eager young scientists whose work could be observed by motorists heading out of town, bound perhaps for the cozy carrels of the country library or Mabel's truck stop for cheap cigarettes, diesel fuel, and warmed-over candied yams. It was a day so numbingly typical that no one would even notice the jeep that had pulled just off the county highway, a camouflaged figure inside peering through binoculars, fixing Justin's image amid sun and shadow.

* * * *

When Kelsey saw she was alone, she closed the door behind her and heard the lock click. The room looked a little like a high school science laboratory, with a large lab table, a sink and a Bunsen burner islanding the center of the room, and a couple of smaller desks pushed off to one side. There was a wall-sized whiteboard in front of the room, and a bank of four television monitors, all turned off, hanging from the ceiling. Ringing the room was a series of cages built right into the walls. Each of the cages had a heavy black cloth covering the front, so that whatever was inside couldn't be seen. The cage fronts were at eye level.

Kelsey approached one of the cages cautiously, her heart beating like the clop-clop of a carriage horse. She kept her gaze locked on that cage, looking for any movement, listening for any hint of life underneath that cloth covering. She slipped a hand through a slit in her Amish gown, reached into a hidden pocket and pulled out a digital camera. The original purpose of the pocket, Sarah told her, was to keep a small Bible handy for any spiritual emergencies one might encounter away from home. Though she knew she was alone, she moved as quietly as she could. She raised the camera, looked at the view screen, framed the cage, snapped the picture. Then she moved closer to the cage, still holding the camera up, moving in for a tight shot, only about two feet now from the cage. She snapped another picture.

No sounds, no signs of life at all in that room, only Kelsey's shallow breathing. For all she knew, all these cages could be empty.

Probably they are, she thought. *Maybe that hissing I heard last time I was here was a steam pipe,* she guessed, looking up to see if there were any pipes visible, or a heating duct that might have been responsible for the sound.

There was nothing but the fluorescent light flooding the lab.

Or maybe it was a fluorescent light bulb that needed changing, she concluded. *Or the television monitors might have been tuned to a test pattern. Could have been lots of things.*

She moved closer to the cage directly in front of her. She was a foot away now, standing still, her head cocked slightly, scanning for the slightest evidence of life within the wiry confines. She stood there, knowing what she needed to do: reach out and pull the cover off that cage.

It looks like a pretty solid cage, she assured herself. *There's no way anything could get out.*

She moved closer, a couple of inches. She was tempted to speak, to call out to whatever might be in there, in a quiet, calming voice. She wanted to show that she meant no harm. *"It's just me, Kelsey, and I'm not here to hurt you. Just take a few pictures, make a note or two. Then I'll be on my way. And nobody gets hurt, okay?"*

She reached out her hand, her thumb and first finger

extended like some fleshy claw. The flap of the cage's cover was hanging loosely, just inches from Kelsey's trembling fingers. She willed herself to grab it. Closing her eyes, she stretched out another inch, then another. She had it now, felt its coarseness between her fingers, squeezed it.

She should have pulled slowly, the fabric sneaking unobtrusively across the cage's frame, a steady unveiling, non-threatening. But her hand trembled, and her heart beat quickly, and she felt a surge of anxiety and expectation that was impossible to combat. She yanked violently at the covering, eyes closed, her fierce tug accompanied by a determined, teeth-grinding grunt.

She opened her eyes and gazed squarely at the empty cage. It was the last thing she saw before the lights suddenly went out and she found herself engulfed in crippling darkness. She thought she was hallucinating at first, or maybe she'd blacked out from all the anxiety. Kelsey never remembered being in such darkness. She raised her hand in front of her face but couldn't see it. A surge of panic convulsed her. Deprived of her sense of sight, she tried to focus. She thought she heard someone breathing. Forgetting she was trying to avoid detection, she shouted out, "Hello…anybody there?" There was no response, but now she definitely heard breathing, measured and not too far away. She stepped backward, tentatively. Her heartbeat filled her head. Her voice quivered when she spoke again.

"Can I please get some light here?"

No response, no light. She couldn't see where to move and wasn't sure what she should do. She thought briefly about bolting for the door, but she didn't know if there was a clear path. Maybe the thing to do was slowly inch toward the door, feeling her way as she went, and then make her break. She took a tentative step toward the door. That's when she heard a sharp hiss.

"WHO'S THERE?!" she shouted, appropriately panicked, realizing that whatever was hissing wasn't interested in having a dialogue with her. But it was all she could think to do.

She waited in silence and then finally moved tremblingly toward where she thought the door was. She remembered there being a small window on the door, but now there was no light coming through.

That's odd, she thought, not knowing that the window had just been taped over. No light was going to get into that room, someone had determined.

Another step, another eruption of hissing, louder this time, and closer. It was like her movements were being tracked. She clasped her hands over her ears and clenched her teeth. She felt like she was about to shatter. She was getting ready to make a mad dash for the door when she heard him.

"Hello, Kelsey."

"Daddy?" she blurted out, not sure why, a nervous reflex probably. Except it was a man's voice, controlled, authoritative. Was this a nightmare she was having? She reached her hand out in the darkness, a gesture that brought about a wild fit of hissing and snarling from a creature that sounded cold-blooded, closing in.

"Please! Please!" she said, panic having now assumed complete control of her nervous system. "What's happening?!"

Grrrrr. GRRRRRR! Hissssssssss!

"Talk to me, please!"

"He is talking—in his way," the man's voice said. "I believe he's saying he's hungry."

Kelsey drew a deep breath and the creature advanced, screeching and scratching. Her eyes were adjusting to the dark, and she could see a little bit ahead of her, and what she saw sent a shiver down her spine. She was only a couple of feet from a pair of red eyes, almost glowing, moving wildly, up and down, side to side. This couldn't be. This just couldn't be.

How could a creature be face to face with me?

It seemed to Kelsey that it was hovering, just beyond her reach, stalking her, its watchful eyes looking for just the right cue to begin an attack.

"OH GOD OH GOD OH GOD!" Kelsey screamed out, crying, her knees buckling, falling to the ground. The creature moved with her. It was very, very close, perhaps just inches from Kelsey's face. She thought she could feel its hot breath, hear its claws extend, sense its raised fur and razor sharp teeth.

This is it, she thought. *It ends here. It started in New Jersey, in the cozy office of Dr. Reeves, and it ends on the floor of an underground research lab in Milton, Indiana.*

She covered her eyes with her hands, sobbing.

She remained in that posture for so long she didn't even realize the lights had been turned on.

"Say hello to Gus," said the man's voice.

Kelsey opened her eyes and was staring face to face into a wire cage containing the body of a fuming creature, about three feet long, glowing eyes, gleaming row of teeth, hissing ferociously, and resembling in every detail the fabled Indiana Corn Weasel. It tore at its cage desperately, claws engaged, trying to get at Kelsey, to inflict itself on her, fulfill its savage purpose. Kelsey was frozen to the spot, afraid to move, afraid to speak. She squinted toward the ceiling and felt sick when she saw who was holding the cage. Major Praeger continued his unsolicited commentary.

"Well, I call him Gus. That stands for Government Undertaking Six. He's got five brothers. This is where they live," he said, his head cocked to indicate the other cages in the room. "Say hello to Kelsey," he whispered to Gus, and the animal lashed out furiously, spitting saliva and reaching a claw through the wire mesh. Kelsey recoiled in terror.

"I take it you're not fond of him? Oh, that's a shame. You've gone to such lengths to make his acquaintance. Are you sure? Maybe you'd like a closer look." He put his hand on the latch at the top of the cage and started to turn it.

"NO! PLEASE NO! DON'T LET HIM OUT! PLEASE!"

"Hmmm. But I thought you wanted to meet him? That's why you're here, right? To get a good look at Gus. You have a camera, right? Here, let me take a picture of the two of you together." He grabbed her camera and settled the cage so that it was lying right next to Kelsey's head, which was still resting on the cold concrete floor. She closed her eyes and screamed.

"Smile!" Major Praeger said, snapping a picture. The flash drove Gus into an even fiercer frenzy, clawing, spitting, and emitting a high-pitched hiss that even Major Praeger found difficult to endure.

"Gus, why don't you rest up for a few minutes?" he said, lifting the cage and putting it on the lab table in the middle of the room. He threw the cloth covering over it and the creature quieted almost magically.

He looked down at Kelsey and shook his head.

"Such a shame no one will ever see that picture," he said, throwing the camera down right next to her head, smashing it to bits. Kelsey had given up any pretense of appearing dignified. She was beaten, she'd lost, she had nothing left. She lay there, whimpering quietly, trying vainly to recover from this assault on her nervous system.

"Since you've made it this far, allow me to fill you in on the rest," he said, reaching down and ripping the notebook out of her pocket, tearing up its pages, one by one, as he spoke. "It's not like anyone will ever find out what's going on here.

"You're currently in a room that doesn't exist. At least, not officially. Right after it was built, it was designated for top secret germ warfare experiments. These cages used to contain animals that would be injected with various substances, and they'd be observed, the effects noted by the researchers who worked here. When more modern facilities were built, these were deemed too primitive for such advanced work. So they shut it down. This lab was kept shuttered until just a few years ago, when some promising results with genetic modification made it necessary to do some field testing in this area."

Kelsey had recovered enough to sit up. She was listening, though she kept glancing at the cage, fearful that she, like the room she was in, might also soon cease to exist.

"You see, Miss Kane, the world has changed. Traditional ways of waging war simply don't succeed any more. Today's wars require a different approach. Tanks and battleships are the stuff of newsreels. The key word now is 'stealth'—drone fighters, satellite-based lasers, and—" he said, pausing for effect and pointing to the covered cage, "Gus."

Her baffled look enticed him to say more.

"Imagine a creature that can live for days or weeks without food, in the most inhospitable terrain, that can get around without being detected. Now imagine such a creature as a weapon of war," he said, sounding excited. "Think about it! If you could train these creatures to obey commands, or respond to an electrical stimulus input, they could be equipped with video cameras to take pictures of enemy positions and troop strength, bury explosive devices, even attack! My God, can you imagine the advantage a battalion would have if they could unleash such a primal fighting force?"

Major Praeger was insane, she feared. He seemed to revel in contemplating the nightmare scenario he was sketching out for her.

"We would be unstoppable!" he explained. "What was needed, however, was a larger and more durable species than was currently available. So we began to make genetic modifications: larger body size for longer periods without food, ability to climb, to leap. We had to modify them for water-based incursions and increase their bite radius to inflict damage on hostile personnel."

"A more durable species," she said softly. "That's what the Indiana Corn Weasel is. A genetically modified government experiment."

"The U.S. Military isn't stupid, despite what your egghead friends think," Major Praeger said. "We knew there was a risk that one of our experiments—Gus, or any of his brothers—might actually escape from our control. We track them all closely—they've got GPS chips implanted at the base of their spines—and we can always find them and retrieve them. But until we do, they can create a bit of a, well, a situation."

"People think they're seeing the Indiana Corn Weasel."

"Intelligence officials knew there was this long-standing myth around these parts, and figured if anybody said anything about seeing a huge vicious weasel, they'd be dismissed as a crackpot. That's why this particular facility was chosen. People have been seeing the Indiana Corn Weasel for hundreds of years. What are a few more sightings, huh?"

It was ingenious, really. And it all made sense. Except one part.

"Why are you telling me this?"

He took a piece of paper out of his pocket.

"Miss Kane, I have something for you to sign. It's a non-disclosure agreement. Sometimes these documents are referred to as 'gag' orders. It stipulates that you will never reveal anything you've seen, or heard, pertaining to this matter. Not to anyone. You can't write about it in your dissertation, can't tell your reporter friend about it. You can't even whisper it to Old Ben Yoder. Now, you can refuse to sign it, of course, That's your right. Though I'm pretty sure your son would want you to sign it."

Justin.

Kelsey jumped up from the floor like she'd been jolted with electricity.

"Where's Justin? What have you done?"

"He's safe. For the moment. But if you refuse to sign—or if you sign but then later change your mind and tell anyone what you've learned here—I can't guarantee his safety. If you'll read the agreement, you'll see that disclosing this classified military information at any time, to anyone, will result in your being arrested and tried on charges of treason. You'll lose your freedom, and your son will be taken into protective custody. Revealing classified information is one of the surest ways to ensure you'll be spending the rest of your life in an underground facility, Miss Kane. Here," he said, sliding the paper towards her. "This is where you sign."

A trembling and unsteady "Kelsey Kane" was now inked on the non-disclosure agreement. It was done, and she knew it would never be un-done. She would not risk losing custody of Justin. At that moment, she wasn't sure if Major Praeger had the law on his side or if he was just further toying with her, but she knew she'd never tell anyone again what she saw and heard. This nightmare would end, here and now.

"Where's Justin?" she asked, pleadingly.

He handed her a crudely drawn map, folded in two.

She snatched it from him. It took Kelsey a few seconds to figure out the map's features, but then she gasped in horror. It was a map of the lake where Kelsey had her near-fatal encounter with the weasel. According to the map, Justin was on the small sandbar in the middle of the lake.

"My God," she said. "How could you do this to him? He's just a little boy,' she said, fury and terror intermingled. "He doesn't even know how to swim."

"Oh that's right," Major Praeger said with mock sympathy. "You're not 'water people.' Well, in that case you'd better get going. When the lake gets choppy, that sandbar gets battered pretty good. Just give that map to the driver in the jeep outside the gate and he'll take you there.

When you arrive, a rowboat will be waiting on shore. I truly hope everything turns out okay, Miss Kane."

She ran out of the room before he could even finish his smirk.

The sight of an Amish woman running madly across the compound must have engendered at least a little head-scratching among the base personnel. But Kelsey wasn't around long enough to generate much notice. As Praeger had grimly promised, there was a jeep waiting to take her to the lake. She jumped in the front seat, handed the map to the driver, who appeared as stone-faced as Ben Yoder had been on her morning commute, and after the grinding of a couple of gears, they were off.

Geographically, the ride was short. The lake was less than two miles away. Kelsey and the driver didn't speak, didn't even look at each other. The only word that was exchanged between them came near the end of their trip, when the lake first came into sight and Kelsey appeared like she was going to jump from the jeep. "Wait," said the driver, sternly. Whether his terse command was intended to ensure Kelsey's safety, or whether he was a student of the Praeger school of manners, wasn't clear.

She jumped out before the jeep even came to a full stop, and ran up to the bank. Before she saw the boat, she scanned the horizon, looking for Justin. The sandbar was about a hundred yards off the shore, a gently sloping rise that was much more prominent during the dry summer months. By late fall, it was more of a protrusion than an island. Through much of the winter and early spring, it disappeared altogether. Kelsey ran in the water up to her ankles, the hem of her Amish dress darkening in the wetness, oblivious to everything except seeing her son, getting his attention, and then getting to him.

Justin was there. She saw him. He was sitting in the sand, arms gathered around his knees, his feet almost at the water's edge. He lifted his head and looked out across the water from his sandy exile when he heard her yelling out to him. And then he started yelling back. It was a grey day and the wind was blowing, making communication almost impossible. Kelsey tried to shout that he should stay put, hold on, that she would be there in just a couple of minutes, but he was shouting back at the same time, telling her he was cold and scared and he just wanted to go home. Neither heard the other as their frantic cries crossed in the wind.

Major Praeger was true to his sadistic word: there was a wooden row boat with a pair of oars waiting for her. He didn't mention the small hole in the bottom of the boat; he thought he'd let her discover that feature for herself. Kelsey yanked the boat from its resting place on shore and shoved it into the water, leaping in clumsily. The momentum of her jump moved the boat away from the fringe of the water and she grabbed an oar and pushed against the muddy bottom of the lake, moving slowly toward her son. It took her a frustratingly long time to figure out how to get the metal peg of the oar she was holding positioned securely into the oarlock. "Fucking boats," she muttered to herself, her dread and ignorance of life on the water tormenting her yet again.

She was trying to keep Justin in sight but this was difficult because she had positioned herself to pull the oars with her back towards her destination. But she wanted to face forward, to keep him in her view, so this led to some rather inelegant oarsmanship as she ended up kind of slapping at the water, more than rowing. Her progress was slow and hard-fought, but it was progress, and through sheer force of will, the boat drifted towards the sandbar.

She was tugging at the oars, which kept slipping out of her hands and out of the oarlocks. She had managed to get far enough along that she could hear Justin more clearly, the distress in his voice carrying across the water. All of that sloppy, choppy rowing had apparently kicked some water back into the boat as Kelsey noticed her feet were now sloshing around as she tried to brace her heels while pulling on the oars. She was making some progress, getting closer to the sandbar, and finding a rhythm when she heard a splash, just in front of the boat.

Kelsey, startled, thought it must be a fish. What else could it be?

She was now more than halfway to the sandbar. She waved to her son, shouting and tugging at the oars.

"Justin, I'm coming! Don't worry! Everything will be fine, I promise!"

Her little guy was now standing expectantly at the edge of the dark, sandy isle, awaiting rescue.

"I'll be right—"

It leapt out of the water, right in front of Kelsey. It wasn't a fish. Its matted fur glistening, its teeth bared, it rose, appeared almost to hover before disappearing under the water. For just a moment, Kelsey froze.

It can't be.

She pulled frantically at the oars but she slipped in the now ankle-deep water in the boat, and one of the oars slipped out of its oarlock and fell, floating just off the side of the boat. Kelsey reached out to grab it but the creature broke the surface again, leaping like a flying fish, emitting that horrible, skin-crawling hiss. Kelsey fell back in the boat, gasping.

"Mommy!"

Justin didn't know what was happening but he saw his mother recoil in fear.

"It's going to be all right!" she tried to assure him, assure herself. She sat back up and grabbed the only oar she had and pulled wildly. It was only a few more pulls before Kelsey realized she was simply spinning now, and that she'd have to pick up the oar and use it like a paddle. "God, I hate boats," she said, paddling.

Another splash, another hiss. Kelsey beat at the water, but it was too late. The creature was gone. But just as quickly it appeared on the other side, breaking the surface and briefly clinging to the side of the boat, its claws scratching the wood while Kelsey screamed and tried to bat it away with the paddle. The creature hissed at her then disappeared.

There was a serious amount of water in the boat now, and even Kelsey, who knew nothing about boats, realized this was not a good situation. She was only about twenty-five yards from the sandbar but because neither she nor Justin could swim, she had to get the boat all the way to the sandbar.

She heard a splash, and then another. She saw the claws of a creature clinging to the bow of the boat while another hissed from her left and still another leapt, breaking the surface about ten feet in front of the boat.

Oh God. What's happening?

Then she remembered: Gus was one of six genetically altered creatures. There were five others.

As she worked out the math, one of the creatures leapt out of the water and into the boat, hissing at Kelsey, She took the oar and swung it but she missed. The animal seized its chance and leapt at Kelsey, who slipped and fell back. The creature's bite failed to land but its claws scratched her arms, ripping a small patch of flesh, leaving Kelsey bloodied and shaken. It hissed at her, almost like it was taunting her, and jumped back into the water. Kelsey stood up in the boat and found she was standing in water. The small wooden craft bobbed in the water as the lake slowly filtered in. In a couple of minutes, it would no longer be afloat.

"Mommy!" His cry was desperate and confused.

She knew what it was to witness the horrific loss of a parent, how scarring and far-reaching such an experience was. She tried to focus, wiped her hair away from her eyes, a bloody smear from her wound mixing with her sweat and the cold water of the lake. Then she heard it, the terrifying chorus of hissing, rising up out of the water. She turned around and saw the grim tableau of churning water, five steady trails in the distance heading right for the boat, which was now listing badly, lake water beginning to pour over the down-turned bow. Kelsey was helpless, sinking, her son within earshot of the blood-curdling hissing, blood streaming down her arm. She squeezed her eyes shut, hoping it was a mirage, hoping to blink it away. But the sound grew louder and more maddening. Kelsey held tightly to the oar, standing now in knee-deep water, the boat resigned to its fate. Her beleaguered mind reeled, defiantly looking for a way out. But it was impossible to think. That hissing sound was torturous. It was as if these creatures were taunting her, toying with her before they came in for the final strike. The hissing drowned out the cries of her son and the manic thoughts in her own head. As they approached in an unbroken line, heads slightly above the water, teeth bared, she held out the oar in desperate defense.

The hissing grew even louder but it had changed, sounding lower now, more steady, more propulsive. It sounded at first like a buzzing, and then, like someone had revved up a chainsaw in the nearby woods. The noise was becoming deafening. Kelsey put her hands up to cover her ears, dropping the oar just at the moment that the boat finally gave way, sinking to the bottom of the lake. In her panic, Kelsey reached out and tried to grab the floating oar, hoping it would support her, though it probably wouldn't matter to the weasels whether Kelsey was still buoyant when they got to her. She was at eye level with the creatures now as they slowly closed in, just seconds away. The buzzing sound was unbearably loud, drowning out any last goodbyes she might shout to Justin, her final words lost on the water. She was about to shut her eyes and plunge underneath, hoping to momentarily dodge the corps of weasely predators stalking her when she had a vision, a mirage. She gasped and then she screamed, still stunned.

"Help me!"

It was a motor boat that had been creating that buzzing sound. It had been racing to her across the lake and was now there, almost on top of her, approaching her from behind. Its loud, rapid approach temporarily disoriented the creatures, who dispersed fearfully, leaving Kelsey bobbing uncertainly on the water, clinging to life on a chipped wooden oar. The vessel slowly turned around, coming up along side her, the boat's pilot now visible.

"I thought you didn't like the water," said Frankie, as he reached down to scoop her out of the lake.

Kelsey was almost too shocked to speak as she exhaustedly reached out to him. She climbed into Frankie's speedboat and he saw immediately her bloodstained clothes.

"Oh my God, Kelsey. They got to you."

She waved off his concern and pointed to the sandbar. "Get him."

Frankie turned the boat, pulled back the throttle and in a few seconds, he was floating as close to the sandbar as he could get. He turned off the engine and jumped in, wading in the fifteen feet to where Justin was, grabbing him by the waist, and carrying him back out to the boat, where his mother helped him climb the aluminum ladder next to the motor. She wrapped her lake-drenched blood-stained Amish long sleeves around him and squeezed until he started dripping.

"I love you," she said through the tears.

Justin said nothing as she hugged tightly his chilled and shaking frame.

* * * *

They didn't talk at all on the ride back into town. Kelsey was too emotionally and physically drained, and her son just seemed to want to stare out of the window of Frankie's car, perhaps wondering what he should tell his schoolmates about what he'd just been through. It wasn't until they all got back to the barn and Kelsey showered, bandaged her scratches, and made herself a cup of tea, that she even began to organize her questions. But before she asked him anything, he made a request.

"Would you bring me that Amish gown you were wearing?"

"Frankie, it's a mess. It's soaked and filthy."

"Please?"

"I suppose I do owe you a favor," she said, and she returned in a minute with the dress, bundled up, and handed it to him.

"Here you go," she said, puzzled. "Now it's my turn to ask you something. How the hell did you know we were out there?"

Frankie lifted his mug of tea and took a sip.

"After our shouting match in the parking lot, I realized how determined you were to see this thing through, so I thought maybe I could still help you out some way. I did a little more digging into Major Praeger's background. I have some sources at the VFW Hall in Oakton. Gulf War vets. I did a feature story about them once. They love me. Anyway, they made a couple calls to some of their buddies who are still in the service. I found out the real deal with Praeger. He was Section-8."

"What's that?"

"It means he had a mental breakdown. They put him in a military psych ward. He was deemed unfit for duty."

"How'd he end up here?"

"Praeger threatened to go public with what he said were war crimes authorized by his commanders. He was going to run to the press and spill his guts unless they revoked his Section-8 classification and put him back on active duty. The generals caved. They didn't want this psycho going all over the country, telling gruesome stories to the press that made our G.I. Joes look bad. So they sent him here, to a military Siberia. That's when he started pushing for these experiments. The military wanted to pull the plug, but Praeger played that war crimes card again, threatening to cry wolf to the national media. Apparently, they didn't know how far out of hand things had gotten here. Praeger never told them what he was up to, really. They figured when they sent him here that he'd spend his days cheating at poker in the Officer's Club. Turns out he was conducting this whole secret program, threatening anyone on the base with court martial if they so much as breathed a word of it to anybody."

Frankie took another sip of tea—the natural storyteller in him enjoying the drama of dragging out the tale.

"When I learned what a nut job this guy was—how dangerous he could become—I realized you were in danger too. I was going to come to you, but as you'll recall we weren't exactly on speaking terms. Besides, I was afraid you'd think I was just trying to protect my job and you'd ignore me anyway. So I did what any concerned ex-lover would do. I followed you."

"You what?"

"I followed you. After you went out to Ben Yoder's, I went there myself. He wouldn't tell me why you went out there. Told me it was none of my business. But after I told him what I had learned about Praeger, and how worried I was about you, he told me about your plan. There was no way I could come along with you, I realized. So I did the next best thing."

Here he unfurled the bundle that was her gown, and searched for the top. He removed something that looked like a button from the back collar.

"Voila," he said. "The next best thing to being there."

Kelsey picked up the small disk, which was no larger than a watch battery.

"What is this?"

"It's a long distance voice transmission encoder. Or as reporters and mafia turncoats call it, a bug."

Kelsey was speechless.

"I didn't even notice this when I put the dress on," she said.

"It wasn't on the dress then. I gave it to Ben Yoder, who gave it to Sarah. She was supposed to stick it on your dress before you split up."

Kelsey remembered now the odd, tight hug Sarah gave her just before they parted ways.

When she grabbed me around my neck, she must have put this on, she concluded.

"Once it was in place, I was able to listen to what was happening. It was pretty rough there for a while."

"Tell me about it."

"When I heard him talk about Justin being at the lake, I stopped listening and got in my car and headed off to the lake myself. It took me a few minutes to get there, but as you know, the story has a happy ending."

"Barely," she said, shaking her head at the stunning turn of events. "And thanks, by the way. For everything." She put down her tea and moved closer to him, kissing him on the cheek and burying her head against his shoulders. He wrapped his arms around her and they stood there for the longest time, neither wanting to break the bond. So it was left to Justin to interrupt things.

"Okay, I'm ready now, Mommy" he announced, dragging a suitcase out of his room.

"Ready for what?" Kelsey asked, Frankie's arms still around her.

"Ready to go home. You found the weasel," he said proudly. "And I won my bet!"

Chapter 14

The early morning service was almost over when Kelsey pulled in to the parking lot of Jesus the Redeemer church. A soaking rain had been falling since dawn. She grabbed an issue of the *Milton Forum* and covered her head as she dashed to the church's entrance. The church was still mostly dark—Reverend Lonnie had a thing against light, apparently. Services in the dark, services outside at night—a lack of illumination seemed to fire his evangelical fervor.

She sat in the same row that she and Justin had sat in on their first night in town.

If I'd only known what awaited me, I think I might have actually prayed. She was amused by the revelation.

Reverend Lonnie was reading a passage from what Kelsey assumed was the Old Testament, full of "thee" and "thou" and other archaic expressions.

The rain had put a damper on attendance. There were only about a dozen people there, mostly with heads bowed. The cleric was holding nothing back though, selling his message as if there were a full house, gesturing intently when he reached the climax of his passage.

"For the book of Proverbs tells us, 'Trust in the Lord with all your heart and lean not on your own understanding; in all your ways acknowledge him, and he will make your paths straight.' Let it be so, brothers and sisters! Let it be so!"

His booming voice echoed in the nearly empty church, disturbing a few bowed heads. He closed the book with a dramatic gesture, tucked it under his arm, and simply walked off, disappearing into one of the side rooms abutting the front of the church. In a moment, all the lights came on. Kelsey walked up to the front of the church against the straggling tide of worshipers ready to now start their day, fortified by the Word.

She probably should have knocked at the half-open door but recent events had emboldened her, so she walked straight in to the small anteroom where he was sitting, arms folded, eyes closed. She stood there, unsure whether he was meditating, or praying, or trying to sleep. He detected her presence, and spoke first.

"Don't worry about coming in late," he said. "I always save the best for the end."

Kelsey laughed. "Yeah, that was pretty good stuff. I liked the 'Let it be so.' Reminded me of the Beatles."

She was being sincere, not irreverent. Kelsey had derived much more spiritual direction in her life from pop music lyrics than from the words of the King James Bible. He took it in stride.

"Yes, Matthew, Mark, Luke and John have been replaced by John, Paul, George, and Ringo. You're not the first to prefer them," he said. "What brings you here this morning, Miss Kane?"

"I came to say goodbye."

"You're going back home?"

She nodded. "Leaving this afternoon. I just wanted to thank you for your assistance, and your time. I really enjoyed our conversations."

He walked over to her and grabbed her extended hand, clasping it warmly.

"It was my pleasure," he said, returning to the desk in

the office and opening a drawer. "I have something for you." He rooted around through a few papers and removed two cards with pictures on them. "It's a holy card," he explained, handing one of them to her. "St. Thomas. The doubter."

Kelsey looked at it and nodded.

"Thanks," she said, tucking it in her purse.

"And this one is for your son." It was a man in a robe, arms extended, surrounded by animals. "St. Francis, lover of animals."

"Justin will like this," she said, taking the card and studying it.

No weasels.

She put it in her purse, and turned to go.

"Maybe our paths will cross again," she said, aware of how unlikely a prospect that was.

"The Lord works in mysterious ways," the reverend said. "And I have a feeling he's not quite done with you, Miss Kane."

She smiled and walked out through the now-lighted church and then back into the sodden, secular world.

* * * *

"I'm sorry, but he's not here. He must be on assignment, but he's not answering his cell phone. Or it might be the coverage," the receptionist explained. "Some of these farms don't get much of a signal."

Kelsey nodded. She'd tried to reach Frankie on his phone too, but couldn't. She was hoping for a final goodbye, though she realized it was probably better this way. The last thing she needed was another emotionally draining scene, and he certainly didn't need to deal with something like that at work. He'd made it clear to her last night that his job, his life, his whole world was here, hard as that was to believe. He'd found a way to make the town his own, something Kelsey thought she would never be able to do no matter how long she stayed. Justin was right: it was time to go home.

"Thanks," she said. "Tell him I stopped by. My name is—"

"I know who you are, Miss Kane," the woman said. "Everybody does."

She remembered Frankie telling her, in one of their first conversations, that there are no secrets in a small town.

"Right. Well, goodbye."

"Have a nice trip. Say hello to New Jersey for us."

In about sixteen hours, that's exactly what she hoped to do.

* * * *

It would take about an hour to drive from Milton to the bus depot. After Kelsey picked up Justin from school—he wanted to say goodbye to his class, which gave him a going-away present, a variety of lichens and mosses, labeled and pasted to the inside of a cardboard cigar box—they cruised one more time down Main Street, past the diner, past the police station, past the bait and tackle shop, and then out onto the county highway, headed to the bus that would take them to the train and then back to New Jersey. "We're on our way," Kelsey said, but Justin just looked out the window, studying the farmland. Kelsey remembered when they first rolled into town, the sense of wonder palpable, everything new and strange, the promise of discovery around every corner.

"We've had quite an adventure, huh, Spinner?"

He nodded, still staring out the window, taking it all in while he could. They rolled on in silence, each lost in thought. When they got to the depot, they pulled their suitcases out of the trunk. Kelsey left the keys in the car—she had told Mrs. Hochstetler that her brother could have the car back, that she'd leave it in the bus depot lot, no charge.

"Don't you want to drive it home?" Mrs. Hochstetler asked.

"It would never make it," said Kelsey.

She and Justin got on the bus and watched Indiana passing by. After what seemed like one long cornfield, they were at the train station.

"Next stop, New Jersey," Kelsey said, as she and Justin climbed on board their train, navigating the narrow aisles to find a seat to call home until after midnight, when they would sleepily disembark at Newark's Penn Station, a cab ride away from their former lives. About half the seats were taken, many by passengers who were already sprawled out, making themselves comfortable for the long ride ahead. As they made their way to the rear of the car, Kelsey noticed two seats, directly behind someone reading a newspaper.

"The *Jersey Examiner*," Kelsey noted as they walked past the passenger. That was her local newspaper back in New Jersey. Since she needed something to read on the ride, she thought she'd find out where he got it.

"Excuse me, sir, can you tell me if they sell that paper around here?"

The man lowered the paper.

"I'd give you this copy, but then I'd have nothing to read but the *Milton Forum*, and that would be torture."

"Frankie!" Kelsey shouted. "What are you doing here?"

When Justin heard Frankie's name, he leapt out of his seat, raced past his mother, and hugged him.

"Hey there, Justin!" he said, tousling the boy's hair. "Fancy meeting you here."

Justin just giggled as the train pulled out of the station.

"So what in heaven's name are you doing here?" Kelsey asked, still stunned.

"I thought it was time to see a little more of the world," he said. "I figured I'd start with New Jersey."

Kelsey stood there, mouth open.

"Do you mind if I share your train?" he asked.

"But what about your job?" she said, settling in next to him.

"You were right, Kelse," he said, reaching out to grab her hand. "I was stagnating. It's time to move on."

"But you were on assignment this morning, working on a story. I went by your office."

"No. I was at the County D.A.'s office, dropping off the tape of Praeger."

"You recorded him?"

"It's automatic. The receiver I have makes a recording of whatever it picks up. I knew the D.A. would be interested—which he was. It's over for Praeger. He'll be lucky to keep his Private stripes by the time the government's done with him. I'd expect a court martial, followed by a dishonorable discharge and some time in the brig."

"Wow. Praeger in a cage. That's ironic."

"But it also means you're off the hook. The D.A. told me that non-disclosure agreement you signed was worthless, anyway. You can publish this story on the front page of the *New York Times* if you want."

"I just want to finish my dissertation," she said. "If you want the story it's all yours."

"Thanks," he said. "I think I'll turn it into a novel. *On the Trail of the Terrible Indiana Corn Weasel.*"

"Catchy title. But I thought you were already working on a novel."

"I was at a dead end. It wasn't going anywhere. I needed a fresh start. The corn weasel just might be my ticket to literary fame."

"More irony," Kelsey said. She leaned her head against Frankie's shoulder as he leafed through his newspaper, an unseen smile curling her lips.

"Hey Kelse—listen to this. It says here that the police received multiple reports last weekend from witnesses claiming to have seen the Jersey Devil."

"You're kidding."

"No, really. The cops say it's a hoax, but the witnesses are pretty adamant about what they saw." He lowered the paper. "My reporter instincts tell me there's a much bigger story here. What do you think?"

Kelsey stared blankly into the distance. As the train surged out of a tunnel, she heard the high-pitched howl of the wind whistling through the window, sounding like the cry of some wild and unknown creature.

ABOUT THE AUTHOR

James F. Broderick is an associate professor of English and Journalism at New Jersey City University. The author of five works of non-fiction, he lives in Glen Ridge, New Jersey with his wife Miri and daughters Olivia and Maddy.

For your reading pleasure, we invite you to visit our web bookstore